REDEEMING VOWS

"Redeeming Vows takes readers on a journey that's steeped in dangerous magic and breath-taking suspense."
~Nights and Weekend

"...filled with suspense, action, magic and of course romance."
~Nocturne Romance Reads

"Catherine Bybee knocked this series out of the park."
~Forever Booklover

BINDING VOWS

"Binding Vows whisked me into an adventure I was sorry to see end."
~Romance Studio

"...full of all the things I love, action, romance, history, and a knight in shining armor."
~Night Owl Reviews

"...you cannot help but feel completely mesmerized."
~Coffee Time Romance

"Catherine Bybee does an exceptional job of making her time travels come to life."

Discover other titles by Catherine Bybee

Contemporary Romance
Weekday Bride Series:
Wife by Wednesday
Married By Monday

Not Quite Series:
Not Quite Dating

Paranormal Romance
MacCoinnich Time Travel Series:
Binding Vows
Silent Vows
Redeeming Vows
Highland Shifter

Ritter Werewolves Series:
Before the Moon Rises
Embracing the Wolf

Novellas:
Possessive
Soul Mate

Erotic Titles:
Kiltworthy
Kilt-A-Licious

REDEEMING VOWS

BOOK THREE

BY

CATHERINE BYBEE

Redeeming Vows
Catherine Bybee

Copyright 2010 by Catherine Bybee

Cover Art by Crystal Posey

Publishing History
First Edition, Faery Rose Edition, 2010
Second Edition, Catherine Bybee, 2013

Published in the United States of America

Dedication

To Carrie, Tommy and Andrea...
Through the good, the bad and the ugly,
I know deep in my heart that you'll always be
there.
Even if only in spirit.

Acknowledgment

This trilogy has been a journey. There have been times I've cried over the process, wiggled in my seat and wondered if I'd ever be able to face my father again after he's read the book, and times I've patted myself on the back and said, "Damn, that's good!" I didn't do this alone and want to take a minute to thank those who helped along the way.

I want to thank Sharon Meyer, who encouraged me to pursue publication of *Binding Vows* and has offered unwavering support for my new passion of writing. Aithne Jarretta helped me with some of the basics with writing and the first book in this trilogy. Sandra Stixrude, your advice and critical eye kept me on track throughout! I can't thank you enough. My editor Fran... I can't find the words of gratitude you deserve. When the day comes that we finally meet in person, the first round is on me! Salute!

Catherine

Chapter One

Liz snapped out of her daydream with Simon's voice ringing in her ears. He wasn't screaming from the front yard about his ball hoping over the fence. No, he was calling her in his head. Something even now, ten months after the first time he'd done so, she'd not grown used to.

Mom, come back to the keep. The shit is hitting the fan again.

Liz shook her head and surged to her feet. *How many times have I told you not to use language like that?*

I'm talking in my head, Mom. It doesn't count!

Liz lifted her skirt, ran to the door, and continued to argue with her son who was over a mile away.

It sure as hell does when you're talking to me.

Simon laughed. *Ha. You just swore.*

That's different, I'm an adult.

Whatever.

Liz could imagine the expression on her son's face. With eyes rolling back in his head and hands on his hips. *What's happening now?* she questioned, knowing he wouldn't have called her if it wasn't urgent.

Birds, hundreds of them. Grainna has to be in the mix. We all feel her evil.

Crap, hold on.

Like a cell phone, Liz tuned out of her son's thoughts and raced to the mare saddled and waiting outside the sanctuary of her hideaway.

"Come on, girl. We have somewhere to be," she coaxed while grasping the reins and hoisting up and into the saddle.

Hurry! Simon's voice pleaded while she watched the Scottish landscape race beside her.

The wind and rain drenched her gown and hair, grown long in her months in the sixteenth century. She searched frantically for a spell to ward away the birds so only the Druid witch remained when she finished her chant.

Liz pushed her horse faster, hearing her son's urgent voice in her head. Damn, she shouldn't have left him, she scolded herself.

Over the hill, the keep emerged strong, solid, and massive under a blanket of black.

Her horse stopped and whinnied at the chaos unfolding in front of their eyes. Crows filled the sky, thousands of them, blotting out the sun.

Liz's jaw hung open. "Son of a bitch!" she whispered before kicking her mount into a frantic run.

She started chanting long before she reached the gates.

"In this day and in this hour, I call upon the Ancient's power. Give us all the ability to see Grainna amongst all of these."

The closer she drew, the more powerful the effects of the chant became.

Birds dropped from the sky, dead, while servants fled the walls of the stone fortress of the MacCoinnichs'.

"Open the gates," she yelled from outside the huge wooden doors that blocked all unwelcomed visitors. "Open the damn gates!"

Stopping short of the wooden doors, Lizzy's horse strained against the reins and whinnied. Careful to hold her seat, and avoid landing on the ground, Liz continued her chant and watched the sky.

Finally, the barrier opened, and she had to still her horse with the dash of retreating people screaming and fleeing the inside of the gates.

Pushing her horse forward, she surveyed the courtyard and found her son standing next to Fin and the entire MacCoinnich family. All of them watched the sky. Tara, Myra and Amber held hands in the shadows, waiting.

Liz jumped off the mare and ran to the women, gasping for air.

"In this day and in this hour..." they all chanted, the only way to fend off the evil coming from the sky. Liz grasped their hands, strengthening and completing their Druid circle.

"Give us the ability," Liz said and waited for the others to repeat her words. "To see Grainna's true self amongst all these."

With each phrase, the sisters levitated from the ground, a side effect of any spell they wove together. No one knew why they hovered above the earth, and none of them knew how to fall back gracefully when they were done. Twice they repeated the words and like a plague, the crows began to drop.

As one, the sisters turned their heads to the sky as an inhuman screech of evil filled the air.

A solitary crow hovered. With one loud screech, it darted away.

Tara squeezed her hand before Liz let her gaze slip from the sky. Slowly the women let each other's hands go and slid to the ground. Myra fell on her behind and extended a hand to Tara to help her up.

Liz hardly took a breath before Fin stepped in front of her with hands perched on his hips.

"Where the hell were you?"

"Out." She turned away, intent on letting that be the end of their discussion, but Fin had other ideas.

His hand darted out and caught her shoulder. "Dammit, Elizabeth, you know better than to leave the keep without someone with you. Are you so selfish that you'd endanger everyone here for your own needs?"

His eyes expressed his anger.

She looked beyond him and over to her son who quickly diverted his attention to his shoes.

"I needed some time alone."

Taking a step closer, Fin lowered his voice so only the women heard. "Then take to a far tower here within these walls. You're of no use to any of us dead."

Liz felt her chest rise and color flame to her face. He was right, and she hated him for it.

Clenching her teeth, she turned and marched from the chaos. She didn't stop until she safely passed the threshold of her chambers. Tara followed her inside and gently closed the door behind them.

Without looking in her direction, Liz addressed her younger sister. "You agree with him, don't you?"

"You agree with him, too." When Tara didn't say more, Liz turned and stared at her.

"What if Grainna positioned that flock of evil over only you? None of us are capable of taking her on alone." Tara stepped closer, taking Liz's hands.

"I'm suffocating here."

"I know." Tara pushed back a strand of Liz's hair and continued. "But stay close, Lizzy. I need you here. *We* need you here. You are the strongest of all of us."

"I'm not stronger than you."

"That's not true and you know it."

"I don't have an ability like yours or like the rest."

Liz referred to each and every one of the MacCoinnichs' gifts. Tara's ability to move and manipulate everything that grows might have been a new power, but it was something Liz's baby

4

sister had already learned to use to her advantage. Tara's husband, Duncan, could cast a flame larger and stronger than anything imagined by twenty-first century fiction writers. Simon spoke to animals. Ian directed the weather with a mere thought. Myra moved objects with her mind. Even Amber, the youngest of the MacCoinnichs, was an empath who could sense events long before they happened.

No, compared to Tara and the rest, Liz felt inferior, like a cast off.

As if sensing her concern, Tara continued. "You are the one who comes up with every chant, every spell that keeps Grainna at bay."

"Any of you could do that."

"Really? I don't think so."

"All of us are Druids, Tara. We all have the ability." Liz moved to the large fireplace and held out her hands. Sparks flew into the hearth and flames leapt to warm the room.

"Look at you. If I had told you a year ago that you were able to start a fire without a match, you would've had me committed. Now you prance around, spread your hands and *voila...* flames." Tara stepped behind her. "I know you're unhappy here. But until this is finished, until we destroy Grainna and find the stones, you're stuck here."

Hearing the words aloud felt so final. It wasn't that she hated the MacCoinnichs; she simply didn't have any control over her own life. With Fin hovering close by, it was as if she couldn't breathe. In order to return to her century, they needed the sacred stones. Grainna had three of them in her possession. The MacCoinnichs held the other three.

"I know."

"Think of Simon. If Grainna caught you alone, killed you..." Tara's voice dropped away. "What would he do without you?"

Closing her eyes, Liz turned. Tara was right. They all were right.

~~~~

Fin supervised the cleanup of the dead birds, all the while dodging the questions posed by the Knights and servants of the keep. Keeping their ancestry concealed was becoming increasingly difficult with every passing day. Todd, his brother-in-law, stood beside him and nodded toward the yard.

"Have you ever heard of Alfred Hitchcock?"

"Sounds like a name of a person."

"It is. I wonder if Grainna watched a lot of movies during the twentieth century."

Fin moved from the shadows and into the sun.

"Did she get this from your movies?"

Todd, a police officer from the century of which they spoke, would know if she did.

"I think so." Todd picked up a dead bird between his thumb and his index finger before tossing it into a pile with the rest. "God I hope she didn't like Freddy Kruger or Michael Myers."

"Who are they?" Fin asked.

"You don't want to know."

Before he could question Todd, Gregor approached them.

"'Tis all there is. Do ye want us to burn them?"

Drawing his shoulders back, Fin answered. "To ashes, Gregor. Let no feather go un-touched."

"Aye, 'tis best to have no evidence."

Fin's eyes narrowed. He nodded and left the yard.

"I think it's time for a drink," Todd said by his side.

"Agreed."

Together they walked into the main hall, past the dogs sitting at the base of the stairs, and through the door to Ian's private study. Duncan and Ian already held glasses in their hands,

6

enjoying what little Scotch remained.

"'Tis done?" Ian asked from behind his desk.

"Aye, Father. The carcasses are being destroyed, and there are no others in the sky." Fin poured two goblets, handed one to Todd and took a seat.

"Where the hell is she hiding?"

"I wish I knew." Ian, laird of the Coinnich land, ran a hand through his graying hair. "I'm not sure how much longer we will keep the village together if this continues."

Duncan cleared his throat. "I've heard of several families fleeing to Lancaster in the past month. Rumors of evil are driving them away."

Ian dropped his drink to the desk. Amber liquid splashed against the side of the cup. "I expected loyalty from my people."

"And 'tis why so many stay. If you were anyone else, your lands would be empty by now," Fin reminded his father.

Ian stared at the men in the room. "If I could raise an army to fight this evil I'd do it. But how do you fight evil magic?"

Fin watched as they all sat, staring into their goblets, each of them large warring men, capable of their share of death and destruction. Each of them powerless against one evil woman. Grainna.

Chapter Two

Leafing through the pages of the book Liz aptly named her Bible of Druids, she jotted down a note within the margin.

We are peaceful people who mean harm to no one. Our maker judges all evil that dwells amongst us. Never should our gifts be used for injury upon another soul.

"Ha!" Liz turned the book over and glanced at the year the book was published. 1998. Selma Mayfair, the author, thought she was a witch. In truth, she was most likely a Druid who didn't know it. She'd capitalized on her heritage and gift of premonitions to help the local police when a child vanished in rural Ohio. After the child was located exactly where Ms. Mayfair said she'd be, the media caught hold of her story and posted it all over the national news. Before long, Ms. Mayfair had every publisher and his brother asking for a book deal.

The first one, *Sixth Sense*, hit the New York Times Bestseller list, which made her an overnight sensation. But that book wasn't the one Liz looked at now. This book was labeled *Seventh Sense*. The book lacked the drama of a child's abduction and consequently didn't do nearly as well in the bookstores as the first. Liz remembered the hype and the syndicated talk shows all blasting Ms. Mayfair's "abilities" when *Seventh Sense* came out. Because the book teetered on a religious fence, most of the spiritual community ostracized the author and called her a fraud.

By the time *Seventh Sense* was in paperback, the only people picking it up were those self proclaimed witches who went around smoking pot and saying "Blessed be."

Before Liz's desired trip back in time, she'd bought the book for her sister. She meant it as a joke. However, it wasn't an accident she'd remembered Ms. Mayfair's plight long after her fifteen minutes of fame were over. It wasn't an accident that while Christmas shopping for how-to books, she came across *Seventh Sense* in the closeout counter. And it wasn't an accident when Liz first touched the *tome of paranormal* that a current of electricity jolted her down to her toes. No, the Ancients knew what the hell they were doing.

"Mom?" Simon's voice bellowed down the hall as he approached her sanctuary.

"In here."

Her son sauntered in the room with newfound confidence. He had grown in the short time they had been in the sixteenth century. At thirteen, he started to look more like a man. His features lost the baby fat of his childhood and his limbs started to fill out. Already his height threatened Liz's.

She couldn't help the proud feeling every time she saw him. He was her life.

He plopped down beside her and nodded to the book. "Still at it?"

"We're not home yet, are we?" She repeated the words daily. Liz wouldn't stop reading and trying new things to rid the MacCoinnichs of Grainna and find the stones that would take them home.

Simon looked around the room built of stone. "No, we're not in Kansas anymore."

Rolling her eyes, Liz laughed. "We never lived in Kansas."

"Yeah well, we're not in California anymore doesn't have the same ring."

Liz reached out and ruffled his long hair. "No,

it doesn't."

Simon cast his eyes to his hands that plucked at the wool fiber of the bedding.

"What's on your mind?" Liz set the book aside.

"I ah, I need to tell you something."

Oh, geeze. Nothing good ever came of that statement. "You can talk to me about anything." And Liz hoped he always would. Realistically, she knew he would hold some secrets.

"I don't want you to freak out."

She swallowed. Hard. "I won't freak out." *Oh please don't let me freak out.*

"I've noticed my powers increasing."

"Okay."

"I mean really increasing." Simon bit his bottom lip, but didn't meet her eyes.

"How, Simon? I know you talk to animals, can feel their desires and needs. What's changing?" Her and Simon's powers changing, morphing as they became aware of them was apparently normal. When she'd first lit a candle without a match, it took tremendous effort. The ease of it now was laughable.

Simon scrambled off the bed. His posture slightly hunched. He stopped in front of the mirror on her vanity table. There he stood taller and met her gaze through the reflective glass. "I think my ability to talk to animals, and make them move the way I want them to, is the beginning of something big. Real big."

I'm not freaking out. But her heart started to speed up, despite her internal chant. "How big, Simon. What's happened?"

Simon's eyes drifted shut, his hands clenched at his sides. "I think of the animal I want to talk to. Think of the way their body moves, the way they breathe." Simon stretched his neck. "I feel their hearts beat. Birds have this—fluttering rate that moves so fast I feel like I need to run to keep up with it. When they take flight, I look down and see the world as they do. The freedom of flight." He sighed. "There's nothing like it. If I try hard enough, and stretch my arms..." Simon lifted his limbs wide, a smile expanded over his face. "I feel myself start to change. If I can focus just a little more, I'll be able to taste it. Be it."

Liz held her breath and stared. The back of Simon's neck moved in a way that wasn't normal. Wasn't human.

I'm not freaking out, I'm not freaking out.

Simon sighed, dropped his arms in frustration, and opened his eyes. The narrow iris of his beautiful eyes stretched vertically and blinked. They opened again and his eyes remained, elongated. Not the eyes of her son, but the eyes of the bird he imagined himself to be.

Liz's lip trembled.

Simon watched her reaction. When he turned to face her, he blinked again. His eyes rolled back and finally returned to normal.

The only thing keeping her on her feet was the uncertainty on Simon's face. He wanted her approval.

"Wow," she said while dragging in one long and deep breath.

"Yeah, wow."

"We knew your powers were going to get stronger." She didn't think they would actually change his physical appearance.

"I know. I've been working on them." He let a smile creep higher. He was proud. Excited. But they weren't talking about an A on his report card. They were talking about her son changing form, species.

Liz turned away, hiding the fear deep in her heart and her mind. His ability to read her thoughts would tell him just how much she *was* freaking out. "Do you feel like you're in control?"

11

"Yes...and no. I mean, I know I'm making myself, change. But I can't make it happen. Not completely anyway."

"When you stop trying, you feel normal again?"

"Kind of. Sometimes it takes a little time to feel completely normal."

Liz forced her lips up. "Okay. Well then, is that it? Nothing else going on?"

Simon's brows came together. "What?"

"You don't have a girlfriend you've met in the village? No siege from Ireland pending?" If she didn't laugh, she was going to break down.

"No, Mom." He rolled his eyes.

Hiding the shake in her hand, she picked up *Seventh Sense* and opened it.

Simon headed for the door.

"Simon?"

He turned.

"When you practice, make sure someone is with you. We wouldn't want you changing into... something, and none of us knowing it's you."

He nodded, smiled, and left the room.

Liz let her eyes fill with tears as soon as she was alone.

~~~~

After drawing energy to the tips of her fingers and using it to charge the iPod, Liz wiggled the earplugs snug in her ears. She turned the volume as high as she could stand it and went through her workout routine in the far tower of the keep, the one she'd been reduced to using for privacy. The snug T-shirt clung to her frame. Sweat formed on her brow from the physical workout. She'd enjoyed kickboxing classes in LA, the one she forced herself to go to after Simon was born. The one she'd do anything to be in right now.

She closed her eyes and pictured a long length of mirror in front of her, other scantily clad women wearing tight leggings and sports bras at her side. Thank God she'd had the sense to bring extra modern clothes for Tara when she'd come here to visit. Otherwise, she'd have to wear some poor excuse for workout clothes instead of the cool cotton she had on now.

Listening to the electric guitar of Nickelback, Liz bobbed back and forth on her feet before lifting her leg in a vertical kick, shoulder height. Her muscles grew warm, free. Her breath came quickly without the tight binding dresses she was forced to wear in this time. God, it felt good.

She pivoted, bobbed, and punched at her invisible enemy.

~~~~

Fin ascended the stairs, expecting to find Elizabeth sitting in front of an open window with one of her famous books in her hand. When he approached the door, he heard a scuffling of feet and a small grunt.

He went on alert and placed a hand to his sword at his side.

Slowly, he opened the door. Ready.

Liz had her back to him, oblivious of his presence. The clothing she wore clung to her every curve, sweat beading down her back, her legs bare for him to see in what she and her sister called "shorts."

He stood tall, no longer fearing for her safety, or his own. Her tiny butt swayed back and forth, causing him to swallow hard. The fabric of the shorts held so closely to her skin he could see every line of her feminine body.

Liz started singing along to the music she listened to.

God it was awful. She couldn't carry a tune to save her life, but it was the most beautiful sound he'd heard all week.

Liz turned and shot her foot in his direction.

Fin snapped out of the trance she'd put him in by simply existing.

She straightened. Obvious surprise marred her face to see him standing there watching. Instead of removing the ear pieces where the music flowed, she bent her knees and put her hands in front of her face, asking to spar.

Fin laughed. "Come on, lass. You can't be serious."

Her chin lifted. "What's a matter, Finlay? Afraid I'll kick your ass?"

He shook his head, closed the door behind him, and removed his sword from his hip. No use nicking anyone by accident. Rolling around on the floor with Elizabeth sweating beneath him was a recurring fantasy of his since they'd met. Of course, this wasn't exactly how he pictured it. But he'd take what he could get.

A pearl of sweat fell down her neck, over her collarbone and disappeared between the alabaster crease of her breasts. He licked his dry lips.

Liz circled, confident. Fin waited for her to make the first move.

He didn't have to wait long.

Her foot shot out. Fin backed up to avoid the blow to his chest. She advanced with a quick step and attempted to hit him with her fist. Fin caught her hand, but didn't take her down. He let go, allowing her to gain her balance again.

Liz's cocky smile slid into something much more serious. Determined.

Fin watched her eyes, quick to catch her right before she made any move. Then something happened. She realized his strategy and managed to sneak in a kick.

Her foot caught him in the stomach and had him stumbling for balance. "Good girl," he whispered, knowing she couldn't hear him over the music in her ears.

Her next two punches came fast and unexpected, one catching him hard on the jaw. And it hurt. His brow rose. The muscles straining on her arms held strength he didn't know she had.

Fin sent his foot out to trip her. She avoided it and waved him toward her. "Come on, Fin. Stop playing."

He turned his back to her, heard her approach, and swept her off her feet. She hit the floor hard. Her eyes opened wide, stunned, but she jumped up and came at him.

Within ten minutes, they were both panting. Liz's punch wavered. Fin caught her fist and pulled it behind her back and her firmly up against his chest. Her breasts heaved, and her breathing strained. The soft curves of her body pressed to his. Liz reached up to the arm he used to hold her and called her Druid powers. Fin felt his skin burn under her touch, and he let go, springing away from her, catching the earplugs and pulling them out of her ears. The device skirted across the floor.

"Not fair, lass."

"Ever hear the term, all's fair in love and war?"

Aye, well, what were they?

When she came at him again he ducked, taking her down to the floor and grabbed her hands and stretched them above her head where she couldn't apply any fire or heat because her fingertips weren't touching him.

Her eyes met his, his body laid on hers keeping her from moving. But this closeness, this contact was torture.

Elizabeth's gaze traveled to his lips dancing dangerously close to hers. He smelled the sweet scent of her breath, knew without a doubt she desired his taste as much as he did hers. He knew that taste, had it once before, briefly.

15

Wanted it even more now.

"You're quite a workout." She breathed the words to him, lifted her lips a tad closer.

"As are you."

They lay there, staring at each other, neither willing to make the first move. Stubborn.

Fin's body responded to her nearness, his kilt hardly containing the effect she had on him. Her eyes grew wider until she shut them, cutting him off. "You're crushing me."

He shifted his weight, giving her room to stand. Liz's face turned red as she looked away from him. He wanted to laugh at her reaction, but cautioned himself against it.

"You move much faster than I expected." Fin lifted onto his elbow, but remained on the floor and willed his body to relax.

"Yes, well. Practice makes..." Her voice drifted. Her eyes glossed over.

"Practice makes what?"

"Perfect. Oh my God, that's it." She ran her hands through her hair, her smile hardly contained. "We're going about this all wrong!"

Confused, he asked, "What are you talking about?"

"Practice. Oh my God, Fin. We've been sitting here, hiding what we are, hiding what we do while Grainna is out there exercising her powers daily. We don't stand a chance if we continue doing what we're doing."

Fin found his feet. "We have to hide who we are. Secrecy is—"

"Bullshit. Secrecy means nothing if we're dead. And that's what we'll be if we don't start playing by her rules."

Her idea went against everything he'd been taught growing up. Druids didn't openly practice their gifts for others to see.

"What are you suggesting?" He knew he

wouldn't like the answer, but he needed to know what she was thinking in order to keep her safe.

"We need to practice. Daily. Like you and the men do with your swords and fighting."

"We do use our skills."

"No, we don't. Not like Grainna does, not without limitations."

"We can't go into the courtyard and start throwing fireballs around, Elizabeth."

She turned from him, her mind deep in thought. "There has to be a way." Tapping her finger to her chin, Fin knew her thoughts were far from the room in which she stood. "When you were a kid discovering your powers, where did you practice?"

"We didn't."

"Please, Fin, any child with a new skill practices."

"We learned to control, more than use, our gifts."

"Grainna uses, practices and controls. *That* is her advantage."

Fin hated to admit it, even to himself, but Elizabeth had a point. "As boys, Duncan and I would ride out into the woods and work our powers. 'Tisn't safe to do that now."

"Alone, no. Maybe if we went out in groups it would be." Liz took new interest in the room where they stood. "I chose this end of the keep to exercise because nobody comes up here."

"So we practice here."

"Tara's gift manipulates plants and nature. Your father can control the weather, Myra the wind. Those things can't be worked out inside these walls."

"And Simon needs animals to see through," Fin concluded before she could.

Elizabeth rolled her eyes at the mention of her son's name and walked away. "Not completely."

"What do you mean?"

She took a deep breath and hesitated before speaking again. "Simon is doing more than seeing through animals. I think he's going to be able to shift or turn into the animals once his power is perfected."

Her words didn't come as surprise, but they did raise fear inside him. "Like Grainna."

"Yeah."

Any other family member, any other Druid, Fin could see this new gift as a way to spy on their enemy and bring them closer to defeating her. Simon was still a boy. Quickly growing into a man, but still too young to venture into battle. His gift could keep him from danger, however. For that reason alone, Simon needed to practice and master his new skills. Elizabeth's ideas on this subject held merit.

"We'll discuss this with the others over our evening meal." Fin picked up his sword and strapped it to his waist. Liz covered her modern clothing with a cloak, and then tucked the music device deep into her pocket.

As they walked from the room, Liz said, "Thank you."

"For what?"

"For not putting down my plans instantly like you normally do."

He laughed. "I only deny ideas without merit. 'Tisn't my fault none you've given before held any."

Her jaw dropped, eyes narrowed. Liz pivoted and stormed away from him mumbling, "Asshole."

Fin's laughter followed her as he watched the retreating woman. Her cloak covered her outfit, but Fin still saw the sway of her hips and the long length of her legs. Once again, he battled down the desire the woman provoked. How long would he deny the physical pull she had on him? Why did he deny it now?

Liz rounded the corner and spoke more clearly. "You're a jerk, Finlay MacCoinnich."

"And you love it, Elizabeth McAllister," he whispered to himself.

Chapter Three

Grainna rested on the top of a tree, tucking her thick black wings to her side. The warrior below sat on his horse, back straight, his ear turned to the sky. He waited several seconds before moving his mount closer to the stream that ran along the banks of Lancaster's land.

Reaching out with her power, Grainna probed into the massive man's mind. His return to Lancaster was early, his time away spent defending allies for his laird. Visions of death filled the far corners of the warrior's thoughts. No remorse for the lives he'd taken lurked in the shadows.

He slid from his horse, stepped aside, and proceeded to relieve his bladder. His hand lingered between his legs longer than necessary. Grainna experienced the man's rush of lust and quickly projected her image into his mind. He stroked himself once, twice and started to harden.

Grainna swept off her perch and landed on mortal feet several yards away. Her raven black hair fell to the length of her back, her breasts pushed forward already aroused and ready for the warrior's touch. Living a life in an old woman's body for so long left her starving for a hard man's touch.

Any man's touch.

This one however, held an air of danger.

She worshiped danger.

Do not be alarmed, she chanted in his thoughts. *I want nothing more than the power between your legs.*

As the man's hand gripped his erection,

Grainna's knees weakened. His lust manifested in her thoughts. A weaker man would already be on the ground with her straddling his thighs. This man, this warrior fresh from battle, wasn't as easy to manipulate.

Turn to me. See what is yours for the taking.

Slowly, he did as she demanded. Grainna's eyes drifted to his hand and she smiled a siren's deviant grin. "Allow me," she sighed, stepping forward until his heat collided with hers.

He moved his hand from his shaft to the clasp holding his kilt together. It fell to the ground. His lips parted when she took him in hand. "Who are ye," he asked against her will. Angering her.

"Only a vessel," she told him. *A fantasy here to relieve your desires.*

Hearing her internal whispers, he clasped his hand to her waist and pulled her into his arms. His mouth found hers, but didn't linger. She didn't want to be kissed, thought the exercise a waste in light of the pleasures his mouth could and would bring. *You will deny your pleasures until I've had mine. Until I tell you when.*

"Aye." He trailed her neck with his tongue and lowered her to the ground.

Grainna forced his shirt from his shoulders, biting along his collar. Nothing about her touch was soft or loving.

Her warrior's mouth sucked her erect nipple.

"Bite it. Hard."

When he did, fluid rushed to her center. As with all the men she'd had since the change, this one's mind started to feel the bone deep chill of her immortal soul seep into him.

Grainna spread her legs wide and told him to take her. His personal will already waned. She felt his will shift and the questions in his brain started pushing forward.

His hands stilled.

"Take me now!"

When his cock pushed into her, the cold ache of her core vibrated, consuming him.

She closed her eyes and looked through his. Her image stared back at her.

He started to move, unable to stop himself now. Grainna took, demanding him to pound into her flesh without mercy. As his lust shot from him, she placed in his mind her true image, evil, old, wrinkled. As she rode out her pleasure, the warrior no longer felt any lust, any passion. Remorse and an empty void where his soul once lived were replaced with her desires. As she rode over the first wave of climax, Grainna roared her success of adding yet one more warrior to her army.

One more body to remove the MacCoinnichs from *her* land.

~~~~

Tara held her son Briac with one hand while attempting to eat with the other. Briac's smile brought laughter and love from each of the family members.

Amber pushed her plate aside and rose to her feet. "Let me, Auntie Tara. I'm not hungry tonight."

"Are you sure?" Tara allowed Amber to take Briac from her arms.

"Of course."

Liz couldn't be more pleased with the support her sister received from the MacCoinnich family. Her thoughts briefly shifted to her own experience as a new mother. At seventeen, with two parents more disgusted than disappointed with the unexpected pregnancy, she had little, if any, support. Simon's father was whisked away by his parents as soon as they found out he'd knocked her up.

When Liz turned eighteen, she and Simon were kicked out as well. That was the hardest year of her life. She'd saved a little money, moved into an extra room at one of her recently divorced neighbors, and found a position at a daycare center where taking care of Simon and earning enough money to live on worked hand in hand.

But it sucked. Big time.

She held no regrets. Simon was her world.

Liz glanced at him while he tickled Briac's fingers, soliciting a smile from her nephew.

Unlike her, Simon was happy living in the sixteenth century. He adored the unity of this family. Fin sat at the top of his list.

"Simon." Fin licked the grease from his fingers and nodded toward her son. "Elizabeth told me you've been experiencing changes in your gifts."

Simon's eyes shifted to her and then to Cian who sat on his right. "They seem to be changing."

"I understand it is *you* who are changing."

"Is that true, son? Is your body making changes when you see through the animals?" Ian said from the head of the table.

Simon nodded once. "Yes, a little." Simon's eyes lowered to the table, obviously uncomfortable.

"That's wonderful." Lora beamed a smile his way.

"I think so too, Simon." Amber patted his shoulder with support.

"You're a brave lad. This gift is rare, only those with deep wisdom have ever been known to have such power."

"You knew someone else who's had it?" Simon asked.

"I've only heard of it, never seen it with my own eyes. Well, except when Grainna..." Ian didn't finish his sentence. They all knew the battle he thought of. Grainna had murdered the man responsible for her return of powers and then shifted into a bird to escape her death by the MacCoinnich's hand.

"It would be best for you to master your new skill. Practice."

Ian nodded. "Aye, I agree."

"Elizabeth has come up with a suggestion, one I think we should all consider."

Fin seldom came to her side in any discussion. To hear him doing so now gave her heart a small jump.

"What is it?" Myra asked.

Liz glanced at each family member before she spoke. "We need to find a way to practice all our skills. Daily."

"But—"

"Wait, hear me out," she told Ian. "Grainna isn't playing by the same rules we are. She's practicing her powers, using them, mastering them. We're hiding them. I know the position we're in and the secrecy needed, but we need to do something to enhance our gifts to have a fair fight against her."

"The Ancients did say it would take all of us to defeat her."

Liz would never forget how the Ancient, Elise, daughter of Cameron, floated around the room, telling them of their destiny. The ghost-like woman, arrived on the eve of their face-to-face battle with Grainna and told them to band together to defeat the immortal witch. Elise also said that their battle had just begun. Now, so many months later, Liz felt the weight of those words. Grainna ruled Scotland, or attempted to now.

"How do you propose we practice under the eyes of my men? Men who are not Druid, who fear all magic?"

"You guys were able to come up with a silence spell to keep the servants from knowing when you came together in Lizzy's room." Todd, the only non-Druid in the room spoke up, "Maybe you can come up with something similar, bigger."

Myra clasped her husband's hand. "I don't know if we have the power it would take to do that."

"You won't know until you try."

"Which is my point," Lizzy expressed. "Practice makes perfect and all of that. Tara, outside of helping out the vegetable garden, have you used your active powers to do anything?"

"Not really. I removed the path to the cottage where Grainna took me." Tara shivered. Duncan put his arm around his wife.

"Amber, have you attempted to read objects? I know reading people is easy for you, but what about things?" Liz asked.

Todd snorted. "You've watched too much CSI."

"I'm not so sure, Todd. As a cop, did you ever hear of psychics helping an investigation? Missing kids?" Liz referred to the author of *Seventh Sense*.

"I've not tried, Lizzy. I could." Amber's enthusiasm matched her youth.

"How would reading objects help?"

"If we came across something that belonged to Grainna, maybe Amber could feel or learn something about the woman we don't know, a weakness maybe."

"Perhaps."

The private conversation ceased with the arrival of a kitchen maid. The family switched topics so fast that if Liz hadn't noticed Alice's arrival, she would have thought Myra was a little crazy when she blurted out something about the pheasant she ate.

"It is delicious," Tara chimed in.

"I'm still not completely convinced tomatoes aren't poisonous."

"We ate them all the time growing up, didn't we, Lizzy."

"Ah, yeah, all the time."

Alice walked away from the table and through the back door to the kitchens.

"Did you see that?"

Fin cocked his head to the side. "What?"

"Everyone switched gears, just like that." Liz snapped her fingers. "No one missed a beat when Alice came in. That is what needs to happen with our powers. They need to be a part of our existence, daily."

Ian set his hands beside his plate. "I think ye're right, lass. 'Tis time we find a way to work with all our gifts. Even I've noticed my aim off with my lightning strikes."

A rumbling of laughter spread among the family.

"Thank God for small miracles." Todd glanced at his father-in-law. "What? Myra warned me about your powers. You can imagine the nightmares I had thinking you were going to strike me down for..."

For deflowering his daughter before they were married. Liz mused.

Ian's eyes narrowed.

"Never mind."

With Todd's abrupt end of his little speech, everyone laughed harder.

Except for Ian, who appeared to bore holes into Todd's skull with a look. Although Todd and Myra were now married, it hadn't happened soon enough for Ian's liking. His eldest daughter was still his baby.

"Tomorrow I will take Elizabeth, Simon, Myra, and Todd to scout out a private location where we can practice."

Briac fussed in Amber's arms.

Tara dropped her napkin in her lap and pushed away from the table. "Let me take him."

"I'll meet you in Lizzy's room after I feed him and put him down."

"You're tired, Tara. Maybe we should try a circle another night."

"You just finished convincing everyone here that we needed to practice our powers more. We've held off our circle for too long. It's time we flexed our magical muscles."

Duncan snorted a quick laugh. Tara glanced at her husband and heat rose to her cheeks. Liz assumed Duncan's magical muscle was of a sexual nature by the look on Tara's face.

Liz could tell they were talking to each other in their heads, keeping everyone at the table guessing about their private joke. The sacred vows they'd shared when they were married connected their thoughts.

"You're bad, Duncan," Tara said.

Yep, definitely sexual. Liz glanced at Fin, whose eyes monitored her every move.

~~~~

"In this day and in this hour, we call upon the Ancient's power." Their circle cast around them, the candles lit, the lavender soothed.

The women hovered.

"Give us strength to help us see..." Lizzy led the chant, waited for the others to repeat her words.

"Where the hell Grainna is, oh, please."

"Come on, Lizzy, do you really think the Ancients are going to appreciate your humor?" Tara's voice had Lizzy opening her eyes.

"I don't care if they like it or not. We're cleaning up their loophole. Grainna wouldn't be here had they vanquished her completely instead of sending her into the future. Besides, I couldn't come up with anything else that rhymed."

The others repeated her words, even Amber who giggled when she used the word *hell*. Every once in a while Liz needed to remind herself how young Amber was. At thirteen, she was the same age as Simon, but the girl's maturity matched the others in the circle. Liz supposed growing up in medieval Scotland did that to the women. Then again, Grainna, and the threat of death daily, made the children grow up in a hurry.

Liz sat, holding her sisters' hands, all of them silent, concentrating.

Moments passed, minutes.

Nothing.

"This isn't working," Myra stated the obvious.

"I know," Liz bit out, frustrated.

"Should we stop?"

"No," Amber's voice sounded distant, yet she sat there among them, holding hands, hovering above the ground.

Liz watched as Myra and Tara snapped their attention to the youngest. Her eyes closed, her grip firm.

"In this day and in this hour, we call the Ancients for more power. Through the night and through the day, grant a plan to send Grainna away."

Liz nodded toward Myra and Liz before closing her eyes to see if Amber's chant would bring them any images.

Liz watched the dots twinkling behind her eyelids as the fire in the hearth cast images beyond her lids. The waves of fire felt fresh and clean like that of the ocean. The smell of salt water and rush of waves reminded her of home.

I need to concentrate. Dreaming of California isn't going to get rid of Grainna.

"Does anyone feel anything?" Tara asked.

"I see something," Amber told them. "I don't know what it is."

"What does it look like?"

"Grass, thick grass. Moving in the wind, I think."

Liz gritted her teeth. The highlands were filled

with grasses blowing in the wind. "Anything else?"

"Blue. Sky, I think. I'm not sure."

"Anyone else?"

"No, nothing. Myra?" Tara sighed.

"Nay."

Liz opened her eyes and stared at the sisters, disappointment shown on their faces. The family would hope they'd come up with something for their troubles.

They hovered in a circle three feet off the ground.

"At least, this time, I don't have to worry about going into labor when we hit the floor." Tara's words had them all laughing at the memory of her holding her nine-month belly every time they came together.

"Still, I sure would like to know what elevated us so we could use the reverse power to bring us down softly," Myra said.

Liz glanced at the floor. "Are you ready?"

A chorus of voices agreed. They let go of their hands and fell to the floor.

"That was a waste of time." Myra extinguished the candles and picked them up off the floor. "Maybe we should try something new."

"We keep practicing. Daily." Liz removed *Seventh Sense* from under her bed. "There's something else we might want to try."

Amber crawled up onto the bed and rolled onto her stomach. "Outside," she said. "That's a good idea."

"I hadn't suggested it...yet." Amber's ability to read people bordered on scary. "But, yeah. Mayfair talks about the connection with the elements all over this book. She believes that with the industrial revolution and the ability for people to live without ever going outdoors, witches and their powers diminished greatly."

"It makes sense to me."

"I'm not sure about the naked thing, though."

"Ah, what naked thing?" Tara's brow rose in question.

"Mayfair insists that on the holy days of witches, the solstice, etc. that witches in a coven come together, cast their circle and become one with nature." She took a breath. "Naked."

Amber giggled, hiding her innocent smile behind her hand. Myra also began to laugh. When Tara started in, it was all Liz could do to keep from laughing herself. "I'm serious. Not that I'm suggesting we run around in the buff. However, I don't think we should dismiss anything we haven't tried."

"So you are suggesting it."

"No, not really. I'm just saying…it's something we haven't tried."

"Summer solstice is past."

"I don't want to freeze my butt off in winter."

Briac's cry bellowed from down the hall. Tara stood and walked to the door.

"At the very least we should try and cast a circle outdoors and attempt to find Grainna that way."

"Agreed." They nodded together as one before walking out the door.

Chapter Four

The sun heated their ride as they made their way past the village and far away from prying eyes. Fin glanced over toward Simon who rode his mount with ease. Every once in a while Simon would appear deep in thought, then a grin would spread over his features. Fin couldn't help but wonder if Simon spoke with the horse he rode. *What does a horse think?* He wanted to ask. Perhaps he could find a moment alone with the lad to find out.

With her dress hiked high, Elizabeth rode with confidence. He remembered her first attempts on a horse. Her concern for her son's safety took precedence over her desire to ride properly. Now, her back stood rod straight, her eyes focused on her destination. Her breasts bounced with the gait of the animal between her thighs. Fin's chest tightened with the memory of her breasts pressed against him. Their one brief intimate encounter in the stable so many months ago etched into his memory as if it were a defining moment in his life. No, he thought. It wasn't anything more than a mistake. Yet somewhere in the back of his confused mind, he knew she thought about that kiss, that embrace, as much as he. Perhaps more.

Sensing his stare, Liz glanced over at him, lifted her chin, and sat straighter in her saddle. Fin couldn't help but laugh. Her subtle dare and determination simply made him desire her more. He wondered if she knew that.

Then there was Todd, a complete surprise to all of the MacCoinnichs, Myra's husband, savior, and when he sat down and thought about it, lover.

Thinking about his sister in terms of someone's lover had his back teeth grinding. Yet on occasion, like at this very moment, Fin realized his sister was a beautiful and desirable woman. One day she would be a competent mother and mistress of her own home. What he didn't see was the warrior he saw in Liz. But they were just that...warriors. Battle bound fighters for the good of all.

The sound of the waterfall redirected his focus and had him pulling ahead of the others. "We're almost there," he called and signaled for their band to follow him.

After diverting into the thick wood, Fin found the clearing and small shelter the family considered far enough off the route to anyone's land, including their own. He slid from his horse and raised his hand to Simon. "Can you sense any other domestic animals?"

Simon closed his eyes and appeared to count. "No, only ours."

Fin took the reins of his horse and brought them to a low-lying bow of a tree.

"What are you doing?"

Fin narrowed his eyes at Simon. "We don't want them bolting."

Simon patted the neck of his horse. "They don't want to leave. Do you, boy?" He lifted his chin to Fin. "Don't tie them. They want to graze over there in the tall grass under the trees. They won't run away."

Liz bit her lower lip. Fin had to give her credit when she kept her comments to herself. Simon's ability to speak with the animals concerned her a great deal. Watching him morph into one would probably give her nightmares for months once it finally happened.

The men relieved the horses of their saddles while Liz and Myra finished opening up the small cabin's shutters and door to air out the shelter.

Once finished, they glanced at each other waiting for the first to speak.

"I guess I should start," Myra said.

"You've practiced your power more than any of us," Fin pointed out.

"Well," Myra waved her hand over a fallen log and the leaves upon it scattered under the wind she called to clear a place to sit. "My power is convenient. Not like yours, Fin."

Liz brought her eyes to his slowly. "What is your greatest power?"

Fin let one side of his lips turn up into what he was sure resembled a smirk. His fingers spread wide and the ground started to shake. The horses neighed in protest when the ground under their feet rumbled. Simon turned and calmed them with a few words. Liz's mouth opened wide along with her eyes. Fin closed his palms and the earth quieted once again.

"That is so cool, Fin," Simon said.

"Impressive," Liz offered. "I'm not sure how helpful it's going to be, but I'm sure we can work with it."

Fin's ego took a dive, as did his smirk. He bit back his retort and glared at Myra when she chuckled.

"Where should we start?" Simon asked.

Liz stepped to the bank of the stream. "I thought it would be best for us to flex some of our firepower here, where Myra can use her skills to put out any flames that may get out of control."

"How do you suggest I do that?"

"Well, can you lift some of the river water out of its path?"

Myra bit her lip and glanced over to the pounding current. "I've never tried."

"Well then, now's a good time."

Her eyes narrowed when her palms reached toward the water. Fin noticed the small twitch in

33

her left eye as she concentrated on her task. A gust of wind blew past him, leaves whipped from the forest floor, but the water seemed unaffected by her efforts.

Her arms dropped. "I don't think I can do it."

"Try this," Liz scooped water into her palms and tossed it in the air. "When it's in the air, move it." She repeated the action and Myra studied the airborne water. A few drops slid horizontally before falling to the ground.

"Again," Liz commanded.

This time a larger amount of water fell under Myra's command.

"Fin, call a flame in a ball and toss it over here. Myra, try and put the flame out with the water I throw."

Nodding, Fin surged heat from his thoughts and his palm rounded the flame the size of his fist. He tossed the orb lightly to aid Myra in her task. Her aim was off and the fire bent to the river to put itself out.

"Again," Liz called out.

Within a half an hour, the front of Liz's dress dripped with water and Myra stood noticeably taxed from her efforts. Yet as his flames reached over the water, Myra successfully extinguished them.

"I think she needs a break," Todd placed an arm around his wife and kneaded her shoulders between his large hands. "You okay?"

"Aye." But she leaned against him in obvious exhaustion.

Liz turned away from the river and sat on a fallen log. "How do you round the flame into a ball?"

Simon took a seat beside her and listened.

Fin glanced at his audience with a smile, his battered ego pleased that she looked to him for guidance. "First you need to be able to call the flame and hold it above your palm."

"How do you do that?"

Fin reached for Simon's hand and turned it palm up. Out of nowhere, a small round ball of fire emerged from Fin's fingertips. There it hovered less than an inch from his skin. "Think of it as you would a ball of string. As it reaches toward your skin bat it away." He handed the flame over to Simon, ready to intervene if the lad wasn't able to control the orb.

He heard Liz suck in a deep breath when the flame lowered onto her son's palm. She didn't say a word when the flame lowered to an uncomfortable level. Simon extended his fingers and the fire bounced in the air.

"Awesome!" He bounced it again. Fin stood back. Pride filled him as he watched Simon's newfound power.

"Now, toss it to the river."

When the heat sizzled in the water, Simon pivoted toward him grinning ear to ear. "Cool. You gotta try it, Mom. It's so easy."

Elizabeth squared her shoulders and held out her hand. Fin clasped his palm to the back of her hand. Although her hand felt cold and rigid in his, warmth spread throughout his arm. "Relax," he told her, catching her gaze. The spark in her blue eyes hit him right below his belt. He inched his fingertips around to her pulse and noted the rapid tat of her heartbeat. "You need to settle."

"I'm fine."

"No, you're not."

Her eyes narrowed in challenge but instead of her usual rebuttal, she closed her eyes and breathed deep. Her chest elevated and the creamy white of her breasts pushed up through the swooping neckline of her gown. For a brief moment, he wondered if the nipples on her breasts were a rosy pink bud or a darkened tan patch. His groin tightened and his heart rate started to climb.

"*You* need to settle," Liz repeated his words bringing his attention to her eyes that were now open and watching his.

Turning away from her feminine curves, Fin opened his hand to another ball of fire. He lowered the fire to her palm as he had Simon's, all the while holding her hand safely in his. As the ball inched closer she attempted to bat it away, but the flame continued to fall. His hand reached forward controlling the ball once again.

"Try again."

She sighed and stared at the fire, determined.

This time she managed to move the ball, but as it came down a second time, it fell onto her palm. Her fingers automatically curled around it. She let out a screech, and dropped it. Fin shifted to retrieve the ball just as her gown caught fire.

She froze and Simon yelled.

Fin dropped to his knees batting at the flames. "Myra!"

"Shit."

Myra spun toward the river; her hands hovered in the air. A rush of wind fell upon them, along with it a waterfall of moisture. Fin looked up to see Liz's hair streaming down her face. The flames were out, and she stood trembling. From the cold or fear of the dead flames, he couldn't tell.

"Are you okay, lass?"

Liz shook herself. Her lower lip quivered. "Again," she whispered.

~~~~

After lunch, Liz found a secluded spot next to the river out of view of the others. They practiced with the ball of flames continuously until she controlled it long enough to bounce it three times.

However, the task had cost her. She glanced over her shoulder making sure no one watched before kneeling to the water's edge. Forcing her hand into the cold stream, her eyes rolled back, and her back teeth ground together. She lifted her hand and stared at the blistering skin.

It hurt like hell. The burn happened when the flames lapped up her gown. Her reaction scared her. She'd frozen, completely unable to help herself, and that pissed her off. She cursed herself, knowing how freezing up in the face of danger could cost any of them their lives. She wasn't sure why she'd done it. At the time, all she could see was her body burning and her son watching.

"What are you doing?" Fin's voice came from behind her.

She stood quickly, pivoted and hid her hand behind her back. "Washing, I was washing up."

"Why are you holding your hand behind your back?"

She let it fall to her side, but hid the damage from his eyes.

It didn't work. He was beside her in two steps, her hand in his palm and under his scrutiny. "When did we do this?"

"I'm fine, Finlay. No big deal."

"Why didn't you tell me you were scorched? We should have stopped earlier." He tugged her back to the water, immersing her hand as she'd done. "Leave it there."

My pleasure. The relief of the cold water brought a sigh from her lips.

Fin clasped the hem of her gown and proceeded to tear at the material.

"What are you doing?"

"Sit back," he commanded.

She watched as he tore a strip of material free, dunked it in the water, and then reached for her hand. Liz sat back and let him tend to the burn. His tight jaw held back words she knew he wanted to say but didn't. He was angry, that she sensed. But at what?

"We knew that playing with fire could result in one of us getting burned."

"I'd rather it had been me than you."

What could she say to that? She didn't know so she opted for silence.

He finished his task of bandaging her palm and then sat holding her hand. "How does that feel?"

"Better, thank you." Instead of letting go, he helped her to her feet. They stood beside each other, neither speaking. Her complete awareness of him trickled down to her toes. She sucked in her lower lip and did her best not to stare at him. His genuine concern for her well-being thrust them to a different plane. When they sparred, it proved easy to stay away from him. But this, this quiet response chiseled away at the wall she'd built up from the first time they'd set eyes on each other.

He held her hand and stared into her eyes. Liz swayed closer.

Simon called them from the cottage. "We should start back."

Fin nodded and walked her to their horses. He refused to let her do anything other than watch as he assisted Todd and Simon with the saddles.

"Are you okay?" Myra asked gesturing toward her hand.

"It's just a small burn."

"I suppose that's to be expected. We'll have Ma put some salve on it when we return. Overall I think this worked well, don't you?"

Liz tore her eyes away from Fin and smiled. "Yeah, I think so, too. Each time we practice, we'll get better. Tasks will come easier."

"'Tis the best we can do."

"We're ready," Simon called to them.

Liz took the reins and winced. Fin let out a curse. "Hold on."

Without asking, Fin lifted her onto her horse

with ease. "Can you manage with your other hand?"

"I'll be okay."

"Stubborn woman. Like ye'd tell me if it were otherwise." That was better. Fin's accent always thickened when he was angry. Anger was a hell of a lot easier of an emotion to concern herself with than anything resembling affection.

They started back to the keep, slightly battered, certainly exhausted, and more importantly, well practiced.

Tomorrow they could do it all over again.

~~~~

Amber sat with her eyes closed while Tara handed her objects.

"What about this one?"

Amber wrinkled her nose. "'Tis from the kitchen."

It was a cloth used to clean and most likely Cian retrieved it from the cook.

"Yes."

"But I can smell it, Tara. That gave it away."

"Oh, well, how about this?" Into her hands, Tara placed a necklace. One she'd brought with her from the twenty-first century. She'd purchased it at the Renaissance Faire where she'd met Duncan. Cassy, her best friend in that time, bought one just like it.

Amber's smile fell. "'Tis yours I think. You wear it with some sadness." Her eyes opened. "Why does it make you unhappy?"

Tara's fingers curled around the chain. "Not sadness really, just the feeling of a memory that will have to be with me for a lifetime. Like one you have when someone passes. You remember them with love and joy, but a heavy heart in that you'll never see them again."

"I understand."

"More importantly, you're right. Reading

39

objects is getting easier than it was when we started."

"Should we do more?"

Tara nodded and handed her a shirt from Simon.

Cian slipped quietly into the far room of the keep with more objects in his hands. After some time, Amber was able to determine whom the objects belonged to.

"What is your greatest gift, Cian? I'm embarrassed to say I don't know."

Having passed his eighteenth birthday, Cian no longer resembled the awkward boy he was when Tara had first arrived in this century. He towered over her to the height of his brothers and father.

"I'm fairly capable of fire, moving the wind comes with some ease although I'm not nearly as good with it as Myra is. My true gift still eludes me. Sometimes I see images I can't explain, and when I concentrate the images change, but I have no idea what they mean."

"What do you see?"

"Circles, lines. Floating particles that all move in one direction. It feels like a type of energy."

"Can you draw a picture of what you see?"

"I suppose I could."

Somewhere in the back of Tara's mind, his description sounded familiar.

A timid knock sounded on the door to their hideaway. "It's me," Lora's voice called.

Amber scrambled to unlock the door and welcomed her mother.

"Are they back yet?"

"Nay, but I believe they are on their way."

"It does feel that way," Tara said almost to herself. "It's strange how easily we all have connected to the point where we know if someone is near or far, hurt or well."

Just then, Amber glanced down at her hand and brought it up to her eyes. "Lizzy's hurt."

"What?" All three of them pivoted in her direction.

She lifted both palms and studied them. "She will need salve, Ma. 'Tisn't serious. A simple burn."

~~~~

Fin lifted her from the saddle under protest. She hated to admit it, but her palm hurt, big time. The throbbing started shortly after they left their hidden spot in the woods and proceeded to increase in intensity during their ride home. To make matters worse, Tara, Amber, and Lora met them in the courtyard. As Fin's squire helped him with his mount and signaled others to follow, Amber descended upon her like a mother hen, which struck Liz as humorous considering the age of the girl.

"Are ye well?"

"It's nothing, really."

"I think not. My first impression wasn't as strong as it is now. Come inside."

Liz held her injured hand above her heart easing some of the pain. Once inside and sitting on one of the many chairs in the great hall, Liz let Amber unwrap her hand.

Under the bandage, more than a simple burn emerged. In truth, the pain in the center was minimal to that on the edges lapping around to the backside of her hand. There it felt as if fire still licked the sensitive surface.

"Oh, Liz, what happened?" Tara asked, concern filling her voice.

"Nothing, we were practicing with balls of fire. I'm fine."

"I think not." Lora stood and left the room, most likely in search of a medieval remedy to help the pain.

Liz took the opportunity to whisper to Tara.

"Do you have any Advil or Tylenol?"

"I knew you pushed yourself too far." Tara stood and left as well.

Amber shook her head. "You don't have to learn everything overnight." She moved to a pitcher of water and poured some onto a cloth before returning to dab her palm with moisture.

"It hurts doesn't it?" Fin stood in the doorway. His face set with anger.

"What is the matter with everyone? It's just a burn."

"No, Elizabeth, it isn't *just a burn*." Fin lowered his voice and stepped closer. "Burns often lead to infection. With infection comes illness. We don't have your medicine here to fix such a thing in this time."

Liz drew back and her gaze drifted to her burned palm. Already the swelling doubled. She hadn't though of that. The convenience of modern medicine wasn't something she'd concerned herself with in the past. Doctors were nothing more than a few blocks away.

"I'm sure it's okay." But her voice wavered. She didn't meet Fin's eye. She couldn't. He was right. She should have stopped when she felt the first twinge of pain.

Lora returned and lathered her palm with a foul-smelling, sticky, thick liquid. Tara offered her two brown pills from the coveted stash of the futures medicine. Fin turned on his heels and left the room.

Chapter Five

Liz picked at her food with her good hand, thankful that Tara had insisted that they eat with utensils. Managing the lamb on her plate would be much harder if she had to eat it with her fingers.

"What's this?" Todd waved the paper in the air to no one in general.

"Looks like a bad science book to me," Simon replied.

"More like microbiology." Tara glanced at it sideways. "I had nightmares for weeks after that class. Anytime someone sneezed I thought for sure I was going to die of some exotic illness."

"Who drew it?"

"I did," Cian spoke from the far end of the dinner table. "Tara suggested I sketch what I see when I try to draw my power. This is what I see."

Tara raised her hand to Todd. "Can I?"

Todd handed her the picture.

"What do you see, lass?" Duncan asked at her side.

"Cells. See here..." She pushed her plate aside and spread the paper out in front of her. "These lines look like veins or maybe arteries. Here are the cells. Oh, man, if I'm not mistaken, these are mitochondria, a nucleus, everything."

"What do you think it means?"

"Can you tell if it's a human cell or animal?" Todd asked.

"I hated micro. There isn't much that actually stuck after the final. I know it's a cell. Because of the shape I'd say human, but I wouldn't bet money on it."

"What do you think it means?"

Liz glanced over to Ian. "You said our heritage and gifts stem from nature. Earth, fire, water, and wind. Yet Simon is experiencing telepathy with animals, maybe even changing shape into one. Amber's empathic powers aren't exactly any of the elements, neither are Lora's premonitions.

"True. But all Druids have some ability over the elements. The others draw from a deeper connection with the Ancients, with the energy surrounding us."

"Didn't some scientist say that humans only use ten percent of their brain?" Todd asked.

"Yeah."

"Isn't it safe to assume your ancestry has learned to tap into the other ninety percent?"

"I think Todd's right."

Liz glanced at her aching hand. "Lora, was there a time when anyone of you have been really sick?"

"Of course. Duncan and Fin both fell ill after the two of them decided to catch fish from the stream in the middle of winter. Had they used traps, they wouldn't have had a problem, but they thought it would be better to catch the fish with their hands."

Duncan raised a brow to Fin who shrugged.

"What about Cian? When was the last time he was sick?"

Lora tilted her head to the side in thought. "Well, he... No, that was Fin." She spoke almost to herself. "I don't recall a time where Cian was ill. Do you remember anything, Ian?"

He shook his head. "Nay, my boys were always healthy growing up."

"Why do you ask?" Fin asked.

Instead of answering, Liz asked another question. "What about injuries?"

"Well, there is an entirely different story. Cian fell from his horse and hit a fallen tree. His shoulder sustained a deep cut. We worried for days about infection."

"But he didn't develop an infection, did he?"

"Nay."

"What about a scar? Do you have any evidence of your fall, Cian?"

Cian's gaze drifted to his left shoulder. "Nay. I've nothing to remind me of that time in my life."

Liz pushed back her chair and walked around the table. She removed the layers of bandages from her palm.

"What are you doing?"

"Humor me." The idea formed in her head about the meaning of the cells Cian saw. Fin stood and gave her his chair beside his brother.

Cian sent her a worried stare. "What is it you want me to do?"

"Close your eyes." Liz took his hands and held them in the air. She placed her non-injured palm under his without it touching. "Think of those cells, those images you see when you draw from your power."

Cian shifted in his chair, his face bunched up. After a couple deep breaths, the worried lines on his face softened. His breathing evened out. "I see the circles and lines."

"Are they moving?"

"Aye. In an even pattern."

"Like a pulse?"

"Mayhap."

Liz lowered her good hand and brought her scorched one under his open palms. Neither touched him during the transition.

The expression on Cian's face changed. His brows came together. "The color of the image is darker now. Black and gray."

"What was the color before?"

"Red, no pink."

Liz glanced at Fin standing over them.

"Try and remove the dark image from your mind and replace it with the one you had before."

"How?"

"Just try," Fin encouraged. "Concentrate only on the color you see."

Liz nodded to Fin. He knew what she was trying to have Cian do.

Silence settled over them as they watched Cian's expressions. Liz closed her eyes and concentrated on the discomfort of her palm, searching for any change. She took several deep breaths and imagined her body healing itself, imagined Cian's energy flowing into her palm.

"Oh my God," Tara gasped.

Liz's eyes sprung open, as did Cian's.

A blue, glowing, pulsating light surrounded Cian's hands. For a split second, the pain in her hand completely disappeared but when Cian's concentration severed, the pain returned and the light faded.

Fin's hand rested on her shoulder. "Did you feel anything?"

Liz's face beamed, her eyes lit up. "The pain went away. For a minute it felt completely normal."

"What does this mean?"

"It means that you are a healer, Cian."

"How can that be? Women are healers, not men." He didn't seem nearly as excited as she was.

"Oh, don't you go getting all sexist on us. Men can be healers, doctors. In fact, in our century there are more male doctors then women. Surgeons, people that save lives on a daily basis."

Cian settled in his chair deep in thought. He glanced to his father, searching for approval.

"The Ancients said it would take all our powers to bring down Grainna. This newfound gift will aid our fight more than any I think. The ability to heal our wounds inflicted by her is a godsend," Ian boasted.

A slow smile inched over the youngest MacCoinnich son.

"Looks like my injury wasn't so bad after all."

"We still need to be careful, Elizabeth. Cian will need time to learn his power."

Leave it to Fin to be a killjoy. Without acknowledging his words, Liz thrust her palm at Cian once again.

~~~~

They stood in a line, shoulder to shoulder, while Grainna paced. One of them held power, enough to keep her from knowing instantly who it was.

Her eyes met the leader of the caravan. For one brief moment, the man dared to lift his chin in defiance. Grainna narrowed her eyes at his and filled his brain with the image of his limbs ripping from his body. His hands reached to his head before he fell to his knees in pain. Blood dripped from the tear ducts of his eyes.

Grainna moved to the next gypsy in line. "You learn fast," she said to the man whose eyes and head dipped in respect to her power. As she moved, heads bowed, children clung to the legs of their parents whimpering. She slid into the mind of every adult as she passed and found nothing.

She pivoted and stalked several feet before facing them again. "Show yourself to me."

The gypsies' nervous glances spread among them, most unknowing of what she wanted. Grainna raised her hand, intent on destroying them all before a small voice called out. "'Tis I ye search for, m'lady."

From behind one of the boys stood a girl no more than fifteen, her ripped clothing and matted hair evidence of her poverty even among her people. As she stepped forward, the boot of the man at her side kicked out and she sprawled to the ground. The girl turned on him and spit at his feet. "I give myself up for me, Uncle. Not for ye."

The child's defiance sparked interest.

"Devil spawn," he cursed.

"Which devil do ye speak of?" The girl scrambled to her feet and walked toward Grainna with confidence.

Grainna attempted to search the girl's mind but wasn't able to penetrate her will. *Interesting.*

Her uncle, however, was a different story altogether. He despised his niece for her mere existence. Grainna dug deeper and realized why. The man had used the girl to ease his lust and in return, the child professed to know how he would die and when. His fear penetrated his thoughts as he looked upon the child now.

The girl stopped a few feet from Grainna, her chin high.

"You do not fear me. Why?"

"Because ye will not kill me."

"How do you know this?"

She glanced to her people; most didn't meet her gaze. "I see the future. In it, I am here, as are ye."

A true seer. No crystal needed to yield the power. "What is your name?"

"They call me Tatiana." Her words sounded much older than her years. Then again, growing up under the hand of her uncle, she had little choice. "May I call ye Grainna?"

A slow smile spread over her lips. "For now," she replied. "Tell me, seer? When will your uncle die?"

The question brought a gasp from those who stood in line.

Tatiana leveled her eyes to Grainna's. "Before the sun sets."

~~~~

Liz sat beside her sister in the small cottage

by the stream. Outside, Fin, Duncan, and Simon worked together with balls of fire. The only evidence of her brush with a burned palm was a faint red mark. Cian hovered over her palm daily, healing the wound. Within a week, he accepted and used his gift whenever he could without notice.

"Wouldn't it be great if he could help some of those in the village? Mrs. Claunch is constantly doubled over in pain with her arthritis."

"Mrs. Claunch wouldn't mind, but my guess is the reaction of the others would result in something resembling the Salem witch trials." Liz pulled her dress from her shoulders. Under it, she wore shorts and a light camisole.

"I'm jealous."

"Don't be, next time you come remember to wear something under the dress to strip down to."

"I will."

The clothing proved more comfortable, but more than that, Liz didn't want the extra material of long skirts to catch fire a second time.

"Are you ready for this?"

"Is anyone?" The time had come to work with Simon and his gifts.

"He'll be fine."

"God, I hope so. What if he changes and can't figure a way back to himself?"

Tara gave a half smile. "Then it's better we are with him when it happens. Come on, Lizzy, have a little faith in your son."

They stepped out of the cottage together in time to see Duncan clasp a ball of fire into his palm and extinguish the flames. Unlike the rest of them, Duncan's body didn't burn when the flame touched him.

Fin caught sight of her. His eyes swept her frame before they returned to Simon. *Does he approve of my choice of clothing?*

"Ready?"

"I think so."

Duncan and Fin stood on each side of her son. Although it would be a while before Simon measured up to these men physically, Liz couldn't complain about their mentoring of her son. Simon's respect for them was unparalleled with any man from their time. She owed them both, Fin especially, though she hated to admit it.

Sensing her worry, Simon turned to her and said, "Are *you* ready, Mom?"

"Born ready."

You're a terrible liar, Simon spoke in his head.

I know. "I'm fine, really."

"What will you try first?" Tara diverted Lizzy's unease.

"A falcon. I think that would be easiest."

"Is there anything you'd like us to do?" Fin asked.

Simon shook his head and glanced at the sky.

Liz stared on and watched her son close his eyes and steady his breath. Inside his head, he started talking to himself, then aloud for all of them to here.

"I hear the wind calling. Calling me to be a part of it. I stretch my arms..." As he called out the small command for his limbs, Liz concentrated on his fingers. He spread them wide and turned his wrists. "In order to fly, I need to push off with my legs until the wind gathers under my wings..."

Simons face grew strained but nothing happened. He lowered his arms, frustrated.

"It's okay, we can try again later."

"No." Simon tugged his shirt off and over his head and tossed it to the side.

He closed his eyes again and started over.

"The wind will carry me to the tops of the trees. I will see the fish jumping in the stream."

Liz swayed next to her sister, Simon's

50

singsong voice echoing in her head.

He rounded his neck in a stretch and the tissue beneath the surface of his skin started to ripple. Liz swallowed hard, focused on his fingers, and bit her lip. As Simon clasped his hands, his digits disappeared with crisp gray feathers in their place.

She grabbed Tara's hand, eyes wide, praying for something, but not wanting to see her son change. Liz felt her body start to rock back and forth. Unable to tear her eyes away from her son, she held her breath.

Blood rushed from her head.

Simon bent his arms, reached them out and for one brief moment, they fluttered in the form of a bird. Liz heard him calling in his head, he flapped his arms again, and they were whole. Human.

"Lizzy?" Tara called to her, but all she could see was her son down a long dark tunnel. He was Simon again, only stars surrounded him.

Fin turned when Tara called Lizzy's name. As her body started to sway, Fin leapt to her side, catching her before she hit the ground.

The pasty color of her skin brought a wave of panic over him. He lowered her to the ground and brushed her hair from her face. Her head fell to the side.

"Mom, are you okay?"

"She's fine, Simon. Fetch some water."

"Maybe I shouldn't be doing this."

"No, you did fine. Your mother will be okay."

Tara drew Simon by his arm and led him toward the water. "Come on, bird-boy. You know your mom, she'll be all right."

"I really started to change, didn't I?"

"Yes, you did." Tara and her nephew turned away, talking.

Fin glanced at Duncan. "She wasn't ready for

this." And watching her crumble to the earth with her eyes rolling in the back of her head wasn't something Fin had been ready for, either.

Liz stirred under his hand. Slowly, she opened her eyes. After blinking several times, recognition flashed over her face.

"I fainted?"

Fin nodded.

"Simon?"

"Is retrieving water for you."

Liz started to sit up only to fall back on her elbows.

"Lay down."

"I don't want him seeing me like this." Her eyes locked with his. "He'll blame himself."

"I'll keep him away," Duncan told them before leaving their side.

"Dammit."

The simple curse brought a smile to his heart. She was feeling better.

"I thought I could handle this."

"'Tisn't easy to watch him change."

Liz sat up with his help, but he refused to let her stand until her color returned to normal, which it hadn't.

"What if he can't change back, Fin?"

Fin reached over and clasped her trembling hand. "'Tis in his nature to be human, not animal. We have to believe he will be able to change at will."

One small tear dropped from her eye. Her fear ripped him apart. How could he protect her, reassure her that everything would be fine? All he could do was drape an arm around her shoulder and tell her to have faith. The fact that she didn't pull away when he drew her close was a testament of just how deep-seated her concern was.

"He scared the crap out of me," she confessed.

"I know." And he did. He kept his own fears

and feelings to himself.

He sat there holding her in his arms until he felt her trembling subside. When Liz lifted her head from his shoulder, her color had returned to normal. Her gaze rested on his lips and hers opened slightly. Was it an invitation? Would she want his kiss?

God's blood, she was beautiful. At times like this, when she allowed her vulnerability to show, Fin was lost. Without thought of the consequences, he lowered his lips to hers.

At first they simply sat there, lips touching, neither pulling away or moving to deepen the kiss. Then Liz sent out a simple tiny mewling noise that roused his passion and had him kissing her completely. Her mouth opened and her tongue darted into his mouth. Fin wove his fingers in her hair and deepened everything. Plunging where he probably shouldn't, touching where he'd wanted to for months but didn't.

A flame built within him at such an alarming rate, he thought he would combust. Liz's hands and nails dug into his shoulders with desire. Fin brushed his hands down her back and rounded to the side of her breast. She arched toward his touch and quivered. Although he knew the kiss could go no further, he tantalized her more, his tongue danced with hers.

His body hardened, signaling to him to end their embrace. Against his will, he removed his lips from hers. Her eyes remained closed, her breathing as sporadic as his own.

"Oh, God. That shouldn't have..."

Fin placed a finger to her lips, stopping her words. "We both feel this way, Elizabeth. This spark between us."

"Yes, but..."

"No *buts*. Don't think on this now. It will only confuse you further." This was exactly what he told himself, even though his mind worked just as quickly as hers to come up with a logical explanation to their attraction. He didn't, however, want her fighting him. At least not right now. Holding her in his arms, feeling her body responding to his touch... That he wanted.

Oh, yes. *That* he wanted more than water, more than air.

The voices of the others returning cut off their intimacy and conversation. Duncan, Tara, and Simon, soon surrounded them, excitedly talking about Simon's change.

All Fin could think of was how soon he could get Elizabeth back into his arms.

Chapter Six

Tatiana gazed upon the corpse of her uncle, unmoved. With his death, came her birth, or so her visions told her long before this day arrived. Closing her eyes, she rekindled the images that revealed her future.

As night time fell on the eve of the Romani's final journey, a powerful darkness would end her uncle's life and deliver her from the hell he made it.

Her redemption didn't come without cost. Her uncle's death would be the first of many, but Tatiana's suffering would be over as long as she stood beside the dark power.

Tatiana lifted her head and opened her eyes. In her path stood Grainna, a woman who appeared more beautiful than any she'd seen in her fifteen years. Yet that appearance only licked the surface. Under the plane erupted Grainna's aura, which took skill to look past. It held a dark fog and enraptured the battered souls claimed by Grainna's hands. These long dead souls opened their voiceless mouths but no sound came. Tatiana wondered if when Grainna slept these souls spoke in her dreams.

"What do you see, seer?"

Tatiana's head started to ache. The talons of Grainna's power started to find a break in Tatiana's mind and worm their way inside.

"My travels are over. I am to stay with ye."

The nameless souls swirled, and attempted to find the very edges of Grainna's aura. Her brows drew together and jaw tightened. "I have no need to keep a child by my side." These words spat out in anger. Grainna's irritation slammed into

Tatiana's consciousness, forcing a vision clouded in darkness.

She stumbled back, reached for the pain in her head, willing it to stop. The vision drew from the past and not of the future. "I am not Druid," Tatiana managed, though her skull felt as if it were splitting in two. "Killing me would not bring ye my visions."

Grainna flew upon her, her breath streamed down her neck.

Tatiana cowered.

"How do you read my thoughts?"

"I do not read ye, Grainna. I see the past." Even as the words tumbled from Tatiana's lips, she knew this was only partially true.

The black of her eyes swirled in thought.

"I can be yer eyes of the future. So long as ye let me live."

Grainna reared back, considered her words. As her hand lifted, Tatiana bit hard on her lip, drawing blood, but didn't cower a second time.

"I can kill you now."

"I know."

But death didn't come when Grainna placed her palm on her head. Instead, numbness replaced the pain her vision brought.

"Thank ye."

"Do not thank me yet, seer."

As Grainna turned away, the Romani, who stood by and watched the entire scene, parted in her path. Tatiana knew Grainna would not be destroying her any time soon.

~~~~

Sweat poured off Fin's brow under the bright afternoon sun. Surprisingly, Todd required his full attention during their routine of sparring. His ability with a sword increased every day. Of all of them, Todd needed this extra training in order to survive a fight. For that reason, Fin held little back. His sister's happiness depended on Todd's life.

A shout bellowed from the tower. A signal rose in the air, telling all who listened that a rider approached.

Fin climbed the steps to view the unexpected visitor. As the rider drew near, the tension in his shoulders dissipated. The amber-and-black mantle claimed the knight belonged. Fin ordered the gates down and instructed his squire to bring his father.

"Who is it?" The question came from Todd.

"I cannot tell. He is too far away."

As the rider drew closer, Fin's hand slipped from his sword at his hip and his lips pulled into a grin.

Logan.

Logan jumped from his horse the second he came to a halt. His bearded face dirty from riding didn't hide his appreciation to be home.

A squire caught the reins Logan tossed his way before addressing him. "God's teeth, 'tis good to see ye, *my lord.*"

Fin's baritone laugh shook the walls. "As a second son, I'll never be your lord, Logan." The men clasped hands with forearms with genuine affection.

"How long has it been?"

"Near three years."

"Is that even possible?" Fin knew it was.

"Aye."

A sharp squeal came from the shadows. Myra's voice rose while she ran into the courtyard. Fin stepped away when she affectionately greeted Logan with a hug. Todd kept a watchful eye on the exchange, but said nothing.

"You're home!"

Logan put her back down. "I would have been sooner if I skirted outside of Lancaster. They kept me there nearly a week."

"Everything is quiet, is it not?"

"Aye, but there is news from your neighbors."

Fin wanted to ask what information he had, but Todd stepped forward and placed his arm around his sister's waist.

Logan's eyes took in the exchange.

"Seems I've missed much."

"Logan Douglass, this is Todd Blakely, my husband."

Logan accepted Todd's hand.

"Ye have a wonderful prize in a bride such as Myra."

"Yes, *I* do."

Fin laughed. Todd's reply and possession was the instinctive reaction of many men when it came to Logan. His fair features and easy smile won him many favors among the women. In truth, Myra probably sat on a short list of women not interested in his prowess.

"Does Gregor know you've arrived?"

Logan shook his head.

"I'll find him," she said before turning back to the keep.

"I hear Duncan has married and sired a son."

Fin walked with him and Todd out of the heat. "We've had a productive year."

Todd snorted by his side, but said nothing.

Inside the cool, stone walls of the great hall, Fin led Logan in and took a seat. "Alice!" he hollered.

Soon the kitchen maid scurried into the room, towel in hand. "Aye?"

"Fetch some ale and food for our traveler."

Alice nodded and returned to the kitchen.

The sound of slippered feet drew from the stairs. All eyes glanced to see who came. When Fin recognized Elizabeth's gown, warmth settled in pit of his stomach. They'd said little since their exchange the day before.

58

"Who is this bonny lass gracing yer home?"

The mirth in Logan's tone brought Fin's eyes to him. The inquisitive stare and lift in his lips leapt in his throat with a passing wave of jealousy. "'Tis Duncan's sister-in-law."

"Mom." Simon ran from around the corner, cutting off Elizabeth's entrance to the room.

Logan leaned over. "Is her husband here as well?"

"Nay, Elizabeth is...widowed." Fin knew where the questions were going and didn't care for them at all. Logan's gaze swept her frame from across the room. The man already calculated his chances with her. Before he could set the man back, Elizabeth stepped into the room with Simon at her side. Logan shot to his feet, wiping a hand over his overgrown beard.

Simon opened his mouth to say something before he glanced at his mother. Fin knew they spoke to each other inside their heads. Liz's eyes fell on Logan and her hand caught Simon's attention.

"Seems we have company, Simon. Perhaps the cottage will need to wait for a day or two."

Fin caught her gaze and gave a quick nod of approval.

"An introduction, Finlay?"

Logan chuckled. Fin extended a hand toward Logan. "Logan Douglass, this is Lady Elizabeth McAllister. Logan Douglass is son to—"

A robust bellow came from the main hall as Ian, Gregor, and Lora added to the growing numbers in the room. They turned and watched Gregor step forward.

"Son, 'tis good to see ye!"

Gregor pulled his son into a fierce hug, smiles and pats on the back came from all sides. Duncan arrived with Tara on his arm. Before long they all stood and welcomed their treasured friend.

Elizabeth and Tara stood to the side and watched. Only when Fin moved closer did he hear a shimmer of their conversation. "...what do they put in the water here?"

"I don't know. Scotland sure grows her men big."

Liz laughed at her sister's comment before realizing that Fin stood near enough to hear. His eyes darted away.

"You have word from Lancaster?" Fin asked.

Logan accepted the ale from Alice with a wink before answering his question. "Aye. Seems Lancaster has finally found someone to take Regina off his hands."

"Who is the *lucky* groom?" Fin's sarcasm grew thick.

"Finlay MacCoinnich, Regina is a fine lass, show some respect," Lora scolded.

Ian laughed. "Fin would be more pleased than any of us to know she's accepted a husband. Perhaps now she'll stop staring at him."

Fin endured the jesting, knowing how true the words were. Regina's attempts to gain his attention in the past weren't exactly subtle.

"Who is the man?" Fin asked again.

"A Lord Brisbane from the south."

"English?" Ian asked.

"Half, methinks. Regina will be his second wife."

"I'll bet she's not pleased with that."

"'Tis Lancaster's arrangement. He's asking all his allies to join him for their festivities." Logan's eyes sat on Elizabeth. His grin spread. The hair on the back of Fin's nape stood up.

"All his allies? Why?"

"There are rumors of an unsettling in the lowlands."

Eyes shifted around the room. Liz slid her gaze to his in question.

"Unsettling?" Ian leaned forward.

"Perhaps we should discuss politics after Logan has settled and a meal can be taken in honor of his homecoming," Duncan said, quickly changing the subject. From the expression on Liz and Tara's faces, their worry far exceeded his. Their battles since arriving in his century had all been magical. Yet he knew from numerous conversations with his brother that their concern over warring with fellow men paralyzed them with fear. Fin wondered if their knowledge of history was the cause.

"Well said, Duncan."

"I suppose that's our cue to leave." Liz stood and drew her sister up with her. "It's been a pleasure to meet you, Logan."

Logan tilted his head. "The pleasure is all mine, my lady."

A blush reached Liz's face before leaving the room. Myra and Lora stepped toward the kitchen and Simon and Amber took the hint and disappeared as well.

"Seems yer household has doubled since I was last here."

"Our family has grown," Ian said simply.

"Now that the women have gone, tell us. Is there trouble?"

"In truth, I do not know. Lancaster didn't seek my counsel but informed me that he wanted yours, Ian. He said it had been far too long since the allies had gathered and the excuse of a wedding would cloak the task."

"It sounds as if he thinks spies are watching."

"Maybe."

"When is this wedding to take place?"

"The end of next month. Brisbane's land is a week's ride."

Fin pulled in a deep breath and glanced around the room. This isn't what they needed with

Grainna's wrath as well.

"Have I missed something? Is there other trouble?"

Gregor lifted a brow. "There have been…strange happenings here."

Fin tensed.

"I'm sure these will pass, Gregor. However, we will need to leave the keep well guarded in our absence." Ian stood, ending their discussion. "Welcome home, Logan. After our evening meal we'll discuss more of your travels over something a little stronger than this." Ian put his cup of ale on the table before leaving the room.

~~~~

"Do we have to go?"

"Of course," Myra explained. "When an ally requests your presence, 'tis expected. Lord Lancaster may have sired worthless children, but he is still a man with great power. We wouldn't want him as our enemy."

Liz's head started to pound. "God, don't we have enough to worry about?" Myra sat beside her and Tara explaining the finer points of medieval etiquette. "What does that give us, four weeks to get ready? Being out in the open where Grainna can find us sounds like too big a risk."

"It does feel like we'll be exposed."

"Will we go alone?" Tara asked.

Myra's eyes grew large. "No! We'll travel in the greatest numbers we can. If Lancaster worries of trouble, and his message sounds as if he's concerned, going alone could prove deadly."

"Then we'll have to step up our practice. I don't want Simon going all feathery in a crowd of people."

"Try not to worry. Lancaster's concern may simply be about what has been happening here."

"Or maybe Grainna's been attacking more

than just us."

"I understand that Brisbane's land is south and closer to the coast. At least we'll enjoy some of the sea during our travels."

Tara sighed, "God, I miss the ocean."

Liz shook her head. "I never thought I'd move from California. I haven't been to the beach since Simon went to surf camp when he was ten."

"Our beach is cold and much more violent than yours."

Liz cocked her head to the side. "No chance for a quick dip then, huh?"

"You mean swim?"

"Yes."

"I doubt you'd want to, even if we could find a quiet cove."

Liz couldn't help but feel a bit more liberated knowing that their trip would get her away from the keep. Having grown up and living her entire life in suburbia, rushing from one thing to another, it would be nice to move around again. The thought of even getting her feet in the sand brought a smile to her face.

"What is it?"

"I'm daydreaming."

"About Fin?"

"No." But Myra smiled.

"Did you see him glaring at Logan?" Tara's question sounded innocent enough, but Liz knew better.

"Was he?"

"Don't play dumb to me. What is going on with you two?"

Liz stood and tried her best to hide the heat flooding her cheeks. It didn't work.

"Oh my God, he kissed you again, didn't he?"

A rebuttal died on her lips.

"Lizzy, why didn't you tell us?"

"What's there to say?"

Tara rolled her eyes. "How about, when? Where? How far did it go?"

"My God, I think we're fourteen again."

"Give it up. We're all sisters here."

"We've had this discussion before, Tara. Fin and I barely get along."

Tara folded her arms across her chest and sent her a knowing smile.

"We fight all the time."

Tara's eyes slid to Myra. Together they said nothing and at the same time, everything.

"It's chemistry. Nothing else." Bubbling over in the flask, chemistry. Spontaneous combustion, chemistry.

"You hated chemistry."

Liz shut her eyes and took a deep breath. "Fin's attraction to me would end the second either of us gave in." Liz knew his type.

"Are you going to give in?"

Good question. "Maybe I should. Scratch the itch and move on." The plan held a certain appeal, kind of like addressing the elephant in the room in order to get around it.

"Hmm."

Liz's gaze settled on her sister's smug look. "What?"

Tara put her hands in the air in mock surrender. "I didn't say anything!"

But you thought something.

Chapter Seven

Liz stepped out of the kitchen, nearly falling over Logan in her path. "I'm sorry."

"'Tis I who's in your way, my lady."

"It's Liz." She didn't think she'd ever get use to people calling her *my lady*.

Logan's brow rose, resulting in Liz wondering if she should have given him the freedom to call her by her given name.

"Such a wonderful name, Liz." Logan lifted a hand and brought it up to her cheek.

For a minute, Liz stood in absolute shock. It had been so long since a man, other than Fin, had taken interest in her on a physical level that she didn't see it coming. But with Logan's blatant stare and her lack of backing away, the man took it as an invitation and moved closer. Liz retreated and let her smile fall.

"I should check on my son."

Logan dropped his hand, but not his cocky smile. His frame rivaled Fin's, wide shouldered and narrow hipped. He was completely easy on the eyes, and in another life, Liz would welcome his advance. Now, she simply saw a man who wasn't Fin.

"Ye have a fine son. It must be difficult caring for him on yer own."

"Simon makes it easy."

"Yer pride in him shows." Logan's gaze dropped to the bodice of her dress, his thoughts clear for her to see. The modern woman in her wanted to suggest the man talk to her face and not her breasts, but thought that maybe she was a being a bit harsh. Considering everyone was making such a fuss over him, Liz said nothing.

"I should check on him." Liz lowered her eyes and stepped toward him, hoping he'd move. For one brief moment Logan didn't. On a sigh he pivoted, giving her very little room to walk around him.

She felt the weight of his stare on her back. She wanted to be pissy about his attention, but her ego had her smiling.

"What's so funny, Elizabeth?"

Fin's tone stopped her cold. "Fin?"

His eyes bored into hers and they were not happy.

Behind her, she heard Logan's retreat. Once the door closed, Fin reached out, took her by the elbow, and pulled her into a vacant room.

The minute they were alone, she tried to tug her arm away from Fin, but found his iron grip impossible to escape.

"What is wrong with you?" he spit.

"I could ask you the same thing."

"Being alone with a man who isn't your kin leaves room for rumors."

Liz felt every breath he took, and they came quickly. His angry eyes searched hers.

"You're not my keeper, Fin."

His jaw clenched and he took a step closer.

Liz swallowed and backed up. Only the wall stopped her from moving farther. The predatory glare in his eye sent a shiver down her spine.

"Logan's attention shouldn't be encouraged."

Fin *was* jealous. And ticked. The combination took her back.

"He's only flirting, Fin."

Verbalizing what they both saw brought a flash of emotion over his features. "Does it please you to have his interest?"

His knee brushed against her long skirt. The heat off his body bearing down on hers brought tiny sparks of awareness all over the surface of her skin.

"It doesn't suck to know someone desires you," she managed.

Fin dropped her elbow and placed his palm on the wall behind her. His other hand brushed along her face with one long knuckle. His touch was slow, calculated. He bent forward until his breath touch her cheek. She couldn't control leaning into to his touch any more than she could control the need to swallow.

"I'll be happy to give you more attention, Elizabeth," his words whispered over her lips, hovering, waiting, until finally they met. The spicy taste of liquor swept into her mouth with his tongue. His massive frame leaned into hers scorching everywhere they touched.

Every coherent thought fled and Liz arched into him with a whimper. This was good. So very, very good. Her body felt alive with excitement and anticipation of where he would touch next.

His hand slid down her waist, kneading her flesh through the cloth. Fin lifted her skirt until she felt his rough fingers touch bare skin. His fevered kiss continued, never letting her up for air. Liz wrapped her arm around his back and pressed closer.

The proverbial elephant in the room was definitely being talked about now, maybe not talked about so much as explored.

Fin moved his lips to the side of her neck. A sharp nibble on the lobe of her ear shot straight to her core and had her writhing with desire.

"Is this the attention you need? Is this what you want?" His words still sounded angry, but his mouth was touching her in a place she hardly remembered was there.

Fin's hand, under her skirt, rounded over her hip and squeezed. "Is it, Elizabeth?"

What was the question?

"Or maybe this is what you want." Fin's nimble fingers rounded in front and met the heat pooling at her center. When the length of one finger slid up and into her body, her knees buckled, bringing her in closer contact with his whole hand. "Oh, God."

Liz's head rolled back, eyes closed, while she writhed closer.

Fin drew circles with his thumb while penetrating her in seductive strokes.

Liz felt his erection strain against the fabric separating them. As her hand slipped down and brushed against his length her breath caught. Fin's fingers and thumb moved faster. Her long overdue orgasm, which started deep in the pit of her stomach, now blossomed with every pass of his hand. His heated breath marched in time with hers until she felt her passion swell.

Her body climbed over the invisible wall and stilled right as Fin pushed her over.

Body shuddering, Liz muffled her cries of release into his shoulder. Her body clenched around his magical fingers.

Fin held her there, pinned against the wall, his breath against her neck as the tremors subsided.

His hand slipped away, leaving her damp and empty.

When she finally worked up the nerve to open her eyes, Fin stared down at her. Knowing. He brought his fingers to his mouth and drew the digit past his lips.

For a moment, Liz felt her body clench all over again.

"I'll give you all the attention you need, Elizabeth."

Fin pushed away and her skirt fell in place. He licked his lips before opening the door and leaving the room.

Liz let her frame slide down the wall until she sat firmly on the floor. Her gaze focused on a simple unlit candle across the room. Before her breath resumed its normal pattern, her adrenaline rose again.

"The gall of that man," she hissed between clenched teeth.

The candle sparked to life. Her eyes flew to another. It too started to glow.

Surprisingly, her thoughts weren't of despair or disapproval so much as irritation over his control. Control over her.

She'd had no control and at the time didn't care that he took it all. What was wrong with her? She should be horrified with her submissive body, but she wasn't. She should be raging war over who had the better control over their bodies, but she couldn't.

She inched up the wall, slimmed her skirts over her frame, and pictured Fin's hands on her again.

~~~~

Preparing for their journey south was equivalent to a move of a household. Ian mandated that the elderly and sick prepare to move into the lower rooms of the keep, a precaution against Grainna's possible attack.

Between the extra eyes and the continued attention of Logan, Liz relished the opportunity of escape to the cottage with Simon. However, Fin made certain his presence was in the mix. Only this time, Ian would join them, eliminating Liz's opportunity of revenge on Fin.

"Do you know of our history, lass? Of what Scotland will endure over the years?"

They were still over a mile from their destination when Ian started posing his questions.

"No, not really. There were a few movies about

Scotland. I do know that the kilts get shorter."

"Ahh, yes. Duncan and Fin said as much from their travels in your time."

"Makes you wonder, doesn't it?"

"I don't follow your meaning, lass."

Liz lifted her lips in a smile. "Well, you sent Duncan and Fin ahead in time..."

"The Ancients told us to send them."

"Either way, they went ahead in time, learned that their clothing didn't fit the image my generation assumed of them and their dress altered because of it. Makes you wonder if the reason kilts shortened is because of Duncan and Fin going forward in time."

Ian's brows pinched in thought. "Time travel holds many responsibilities. 'Tis why we were concerned when you came with Myra."

So many months ago when she'd forced Myra to bring her and Simon to visit Tara after Liz learned the truth about her sister's disappearance. Fin didn't welcome her at all, Ian only marginally.

"I think the Ancients wanted Simon and me here."

Ian nodded. "Agreed."

"Will we bring the stones with us when we travel?"

"I've considered that. Leaving them poses a threat, so does taking them. If either results in Grainna obtaining them, the consequences could be devastating."

"Maybe we should take one, leave one, and hide the other," Simon suggested.

Ian slid into a rare smile. "You know, lad, your astute wisdom will take you far."

Simon sat straighter in his saddle with Ian's praise. Liz's heart lifted when her son's smile beamed. The MacCoinnichs were a good influence on him.

"Where do you suggest we hide it in the keep?"

Fin asked Simon, further widening his grin.

Before answering, he appeared to consider all the options. "Well, I don't think it needs to be in any kind of safe, or under a bed. If I were Grainna that would be the first place I'd look. I'd hide them in plain sight. You know, a paperweight on a desk or something simple like that."

Liz thought back on the silly craft projects she'd put together in the mindless hours of entertaining the kids at the daycare. "We could always paint one with dye and make it look like a Father's Day gift from Amber."

"Oh, yeah. I remember painting a face on a rock and giving it to you, Mom. You called it a pet rock."

Liz laughed. "Yeah, I did." She'd kept that rock nestled into the far reaches of her nightstand in her apartment. Of course, her apartment was most likely turned back over to the landlord by now, her belongings sold to make up for lost rent. She and Simon were probably on some missing person's list along with Todd and Tara. Returning now would result in countless questions and explanations.

They neared the cabin and went through the ritual of setting the horses to graze while opening up the shelter. Without another woman in their company, Liz felt a little awkward stripping down to her usual shorts and T-shirt and opted to stay in her full-length dress. Ian's propriety really didn't allow for twenty-first century clothing anyway.

Then there was Fin.

They didn't breathe a word of their encounter. But images of him flooded her mind constantly. Branding her. Even now, he glanced her way long enough for Liz to feel his eyes on her before skirting his gaze in the opposite direction. He thought he was being coy. She knew better.

"Shall we try the fireballs again?" Fin asked

71

once everything settled.

Liz caught Simon out of the corner of her eye, his shoulders fell with Fin's suggestion. He wanted to try shifting again. He kept the words from his mind and therefore didn't tell her his desires directly, but she knew he wanted to. On the same level, Fin appeared to be putting off the inevitable. Probably because of how she'd reacted to Simon's change the last time.

"I'd rather work with Simon."

"Are you sure?"

Liz took a deep breath and one firm nod. "Yes." Although her pulse climbed, it wasn't like before.

Ian stepped in and placed a hand on Simon's shoulder. "If you do change, Simon, don't fly farther than that branch there." He pointed to a nearby tree, its first sturdy branch no more than twelve feet from the ground. "If you were to change back outside of your will, a longer fall could be quite painful."

Liz hadn't thought of that. From the expression on Simon's face, neither had he.

"Good point."

Ian stood back.

Fin took a position beside her. Although they had an unresolved battle to fight, now wasn't the time. All eyes centered on her son.

Simon removed his shirt and closed his eyes before opened his arms wide. Small mumbled whispers trickled out from his lips. His thoughts sang in her head. *I'm a bird. Big and powerful. My talons stretch and want to claw into the top of that tree.*

Liz's gaze drifted to the top of the tree. It was forty feet high. She must have flinched because both Ian and Fin rested a hand on her arm in reassurance.

When she glanced back at Simon, she felt his hesitation, his concern for her.

You can do this, Simon. Your big, powerful with wings the size of an airplane. You can do this!

He stood taller and started over.

Liz chanted with him. His neck bubbled as it had before. A mirage blurred in front of her eyes as Simon moved his arms like that of a bird, feathers sprang forth and then disappeared.

He tried again.

Fin's grip on her arm tightened. Concerned, but saying nothing.

Simon chanted again and everyone held their breath.

As the skin on his back bubbled, Liz coaxed him again. *Let go and become the bird.*

And he did.

One minute he stood there, then the rest of his form shifted, morphed into that of the falcon he wanted to be. His pants fell from his taloned feet and pooled where he once stood. For a brief second, Simon simply stood there as a bird. Then, without warning, he let out a screech, spread his wings, and took flight.

"Oh my God." Liz leapt to follow him fearful he couldn't hear or understand her. Ian's arm slipped from hers, but Fin held tight, grasping her fingers. Simon whirled above her head, Liz was desperate to catch him.

"God's teeth, Lizzy, what are you doing?"

She looked over at Fin who yelled his question. Only he was below her by a foot, his hand still managing to hold onto her hand. Dear lord, she hovered in mid air. Just as all the sisters did when they came together in a circle.

In a flash, all thoughts of Simon disappeared, her concern shifted. She fell to the ground and stumbled to her knees.

Are you all right?

"I'm fine," she cried before realizing Simon posed the question in her head. "You can hear me?"

Oh, man this is so friggin' awesome, Mom. Wow!

Simon swooped down and back up again.

"Is Simon talking to you?" Ian asked.

"Yes. Thank God!"

Fin's eyes skirted away from her, but only briefly. "Ask him how he feels."

I feel great. I can see everything from up here.

"He's fine. Excited to be flying."

"You understand us?" Ian turned in a circle, keeping Simon in sight.

Simon answered in a squawk before landing on the designated perch.

Can I go higher, Mom?

"Please don't, Simon. I know you're excited but let's play this safe."

Okay.

His lack of an argument surprised her.

I did it.

"You did it."

Fin helped her to her feet and held her arm.

"Is your vision sharper, Simon?"

Simon peered toward the stream and back to them. *Oh, yeah.* He took off again, aiming toward something just above the water. He swooped down, caught a large fish, and returned. *Lunch is on me.*

Liz started to laugh. Ian clapped his hands together one time and cheered.

"I can't believe it."

Simon flew over to a fallen log before hopping to the ground. *I'm gonna try and change back.*

"Good idea." Liz told the others his intentions.

Her son's voice echoed but only twice. *I'm human again. With legs to run with and hands and feet.*

His change back came quickly. Had she blinked, Liz would have missed it. But she hadn't. His pink skin glistened as if the feathers had never been there. He was whole.

Liz started running toward him before he cried in horror, "Mom, stop looking! I'm naked!"

She scrambled to a stop and turned her back to him. His delicate teenage modesty needed some privacy. She had to laugh. Her son had shifted into a bird, flew into the trees, caught a fish with talons and not a pole, and now stood worried that she'd see his private parts. Parts she'd diapered and bathed too many times to count.

She laughed harder.

Her pulse returned to normal while she listened to her son gathering his clothes and putting them on. He did it. Really did it. The possibility held nothing to the reality.

Simon, her son, was a shifter.

"Okay, you can look now."

His smile reached to the far corners of his eyes. Fin clasped his back beaming with pride.

"It was amazing up there, Mom."

"I'll bet. How did your body feel?"

Simon cocked his head to the side. "Normal, I guess. I didn't really think about it once I changed." Simon put a hand to his stomach. "I'm starving. Are we gonna eat that fish?"

"We just got here."

"Yeah, well, I don't like sushi."

Simon walked over to the small ring of rocks and tossed his hands toward the half-burnt logs. Inside a large flame leapt to life. He stepped back to avoid the fire reaching toward his long hair.

"Wow. I didn't mean for it to be so big."

Ian tossed the fish to Simon. It slipped through his fingers a few times before he caught hold of it. "Once your true gift is realized, your others enhance. Be careful in everything you do."

Simon nodded.

Ian helped Simon with the dead fish while she stared on.

"What happened back there?" Fin whispered in her ear, his breath a warm caress on her neck.

Liz glanced over her shoulder. "I don't know."

"You were hovering above the ground. Your hand tugged against mine. Had I let go, you might have flown as high as Simon."

A chill shot to her head. "I'm sure it's a fluke. I didn't try to make it happen." Even as the words left her mouth, Liz knew they were only half-true. She hadn't tried, but it wasn't a fluke. Just as Simon said morphing into an animal felt normal, so had hovering above the ground.

Fin grunted in disbelief. "I think not."

"Still, I don't think I could repeat it."

"Perhaps you should try."

"Not today. Today is for Simon."

Ian laughed at something Simon said before placing the fish on the fire.

"He did well." Fin stepped in, placed a hand on her back.

She flinched on impulse.

"I won't hurt you." Fin rested his hand more firmly, his fingers fanned out to small of her back.

When her knees weakened, Fin chuckled.

Liz scrambled away from his arm and rounded on him, angry with herself for her feminine desire, angry with him for his candor.

"Listen," she hissed. "I say when and where if I want to be touched."

"Really?" Fin's hand fell, his brow lifted in amusement.

"Really!"

"So you did want my touch the other day."

Oh God, yes. "No. Yes."

"Which is it, Elizabeth?"

His cocky smile infuriated her. Damn him. "I have needs too, Fin. Only I say who has the right to fulfill them."

His smile fell. Confusion passed over his face.

"'Tis Logan you wanted?"

Liz rolled her eyes and held in her instant denial. The longer she said nothing, the angrier he became. Satisfaction at his obvious discomfort kept her smiling.

"Well? Is it?"

Watching his body tense nearly had her laughing. When she turned to walk away, Fin caught her arm in his firm grip.

"I asked you a question."

Trying not to call attention of them, Liz grasped his hand and squeezed. "The next time you touch me...*if* you touch me, it will be when I choose."

"Hey, Mom? Come here," Simon called from the fire pit.

Fin let her arm go but kept her eyes glued to his.

"'Tisn't *if*, lass. 'Tis when."

Chapter Eight

"They're traveling?"

"'Tis what I see."

Grainna slid a wicked grin over her lips. "Where do they head?"

"West."

Simple direct answers. If only all her minions would follow Tatiana's example. She knew most stuttered and rambled out of fear. Little did they know how close to death they came when they couldn't answer a simple question.

"Who guards the keep?"

"I do not know. My visions only show the family."

Grainna barged into Tatiana's mind to see if she lied. Though she had no reason to, Grainna searched anyway. To the girl's credit, she didn't flinch with the pain Grainna's intrusion provoked.

Tatiana's shoulders slumped, she sighed in relief once Grainna left her mind.

The girl's appearance improved in the short time she'd been under her thumb. A simple bath and clean clothes worked wonders. The girl had worked hard to disguise her beauty when her uncle was alive. Now, without the threat of rape and abuse, she took better care of herself.

With a wave of her hand, Grainna dismissed the girl.

Tatiana hesitated.

"What is it?"

"I...I have a request."

"Oh, really?" No one requested anything of her. They wouldn't dare.

"Aye."

"Be quick then."

"The knight, the one ye call Sampson."

"What about him?"

"He, he watches me."

Grainna tilted her chin high. "You mean he lusts after you."

Tatiana swallowed and held her hands tight to her side.

Funny, the girl feared the man, but not the witch.

"Why should I care?"

Horror flashed and dread filled Tatiana's aura.

"Please. I beg ye not to let him touch me. I will have no man touch me."

"Then stop him."

"How? He is bigger, stronger. How can I stop him?"

Grainna stood and reached her hand out. A dagger from across the room flew to her hand and landed safely in her palm.

"If he comes to you, wait until he is close, then use this to ward him off."

"What if I kill him? What if he uses the knife on me?" Her face went pale.

"I need all my men. Kill him and I will kill you! Cut him, make him bleed." Grainna bent close and whispered her next words. "Cut off his manhood if you must. He will not touch you again."

Tatiana's fear slammed into Grainna's senses. Warmth spread over her body.

~~~~

After a full day's ride, Fin oversaw the squires and the few servants they brought along for their comfort. Accustomed to the outdoor accommodations, the knights sparked a fire and gathered around it while a meal was prepared.

He glanced over to where Todd and Duncan were helping erect a tent for the women. The men would sleep under the stars. Thankfully, the weather cooperated with their journey. Then again, perhaps his father helped with the lack of rain. Fin wondered if any of the knights noticed that the journeys with the family were met with perfect accommodations from above. No one said a thing if they did.

Myra laughed at something Todd said. Her smile warmed his heart. She noticed his attention and walked his way.

"What is it you're smiling about?" she asked.

"Nothing."

She rolled her eyes, a gesture she picked up from either Lizzy or Tara. "I know you, Fin, better than you know yourself I'd venture. You are smiling for a reason."

"I'm pleased you're happy." He nodded toward her husband. "'Tis good you found each other."

"So you do approve?"

Fin's eyes pinched together. "Of course. I like Todd."

"Considering you introduced yourself to him with your fist, I wondered if you supported our marriage."

"Yes, well, Todd deserved it." The man was lucky Fin didn't do more than blacken his eye. He had taken Myra's innocence. 'Twas up to him to put the man in his place. Never mind the fact that Myra loved him and hadn't been forced into his bed. A man should never take advantage of a woman in Myra's position.

Myra scoffed. "All is right now. Well, mostly." Her eyes skimmed toward Lizzy and Simon. Both sat next to the fire and appeared tired from their long ride.

"Why do you say that?"

"It would be nice to have Grainna behind us. Then perhaps everyone could settle down."

Fin forced his gaze from Liz and focused on his sister. "I believe everyone is settling in nicely, considering the circumstances."

"You think so? I know Simon is comfortable here, among us and in our time. But Lizzy is constantly talking about how her life will be once she returns to the twenty-first century."

"Without the stones, Liz isn't able to return." Not that he needed to state the obvious, but saying it aloud comforted him. He would deny why, if asked, but Myra spared him that inquisition.

"We'll find them. And when we do, I think she'll leave, unless of course, she finds a reason to stay."

"Her family is here. Isn't that reason enough?"

"Perhaps."

Deep in the pit of his stomach, an empty ache started to grow. He pushed the uncomfortable feeling aside and left his sister to assist with the tent.

~~~~

With the camp set, and the fires burning, the hearty scent of simmering food wafted in the air.

"God, I'm hungry," Liz said while rubbing her palms over her backside. "And my ass is so sore. I think I may opt to walk tomorrow."

Tara glanced up from where she sat nursing her son. "Try carrying this one around with you."

They pulled a small wagon along with them, in which they took turns riding. A small bed lay inside the wagon, giving Briac some time out of Tara's arms. A sling helped keep him close when she rode her horse.

"I'd be happy to carry him tomorrow," Liz offered.

"I'll take you up on it."

Liz paced the confines of the tent. The mumbling of voices outside grew to mere whispers when the sound of a flute filled the night.

"Who's playing?" Tara asked while folding Briac's sleeping form in a blanket and setting him into his bed.

Liz peeked through the tent. The campfire illuminated the faces of those sitting opposite of where she stood. Whoever played had his back to her. "I can't tell."

The musical notes danced in her head, lifting her spirits and bringing a smile to her face. "How can such a simple tune sound so full of life?"

Tara made her way to Liz's side. "Ever since I traveled in time to get here, I've asked myself that question. Life in general is simple here. Survival, family, and love. No one is worried about the ozone layer or how much the price of gas is going up. They don't care if China is filling the stores with plastic products to undercut the competition." Tara sighed, placing her head on Liz's shoulder. The contact warmed her heart. "Every single day of their lives is a gift. They don't need a rock band blasting from all sides to drown out their internal voices."

As the musician finished the small audience clapped their approval.

Duncan turned, flute in hand, and smiled at his wife.

"Duncan?" Tara and Liz both said together.

"I didn't know he played."

"Neither did I," Tara echoed before stepping out of the tent to join her husband.

Liz stayed behind, wrapped her hands around her suddenly cold arms, and watched. "You're lucky, sis."

A few scattering clouds filtered over the crescent moon in the star-filled sky. Liz couldn't remember seeing so many flecks of light. Even at the keep, the ambient light of lit torches blocked out some of the farthest stars.

Frigid air raced up the back of Liz's neck, halting her thoughts of stars, the moon, and simple music. In slow motion, she turned into the tent.

Tara's son moved in his sleep, his chubby cheeks made subtle sucking noises as if still attached to a breast. Behind him, hovering in the corner, was the iridescent ghostly image of Grainna.

"No!" Liz wailed. At the same time, she leapt to Briac. Her feet left the ground as she flew across the room to keep her nephew from harm.

Liz covered Briac with her body while wind blew objects around the tent. Gathering him close, she closed her eyes and lowered her head to avoid a flying cup.

Within seconds, the tent filled with concerned voices, Tara's among them. "Briac."

A muffled cry escaped his mouth.

The wind stopped.

Liz opened her eyes. Surprised that she'd closed them. It wasn't like she could hide from their enemy.

"What happened?" Tara asked, taking her son in her arms.

Duncan stood by her sister. Ian and Lora were at the mouth of the tent. Fin pushed past them with Simon right behind. Every well-placed item in the tent now sat askew. Liz began to shake.

"She was here."

Duncan drew his sword. "Where?" he bellowed.

Liz motioned to the back of the tent.

Duncan ran past his parents in obvious search for their enemy.

Ian turned to the men who gathered around. "Search the area," he ordered. "Report anything you see."

Fin's deadly stare met Liz before he turned to leave the tent.

"Wait." Liz stopped him.

"What is it?"

A few unsteady steps in his direction brought

her close enough so she could whisper and avoid anyone's unwelcome ears. "She appeared like a ghost, Fin."

His eyes narrowed before he nodded and left her side. "Cian, stay here with the women and Simon."

"Aye."

Amber cooed soft words to Briac who now fussed with the rude intrusion of his rest.

"We need to cast a protective circle, like we did at the keep."

"One that moves with us," Amber added.

Myra ran into the tent, breathless, her hair mussed with a weed sticking to the side. "What did I miss?"

"Where were you?"

"Ah." Myra glanced toward her brother and Simon and shook her head. "That isn't important. Fin told Todd to come with him. Everyone's on alert."

Cian stood before the opening of the tent and closed the flap. "Grainna was here."

"Which means we need to be a lot more careful." Liz shook off her early jitters and started cleaning up the mess Grainna left in her wake.

"Did she say anything?" Tara asked.

Liz shook her head. "No."

"What did she do?"

Liz swallowed not wanting to upset her sister. "She—she watched Briac sleeping."

Tara's eyes swelled with unshed tears. Liz knew that confession would cost her sister many sleepless nights. As a mother, she'd want to know if her son was in danger. "It's okay, Tara. I didn't let her near him."

Tara bit down on her lip.

"Cian, look outside and see if anyone is close. Quickly." Myra lifted her hand. The candles blown out by Grainna's presence lit once again. Myra used her gift, elevated the candles with her mind, and set them in a circle.

Cian poked his head back inside. "No one is close. The maids are by the fire attending the food."

"Hurry." Myra motioned for the women to join the circle. "Put Briac in the middle."

"Are you sure?"

"We have to try."

The women sat. Tara placed her son lovingly down and joined hands with Liz and Amber.

Myra cleared her throat. "In this day and in this hour, we ask the Ancients for this power. Keep this child from harm's way, every night and every day. Repel any object and any charm, cast his way which means to harm."

"Someone's coming," Simon whispered.

"If the Ancients will it so, show us proof so we will know."

The women repeated the words and opened their eyes. Like always, they hovered above the ground. Briac flailed his tiny hands in the air and giggled. He hovered two feet above the blanket he'd been laid on.

"Hurry," Cian sent a hurried whisper.

"Ready?" Liz asked.

Tara reached toward her son with her hands still entwined with the others.

"Now."

The women fell to the ground. Tara's jerky movement and attempt to catch her son was too late. Instead of falling, Briac floated peacefully to the soft blanket.

"It worked," Liz sighed.

"Thank God."

Fin's large hand opened the flap of the tent. He glanced in the room, met Lizzy's gaze and then pivoted and said. "They're fine, Logan. Let us find my brother."

The flap closed before Logan could witness their guilty faces.

Before long, the men returned, reporting nothing out of place.

"None of us should venture anywhere alone," Ian reminded them once the camp quieted for the night and the family could gather inside the tent to talk privately.

"We move in pairs already."

"Not always. We've grown lax as of late, seeking privacy for our basic needs."

Liz would have laughed if the situation wasn't so shitty. Men from the twenty-first century grumbled when women left in pairs to go to the ladies room. She wasn't a prude, but at least in her time public restrooms had doors separating the toilets. Lord, did she miss toilets.

Hell, she'd settle for an outhouse.

"We sleep in shifts." Ian continued to issue orders which none of them countered. "My men will watch the camp, but in here, you ladies need to be aware of Grainna's presence should she return."

"I think one of us should be in here at all times." Duncan said before glancing down to his sleeping son.

"That may raise questions."

"Forget the questions. I think Duncan is right." Fin crossed his arms over his chest, his eyes wandered over the tent covering them. "Grainna could return at any time. The women need their sleep."

Liz met Fin's eyes. In them, she saw him waiting for her to protest, to give him and the others a "we can stay awake as easily as you" response. When she said nothing, his eyes narrowed and a slight lift in his brow displayed his surprise.

"We are trained to stand watch. The women

are not," Fin said. "I'll take the first watch."

"I'll take the second." Todd turned to Myra and kissed her quickly before walking from the tent.

Dinner was a quiet and swift affair. Although Liz pleaded hunger before Grainna's brief appearance, she couldn't consume all that much. The nervous twist in her stomach and the worry of the witch's return was the cause.

Liz watched as the women settled into their blankets. Fin perched beside a trunk and laid his sword across his lap.

Myra extinguished the last of the burning candles and cast the space into darkness. Before long the deep, even breaths of the family filled the silence. A fire still crackled outside the tent where the knights who kept watch could keep warm and alert.

Liz forced herself to close her eyes and try to sleep. When she did, all she could see was Grainna's floating image hovering above her nephew. She rolled onto her side, and tried counting backwards in her head. Once she reached sixty her mind wandered to images of the nineteen sixties, tie-dyed shirts, and Woodstock. Not that she'd lived in those times, but the heavily documented history made it easy to picture living in them. Grainna would have lived in the sixties. According to the Ancients and legend, Grainna had lived in modern times for nearly seventy years. The witch probably loved all the war and chaos she'd witnessed in those times.

Fin shifted, catching Liz's attention. "Can't sleep?" he whispered in the dark.

"No." And trying to wasn't helping. Liz gave up and dragged a blanket over to where Fin sat.

"You should try and sleep."

"I have been for over what, an hour now? It isn't working. I might as well help you stay awake." She sat beside him, using the trunk as a backrest but was careful to keep herself from touching him.

"I won't fall asleep."

"I'm sure you won't mean to." He stiffened by her side. Even though she couldn't make out his face, she knew she'd insulted him. "That didn't come out right."

"Most of what comes from your mouth doesn't come out right."

Liz muffled a laugh. She'd have been insulted if what he said wasn't true. "I might have to make you pay for that remark," she managed.

"I'm sure you will."

Well good, at least he knew where he stood.

"Why didn't you protest when Duncan suggested a watch in here?" he asked.

"I'm stubborn, not stupid." Liz glanced up at his shadow. His face angled toward hers.

"No one could accuse you of stupidity."

It was as close to a compliment as Fin had come in a long time. A pool of warmth spread over her as if he'd just praised her. Perhaps talking with him in the night wasn't such a wise decision. Everyone in the tent slept and the two of them sat under hushed whispers like two lovers engaging in a little pillow talk before sleep could claim them. Not that she'd had much experience with pillow talk. The lovers she'd taken over the years never amounted to that many and with a son to raise, he didn't afford her the time to spend long nights and easy mornings.

"What has captured your attention?" Fin's soothing voice asked as if he truly wanted to know.

There was no way in hell she was going to reveal her true thoughts. Slipping Fin into the image of a man in her bed came to easily lately. Having him discover that wouldn't bode well for his inflated ego, or her resolve to keep her distance from him.

Liz didn't answer his question, instead she asked her own. "Do you think Grainna will come back?"

For a moment, Liz thought she saw Fin smile in the dark before his head turned toward the small bed holding Briac. "We have to assume she didn't get what she came for. She will be back."

"That's what I thought you'd say."

"We need to be prepared for her return."

"How can we be?"

"We've been honing our skills."

Liz nodded toward her son. "And discovering new ones."

"And we've learned her strategies or some of them anyway."

"Which ones?" She hadn't thought they'd learned much in the way of Grainna's tactics.

"She uses the weakest link to draw us in. She kidnapped Simon and attempted something tonight with Briac."

"Which means she might try with Amber or Cian." She hadn't thought of that.

"Or any of you women. Don't forget about Tara's abduction."

"You're right." Liz would love to counter him, but couldn't. She realized her shoulder had nestled up against his during their conversation. Pulling away would make her look foolish. And in truth, she didn't want to. Not yet anyway.

"Does it hurt to say that?"

"To say what?"

"That I'm right?" he chuckled.

Quiet laughter shook her frame and the terror Grainna had placed in her earlier that evening finally started to drift away. "It pains me deeply. And if you go around telling anyone I said that, I'll deny it to my death," she joked.

"I'm sure you will."

Their laugher ebbed and silence followed, not

an awkward quiet, but a peaceful one.

Fin reached up and drew her head to his shoulder. Once there, Liz felt her eyes start to drift closed. She should move back to her bed, but couldn't find the strength.

Liz felt the pad of his thumb stroke her cheek. "Sleep," he whispered. "I'll watch over you."

Chapter Nine

"My ass is so sore from sitting on this horse I could scream. Somewhere in my sick, twisted mind, I looked forward to getting away from the keep. Now at least I'll know what I'm talking about when someone suggests a visit to the coast." Tara's complaints matched Liz's thoughts exactly. They'd been riding for four days, four long, tiring days. It didn't help that sleep didn't come easy with the threat of Grainna hanging in the air. She hadn't come back, but everyone knew it was only a matter of time before she did.

"I could use a bath," Liz added her own complaints.

"Duncan thinks we'll be camping by a river tonight. We can bathe there."

The thought of clean water, even cold, frigid water brought a smile to her face. "Maybe Duncan could stand upstream and heat the water."

Tara rolled her eyes. "Yeah, right. Like no one would notice that."

Still, the thought had merit. From her sister's expression, Liz knew Tara considered how her husband's gift might aide her in a warm bath.

Up ahead, Simon rode alongside Cian. Lizzy's son appeared asleep in the saddle, a term she'd only heard of in old westerns until she'd nodded off herself after the first night on the road. Now she knew a person could actually sleep while riding a horse. Not a peaceful sleep, but a few minutes of shut-eye helped break up the day and rejuvenated what the night neglected.

It was crazy how she no longer stressed when her son rode a horse or lifted the sword he had strapped to his waist. And to think she balked at a pocketknife back when they'd lived in California.

Simon's head jerked up, as though he'd awakened suddenly. His gaze shifted above him where Ian's falcon soared. Even from her distance, Liz noticed Simon's shoulders stiffen.

He turned in his seat and met her eyes over the riders separating them.

Mom, his voice sounded in her head. *Someone's coming up ahead.*

Just then, the falcon squawked. Ian's eyes shot to his flying weapon.

Grainna?

I don't know.

Liz watched as Simon attempted to get inside the falcon's head and see through the bird's eyes.

What do you see? she quizzed him.

Riders, oh geeze. I can't hold on. They have swords like us. Lots of men.

"Dammit."

"What's wrong?" Tara asked, unaware of her silent conversation with Simon.

Liz glanced over her shoulder, noticed Gregor riding up alongside them, and thought better of voicing her concerns. "I, ah, need to use the little girl's room."

"Again? We stopped less than an hour ago."

Gregor rode ahead, unconcerned with their conversation.

"Tell Duncan to stop us," Liz told Tara in a hushed whisper. "Simon sees people ahead."

Tara's eyes grew large, her eyes focused toward the beginning of the caravan. After a few silent moments, Duncan glanced over his shoulder then up again to the falcon flying. Duncan said something to Fin, who quickly rounded his horse and drew up beside Liz and Tara.

"How are ye faring?" he said in a voice loud enough for the surrounding men to hear them.

Tara took the lead and cradled an arm around Briac's sleeping frame. "I need to change my son, Finlay. Can we stop for a short time so I can see to his needs?"

Liz jumped in to be sure they had more than a few minutes to assess what lay ahead. "I could use a break, seems the sun is wearing on me." As if that were possible. The sun barely peeked beyond the clouds and the mist had hardly lifted from the land since they woke. Still, Fin understood and signaled for the caravan to stop.

Within seconds, Simon stood beside his horse, Ian drew up alongside him, and both spoke with their heads close together. Tara ducked into the wagon with the ruse of changing her son. Several knights took the opportunity to dismount and see to their needs.

"Someone is coming," Simon told Ian.

"What color do you see on their flags?"

Simon shook his head. "I can't tell."

"How many men? Do you see women?" Fin asked.

"I think so. There's a lot of riders."

Simon shot his gaze back and forth between Ian and Fin, his feet shuffled beneath him. "I can see better for myself. When I look through the falcon the colors aren't as clear."

Liz stepped forward. "That could be dangerous."

Fin was shaking his head, too.

"I'll just reach the top of the trees to see if they are a traveling party like us or...something else."

Ian let a rare smile slip from his lips. His hand clasped Simon's shoulder. "You would be in far more danger to be in the middle of a battle."

Liz tilted her head back and noted the height of the trees. Her stomach started to turn. Simon had changed into a bird twice since the day at the river. Each time he shifted back into his human form without incident, but she still wasn't ready to have her son scouting for this army of medieval men.

"I'll only go as high as that tree," Simon said while pointing to a nearby cluster of birch trees. They stood on the edge of a rise of hills that would give him a decent view of the party coming their way.

Liz narrowed her gaze to Ian who seemed to be waiting for her approval. Surprisingly, Fin held his tongue, his eyes traveled to the trees and beyond.

The decision was hers. Something she'd never truly been given since arriving in Scotland. Her heart flipped in her chest and squeezed with uncertainty.

"Okay," she breathed her consent. "But you and I have to talk the entire time." Liz tapped the side of her head several times.

Simon squared his shoulders and nodded to her once.

"I'll escort him into the brush for the change," Fin said.

"Cian?" Ian called his son over. "Go with them and keep watch."

Cian turned on his heel and followed.

Liz watched the backs of her son, Fin and Cian as they disappeared into the thick of the surrounding forest.

Ian patted Liz on her back and glanced around him. Some of the men seemed anxious to continue their journey. More than a few watched the trio walking away from the group. "I'll send Lora to your side and divert the men."

Ian walked away, ushering orders to his men.

"Is everything well?" Myra walked alongside Lora, oblivious of the problem.

Lora glanced over her shoulder. "Ian suggests we take the time to see to our needs." With a dart of her head, Lora motioned toward the trees, a short distance away from where Simon and the others slipped. Alone, they could talk easily and Liz could concentrate on Simon's inside voice without worry.

"Good idea."

Walking with purpose, Liz led the women to a hidden section of trees where the MacCoinnich caravan would think the women in need of relieving their bladders. Lora filled Myra in with what was happening.

I'm ready, Mom, Simon spoke in her head.

Liz picked up her skirt and walked faster. *Are you sure about this Simon? You don't have to do this.*

I'm sure.

The women ducked into the shade of the trees and away from prying eyes.

Be careful, Liz told her son.

"Can you hear him?" Lora asked.

Liz nodded, waiting for her son's voice to reach her ears again.

I'm a bird, Simon chanted. His thoughts flowed into her head like water from a faucet. *A big strong winged bird... Ah, yes.*

He'd changed. Liz didn't even need to glance to the sky to know her son soared above them. His ease into the change morphed faster this time. Easier.

I'm up. Can you see me?

"He's in the air," Liz told Lora who she knew spoke to Ian in her head. Glancing at the sky, Liz searched for her son. The thickness of the trees made it difficult to see him.

Where are you? he asked.

Don't worry about me. What do you see?

Hold on.

Liz held her breath, waiting for his next words.

Green. The flag they carry is green with white

edging.

"The flag is green-and-white," she relayed to Lora.

"Are there women?" Myra asked.

Are there women with them?

Yes, three... No, make that four. They have a wagon like us.

What about Grainna? Is she there?

Two seconds passed then three. *No. No sign of her.*

Liz told Lora what Simon saw. Instantly, Myra and Lora smiled and relaxed their stance.

"A traveling party. Probably en route to the Lancaster wedding."

"MacTavish has a green coat of arms," Myra said to her mother.

"Friend or foe?"

"Ally."

The lack of description didn't go unnoticed by Liz. She'd have to see for herself if the clan coming toward them could be trusted.

Is everything okay, Mom?

Everything is fine. Come back and change. Ian has everything he needs.

Okay.

Liz looked above her, wishing she could see her son. *Simon?*

Yeah?

You did a great job, sport.

~~~~

The oldest, unmarried MacTavish son had been eyeing Lizzy for the past several hours. Logan offered to fetch water for her at their last stop. And even his own father appeared to soften his look and tongue to the lass.

Not since the first night had Fin found even one moment alone with her. With the MacTavish clan adding to their numbers, he'd have to wait until after they'd settled at the Lancaster gathering to find time to slip away with her. Not that she'd go willingly.

Fin let his eyes wander to the women in question. Lizzy sat rather slumped on her horse. Their journey would push any woman past the point of comfort. Considering where and when she'd come from, he thought she'd held up remarkably well. He remembered her small apartment in the twenty-first century, remembered her ease behind the wheel of her car. Her world ran fast. Faster than the speed of a single horse running over the Scottish hillside. With all the comforts her world held, no wonder she was so determined to return. Not that she could.

That single thought made him smile.

She had no choice but to stay in his time, his world.

Lizzy reached over and found the hem of her skirt. She lifted it well above her calf to scratch her leg. Her alabaster skin had lightened since he'd first glanced upon her. The lack of sunshine made it impossible for her skin to tan as it had in California.

Beside him, Logan muffled a groan. Fin caught his gaze and realized he'd witnessed Lizzy's act.

"The lass has little thought to her affect on men," he said, bringing to words Fin's exact thoughts.

Actually, Fin thought Lizzy knew exactly how she affected the opposite sex. And reveled in it.

"She's tired of the ride and has obviously forgotten where she is."

Logan shifted in his seat and allowed his eyes to travel to Lizzy again. This time his face softened and his desire for her swam in his eyes.

The hair on the back of Fin's neck stood on end. His jaw tightened and fist clenched at his side. Mayhap it was time to stake his claim. Or at least his desires.

And his desires didn't include Elizabeth in the arms of Logan or any of the MacTavish men.

"Logan?" Fin directed his friend's attention to him. "Elizabeth isn't..." Isn't what? Available? Isn't interested? Damn the woman. She wasn't his. Wasn't even a bedmate he could claim. And if she were, would he tell anyone of their time together?

Logan forced his eye to Fin and waited. "Isn't what?"

In seconds, Logan's lips slid into a knowing grin. His gaze swept over Lizzy again, this time with more interest. "I see."

Did he?

Logan returned his attention to the road ahead of them. The smile never left his lips.

Without any words at all, Fin staked his claim.

"If ye change your mind about the lass, let me know. She's too fine a woman to be left unprotected for long." Logan pushed his horse ahead.

A small weight lifted from Fin's shoulders.

One down.

He drew up beside Lizzy, reached over, and forced the hem of her skirt to cover her leg. She shot him a look of sheer disdain.

"The men are taking notice," he told her.

She glanced ahead and nodded toward Logan.

"You mean Logan."

"And others."

"Really?" She appeared to enjoy the attention. Her back straightened and a smile he hadn't seen in several hours flashed on her lips. "Which ones?"

Instead of letting her win and rising to her bait, Fin waited until she stopped looking around to find who watched her ride.

Only when her eyes leveled to his did he say,

"This one." He pointed a single finger to his chest. Her teasing smile fell into a complete expression of shock.

He'd rendered her speechless. And that almost never happened.

Fin kicked his horse and left her to ponder his words and their meaning.

Chapter Ten

"They travel closer to us, yet have no idea we're here." Grainna voiced her knowledge only to Tatiana.

The girl weighed a good ten pounds more than she had when she'd arrived. She didn't go out of her way to attract attention to herself by wearing flattering clothing, but she had at least grown accustomed to bathing, something Grainna insisted she do.

Never again did she want to smell the stink of unwashed flesh. Death and decay she could tolerate, but filth was another thing all together.

"They will be close for several weeks."

"Obviously." Weddings and the celebrations surrounding them took time.

"I see time as yer friend. Time and patience."

If there was one word Grainna would love to never hear again, it was patience.

"What else do you see?"

Tatiana closed her eyes and drew a full breath into her lungs. Her brows pitched together as she angled her head to the side, searching her thoughts.

Grainna waited for the girl to speak. She'd learned to hold back from entering the child's mind while she searched her visions. The pain caused by invading her head overran the images and kept the girl from seeing.

"The infant is protected," she said quickly. "Your next attempt to overpower the child will cause you pain."

"What of the others? The youngest daughter and Simon?"

Tatiana shook her head and held her body still. "Nothing. I see nothing."

"Look harder."

She opened her bloodshot eyes. "I only see a deep fog when I search for a weakness with the children."

Protection from the Ancients, most likely. The old ones had a way of watching over the young. Yet they hadn't masked the encounter with Briac. Taking the child would draw the MacCoinnichs to her. Their pain will cause carelessness. A weakness Grainna would extort.

Any pain caused by the abduction of the child would be worth the price. Grainna would heed Tatiana's warning and wait until the MacCoinnichs were preoccupied. Their watch while traveling didn't leave room for her to strike. But once the wedding festivities began, and the men sat in endless hours of counsel with each other, the women would be alone, the children unsupervised.

Sweeping her hair behind her shoulders, Grainna stepped to the doorway and peered beyond the walls. Several men trained for war, their minds completely in her control. Her small army numbered those that traveled with the MacCoinnichs.

Time had come to turn the wheels of doubt and fear among the MacCoinnich's and their people.

Time to weed out the weak.

~~~~

The sweat of her hands made the reins uncomfortable in her palms. Liz glanced up, noticing the amber-and-black flags flapping in the breeze coming off the ocean. She could smell the salt air, but had yet to touch the sea. She couldn't wait. The thought of dipping her feet in the sand, even if it were as cold as the MacCoinnichs had told her, sounded like heaven.

The special tack on the horses and the elegant dresses the women were told to wear, drew the occasion of arriving to Brisbane's keep to an exclamation point. They walked their horses toward the center of activity with their heads held high.

Tents littered the grounds surrounding the walls of Lord Brisbane's keep. Flags of many colors flew high, telling everyone whose men resided underneath. Lizzy had been told that there would be rooms inside for many of them if they desired, but with the crush of people, they might prefer to hoist individual tents to ensure some privacy.

Tara voiced her concern about sleeping in close proximity to Matthew of Lancaster. Even though the man remembered nothing of abducting her, she had the misfortune of not forgetting. Duncan agreed to raise several tents to secure them all and have their men close at hand.

A nervous knot formed deep in Liz's stomach.

She felt like a fraud. Like she didn't belong.

Liz's eyes swung to Simon whose face held a smile as his eyes took in the entire scene. Hundreds of people scurried about.

At the gates, Laird Ian's men held back and let him and Lora proceed with the rest of the family trailing.

A stout man with wide girth extended his arm to Ian once he was free of his horse.

"MacCoinnich, 'tis been too long," he said, his voice hissing slightly on his exhale.

"Since Duncan's nuptials." Ian shook the man's hand.

"Ye've become a grandfather, I've been told."

"Aye. Duncan and Tara have a brawny son, Briac."

Ian glanced toward Duncan, who was helping Tara from her horse, Briac in her arms. Tara's eyes kept shifting to the eaves of the courtyard, probably in search of Matthew.

Another man approached, this one nearly as wide as the last, but much taller.

"Lord Brisbane, I'd like ye to meet my neighbors and friends, Laird Ian MacCoinnich and his family."

Brisbane shook Ian's hand. "I've heard much about you. I do hope your journey was pleasant."

The man's accent was clearly English. For some reason, this comforted Liz as she slid to the ground and allowed one of Ian's men to take the horse away.

Simon stood next to Cian and Amber while Myra and Todd received introductions. Liz found her feet planted firmly in place and listened. Simon shook hands with the men, somehow making certain they knew he was there. And belonged. She, on the other hand, didn't at all feel as if she belonged. If it were possible to slip into the eaves of the keep, Liz would have.

"Hiding, Elizabeth?"

Fin's voice was surprisingly close to her ear.

"Maybe."

Fin chuckled before placing a hand to the small of her back and ushering her forward. "Laird Lancaster, Lord Brisbane, this is Lady Elizabeth, Lady Tara's sister and mother to Simon."

Brisbane reached for her hand and kissed the back of it. "What of yer husband?" Lancaster asked.

Lancaster eyed Fin quickly.

"Long since gone I'm afraid." The lie slid from her lips easier each time she'd voiced it.

"I'm sorry, my lady. Seems he left you with a fine son."

Liz smiled with pride. "He did."

The conversation quickly turned to their journey and the days they'd traveled. Their party moved like a hovering cloud toward the open doors of the massive home. Fin's hand continued to guide her forward, as if knowing she'd back out if given a chance.

Once inside, maids gathered around them, helping with their cloaks and handing over refreshments. Noblemen, knights, ladies, and children packed the room.

One woman in particular appeared to be the center of attention. Her deep chestnut hair and creamy alabaster skin sparkled when she spoke with the people in the room. Her attention centered on them and her gaze rounded quickly to Fin.

For a moment, Fin's hand felt firmer on her waist. If she didn't know any better, she thought he pulled her closer to his side. Possessive...or maybe a better term was possessed.

Regina. The one Tara told her about, the soon-to-be wife of Brisbane. The one who really wanted Fin as her husband.

"Hiding, Fin?" Liz snickered when she asked.

His eyes rounded to hers, his cocky grin flashed that damn dimple, the one that did a number on her stomach.

"Maybe."

Liz looked up. "She's walking straight toward us."

He drew her closer. This time leaving little doubt as to what he wanted this woman to believe. For a brief moment, Liz thought of wiggling out of his arm and leaving him to fend for himself.

"Don't even think about it," Fin whispered.

"Finlay. Ye came."

"Of course, lass. Ye know we wouldn't miss yer wedding."

Myra turned to the woman's voice and immediately intercepted her. "Congratulations, Regina. Lord Brisbane seems so nice."

Regina hugged Myra and sent a hard stare to Fin. Something told Liz that Myra had intercepted many an awkward moment in the past.

"This is Sir Blakely, my husband."

Regina curved a brow in Todd's direction while her eyes swept his frame. The smile she'd placed on her face fell a fraction.

Regina Lancaster didn't wear jealousy well. "A pleasure." But her words sounded forced.

Todd kissed the woman's hand, following what everyone else had done. "Congratulations," he said, but Regina didn't appear to listen.

"Hey, Mom. Cian, Amber, and I are going to walk by the beach. Is that okay?"

"Mom?" Regina asked. The smile on her face pulling at her lips again.

"I don't know, we just got here." Liz glanced up to Fin, silently asking what he thought. Was it safe? With so many people, would Grainna strike?

Fin tapped his fingers on her hip, his eyes deep in thought. "Cian, have someone with you."

Someone meaning one of the knights.

You need to be careful, Simon. Grainna could be anywhere, Liz told her son with her mind.

We know, we won't be far.

Liz nodded toward her son.

"I'll watch out for him," Amber said before running off behind them.

Regina pivoted toward the fleeing MacCoinnichs and Simon. "And who would ye be?" she finally asked.

"Oh, how silly of me," Myra said, quickly introducing Liz the same way she'd been introduced to the others. Only this time, Myra added the lie about Liz being a widow.

From the strange expression on the other woman's face, Liz didn't think for a moment Regina was fooled.

"A widow? How sad. It must be difficult

raising a son on yer own."

"A lot of women manage," Liz told her.

"Oh really? I hadn't noticed."

No, chances are Regina hadn't noticed anything other than her life of privilege. Moving from her father's home to Lord Brisbane's wouldn't be a hardship. Although from the glances Regina sent toward her fiancé, Liz didn't think she was all that excited about it.

Either luck or design moved Regina's attention away from them and onto Tara, Duncan, and the others.

Todd found his way to Fin's side. "You're going to have to keep an eye on that one."

Fin laughed. "Tell me about it."

"Don't worry, Todd. Fin has been dodging Regina since he was Simon's age. He's gotten rather good at it."

Liz pulled away from Fin and stood beside Myra. "Maybe Fin likes the attention."

Fin growled, causing them all to chuckle.

"Are you sure it's okay that the others went to the beach?" Liz asked Fin.

"We can follow behind them if you like."

"I'd love to." Liz turned to Todd and Myra. "You guys should come too."

Fin pushed toward Duncan and the others and gave their excuses.

Chapter Eleven

"Come on, Amber," Simon yelled over the sound of the waves crashing along the cliff. The bluff darted out into the ocean all around them. The beach, if you could call it that, was smaller than any Simon had been to in his life. It looked nothing like the beaches in Orange County. From above, the ocean felt massive, but from down here, it was secluded.

But it was the ocean, and he had missed it almost as much as his mom had.

Laird Ian's man stood far above them, watching. He seemed a bit pissed for having to accompany them to the beach. But he was far enough away for the three of them to talk candidly, which none of them had had an opportunity to really do since they left home.

Amber lifted her dress so she wouldn't trip and carried her shoes in her hand.

Cian stood beside him, watching the waves crash on the sand.

"Is this like your home?"

"No. Not at all. The sand is whiter, the ocean bluer. And it stretches for miles like this." Simon pointed to the water's edge. Simon sat in the sand, rolled up his pants and walked toward the sea.

"Shit. That's cold."

Cian laughed.

"You shouldn't cuss," Amber scolded.

"Oh, yeah. Come here and feel for yourself." Simon crooked his finger in her direction.

Amber tilted her head to one side, tossed her slippers to the ground, and marched toward him. As soon as the water reached her toes, her eyes widened and her lower lip quivered.

"I told you it was freezing."

"You said you used to swim in the ocean."

"Yeah, well, it isn't this cold back home."

Cian's feet were wet and all three of them danced around the crashing waves.

"Do you think you'll ever go back?" Cian asked.

"If my mom has anything to say about it we will."

"We need to find the stones before it's even an option," Amber reminded him.

"Do you think we'll find them?" Simon asked her. If any of them could know what the future held, it would be Amber.

"I believe we'll find them."

"Have you had a vision, Amber?"

"Nay, simply a feeling."

Simon looked up to Cian, who had been his mentor since he'd arrived in the sixteenth century. "I think I might hide them from my mom to keep her from making us leave."

"Once found, it would be noticed should they go missing."

"Yeah, well...I gotta do something. I'm not going back." The thought of Mr. Price's algebra class and all the meaningless hours playing video games just didn't seem right anymore.

No longer interested in playing in the water, Simon sat in the sand away from the water's edge.

"You don't need to be so glum, Simon. We haven't found them yet. Lizzy isn't forcing you to leave today." Amber patted his shoulder.

"By the time we find them, you may well be old enough to make the decision on your own," Cian added. "Besides, Lizzy wouldn't leave now even if we had the stones. Not with Grainna threatening all of us."

Simon tossed a rock into the water. "I know."

"So, Simon, have you tried to change into

something other than a bird?" Cian asked.

"No. Do you think I should try?"

"I would if I could do it."

"Why not try to be a fish." Amber glanced at the ocean. "I wonder what it looks like under the water."

Simon considered scales for a few minutes. The thought of a shark coming along and swallowing him in one bite forced the image from his mind. "No thanks. I'd have to become a whale and they don't move very fast."

"What about a wolf?"

"Maybe."

"Or a horse?"

"That could be useful."

Amber glanced up the side of the cliff. "We'll have to find a way to be alone to try."

"That may be a while. I don't think we're going to be left alone for some time," Cian told them. "Weddings like this go on for weeks. My father said there were going to be several gatherings to firm up our alliances."

"Then we'll have to try and sneak away."

"Since when do you think like that, Amber? It isn't like you."

Amber brushed her long black hair away from her face. "I feel like Simon needs to reach higher than he has with his gift. He needs to know what he's capable of."

"If you feel strongly about this, we should tell the others and work together."

She looked over her shoulder again. Simon followed her gaze. Walking down the cliff side was his mom, Fin, Myra, and Todd. The knight posted was gone. Even then, Simon didn't know if he was ready to get naked and shift in front of Amber and Myra.

"Hey, sport," his mom called out to him at the same time she stumbled. Fin caught her arm and kept her from falling. Instead of her normal scorn for Fin touching her, she actually said thanks. Maybe they were finally getting along. It seems like all they ever did was fight, mostly about him.

"Hey, guys."

As soon as his mom reached the bottom, her shoes were off, her dress hiked, and she was walking toward the water.

"It's really cold," he warned her.

"How bad can it be? Ah, man!"

I told you!

Fin laughed when she jumped away from the water.

"It is freezing," Todd exclaimed.

Myra squealed, just as Amber had. Todd kicked water toward her, causing her to giggle and kick back. "Watch it," she warned.

Todd didn't listen and kept teasing her. Before long, they were running after each other away from the others. When Todd caught up to Myra and started kissing her, Simon stopped staring.

"Too bad it isn't warm enough to swim in," his mom said.

"'Tis only fitting for fish." Amber nudged Simon's arm and nodded toward his mom.

"Speaking of fish..."

Liz stared over the water, not hearing him. Or so he thought.

"What about 'em?"

"Ah, well, Amber thinks maybe I should try and shift into something other than a bird."

That got Fin's attention before his mom managed to turn in his direction. "Not a fish."

"I agree with Fin. Not a fish."

"I didn't really mean I wanted to try to be a fish. But maybe a horse or maybe a wolf."

Fin glanced toward his mom, who stood staring back at him.

~~~~

"I was just getting used to him flying." Liz sat on the grass, overlooking the bluff. The tide forced them to higher ground. She'd told Simon she'd think about it. In truth, there was little else she had thought of since he brought up the subject.

"We should have seen his desire to be something else coming." Fin sat beside her.

"I guess a wolf is safer than a bird."

"And if Amber feels he needs to practice other shapes, then he should probably try."

Liz glanced over her shoulder, and noted the number of tents and people milling over the hillside. "How are we going to get away from all these people?"

"Things will settle. It isn't uncommon for small bands of people to wander off for a while during the festivities. For hunting."

Liz thought back to when Myra and Todd left their side shortly after they found their way to the beach. People didn't only hunt when they drifted away from the masses. Myra was getting lucky. As much as Liz was happy for her friend, she was a bit pent up herself. All by themselves, her eyes shifted to Fin. He stared at her, searching for her thoughts. God, she hoped he wasn't able to read every thought milling about in her head.

"I wonder where Todd and Myra wandered off to."

Liz's cheeks grew warm. "I'm sure the honeymooners are making the most of some alone time."

Asking Fin to keep his mouth shut after that one would have been asking for too much, and Liz knew it. "What of you, Lizzy. Would you like to make the most of some *alone time*?"

A quick burst of laughter caught her off guard. "Oh, MacCoinnich, you really do need to work on your pickup lines."

Fin had the nerve to actually look wounded by

her mirth. "My pickup lines, as you call them, are fine."

"Oh really? I guess that's why the women are falling all over you here." Liz made it a point to look around them. Several people milled about. Tents were everywhere and several merchants had set up shop between the village and Brisbane's home in order to capitalize on the gathering of people. Several women had eyed Fin, but none had gone out of their way to be by his side. However, she'd been by his side nearly the entire time they'd been there.

"If it's women you want to see falling all over me, love, it can be arranged."

"You know what your problem is, MacCoinnich?" Liz stood and shook the grass from her gown. She slid her hand over her flat stomach before waving a finger in Fin's direction.

"I have no problem."

Ignoring his words, Liz kept going. "Your problem is the vibe you're giving out."

"What vibe is that?"

"You're not exactly oozing with availability." She waited a breath or two to see if he would rise to her bait. "I mean, I get what all that was about back there with Regina. The woman wasn't exactly subtle." And truth be told, Liz didn't really want to see Fin get caught in the middle of a cat fight between Regina and her hubby to be. From the way she eyed Fin, the woman was already trying to figure out how to land Fin on the side, if that even happened in these times. "I've got to hand it to you, Fin, Regina is a bit of a hottie. I'll have to give you kudos for not knocking boots with her all these years."

Fin caught her meaning and blessed her with a double shot of dimples. "I'm humbled by your compliment."

"Still, she isn't standing here now, so there's

no reason not to let some of the single women here know you're available."

Fin glanced around with interest. "Who would you suggest?"

The smile on her lips started to wane. "Oh, I don't know."

He motioned toward a woman about Myra's age who stood several feet away talking with an older man who was probably her father. "What of her?"

"Too young." Liz quickly dismissed her. "How about the brunette to her right?" She knew he'd balk at her pick.

"I do like a woman with curves."

"That many?" she shot at him.

"Perhaps you're right. She is very much a woman."

Liz placed a self-conscious hand to her slim hips. Maybe slender was quite the *in thing* during the sixteenth century.

They walked past the crowd, discussing the merits of the women among them.

"How about her?"

"Not with that nose," he replied.

Liz laughed, agreeing.

They neared the edge of the encampment and the last of the guests were securing their quarters for the evening. A very attractive woman slipped away from one of the tents, running after what looked to be a sibling. "What about her?"

"She's blonde," Fin said, almost as if it were a bad thing.

"What's wrong with blondes?"

Fin watched the retreating woman, cocked his head to the side, and frowned. "I don't know. It just doesn't seem right."

"What's wrong about them?"

Fin rounded his eyes to her and looked over the top of her head as if he'd just noticed for the first time that she had blonde hair. "I didn't say there was anything wrong with blondes."

"No, you said they didn't seem right. So if they're not right, they're wrong. What's wrong with blonde?" Liz had heard every blonde joke known to man, and did her best more times than not to blow away any stereotype one could label on her. So what was Fin getting at? Did he really have an aversion to blonde women?

That's when she saw it. The smirk hiding behind the hard lines on Fin's face.

"Someone is a mite defensive."

"And someone's being a jerk," she said, pushing against his chest. And he'd had her going for longer than she'd like to give him credit. Maybe there was more blonde in her than she knew.

Fin caught her hand and held her still. "There is only one blonde I'm interested in, Elizabeth."

His eyes glanced to her lips and back to her eyes.

She stood still, unable to look away. Her breath caught in her chest. Part of her wanted to run away, tell him they were a bad idea. A mistake with a capital M. Another part of her wanted to jump into his lap and lick him up one side and down the other.

Fin stepped closer. His free hand reached into her tresses and held the back of her head.

"This is a bad idea, MacCoinnich." But the words weren't convincing, even to her ears. And how had her hand managed to snake around his waist without her knowing it?

"I used to think so, too."

His hard torso leaned into her, his lips mere inches from hers.

"Maybe we should stop." She tilted her head up toward his and licked her lips.

"Maybe we shouldn't."

His lips were soft, warm and oh, so inviting. A

part of her melted into him, if that were possible. He stood there kissing her, slowly, as if he had all the time in the world to do so and wasn't going to be rushed. His fingers kneaded the back of her head before descending on her neck to coax her head farther back. Only then did his tongue find its way into her mouth to start a slow, lazy exploration there.

Warmth spread quickly throughout her body, making her completely aware of how long she'd wanted to be back in his embrace.

Lord, he felt good. Liz wrapped both arms around his firm body, avoiding the sword strapped to his waist and pulled him even closer. Under the soft fabric of her dress, her nipples pebbled, aching for attention. Fin made no move to touch her more than what he was doing right then. He kissed her so thoroughly she literally had to break away to breathe. Only then did he move his lips to her jaw and feathered his way to the lobe of her ear. When his teeth nibbled on her sensitive flesh, Liz's knees threatened to buckle from under her. "Oh, Fin."

He found her lips again. More urgent this time. His hand slid past her hip and rounded over her butt. When he pressed her into his frame, Liz knew how aroused Fin was. The hard length of him pressed against the folds of her skirt and nestled against her core.

"I want you, Elizabeth," he managed between kisses.

Her hand swept over his back, wishing she could lift his shirt from his shoulders and touch his naked skin. "Feeling's mutual, Finlay."

He chuckled before reaching for her lips again.

Liz sighed and allowed Fin whatever he wanted to take. He started walking her backwards to what Liz hoped was more privacy. Although they were outside the general camp, they were still very exposed.

Before they moved far, the sound of someone calling Fin's name stopped them. Liz opened her eyes to find Fin covering her frame with his, as if to protect her from prying eyes.

Logan strode to them, his eyes focused on Fin. "Sorry to interrupt."

Fin turned toward his friend, keeping Liz directly behind him. Liz glanced down at her dress, surprised to find the bodice askew. She reached down and straightened her dress.

"Yer father asked that I bring ye back."

"Is something amiss?"

"Nothing eminent, but lairds are gathering to discuss several areas of concern. Ian asked that ye be there."

Liz placed a hand on Fin's arm. "You should go."

Logan widened his smile toward her before turning on his heel and leaving them alone.

"Do you ever get the feeling that we are never going to be alone?" he asked.

"Maybe the gods don't want us alone."

Fin swept a hand around her waist and quickly tilted her back for one more kiss. Breathless, he pulled away and said, "Now that I've tasted ye more thoroughly, lass, I'll not be gone long."

Liz lifted an eyebrow. "Promises, promises."

He growled, kissed her again, and then set her back to her feet. "Come, let's find out what is happening."

Chapter Twelve

Long tables filled the hall, reminding Fin of more warring times. Times when gatherings like this happened in the home he'd grown up in. Duncan and Todd sat to his right, Logan to his left. His father sat with Lancaster, Brisbane, and many other heads of households and lairds of the highlands. The only women in the room served ale and dodged the hands of men.

They knew by the kind of invitation sent to this event that there was more to the gathering than the celebration of a marriage.

"I've lost more men in the past year than in our last battle," Brisbane told the council. "Married men with no desire to leave on their own accord." Brisbane's voice boomed over the rumblings in the room.

"Where did ye find their bodies?" someone asked.

"No bodies were found. These men disappeared without a trace. I hoped to find out from you if men had joined your ranks. If anyone else is having such trouble."

"There have been several villagers fleeing outside our home." Fin recognized the man speaking as a distant neighbor to the Lancasters. His land was small by comparison, but his men were known as some of the bloodiest on the field.

"What of your knights?"

"Nay."

"Two of my men are missing."

Fin leaned over and whispered into Duncan's ear. "Grainna."

"Must be," he replied.

The room erupted into many voices, all speaking at once. Several knights were unaccounted for. One had managed to disappear during their recent travel. The numbers were much larger than Fin expected.

The English in the south were suspect, but according to several of Brisbane's friends, they too were missing men. The need to gather all the men in the room now was to keep peace and to merge their minds to find a solution.

"Something else concerns me," Lancaster spoke over the men, quieting them down. "Other happenings have been overshadowing the happiness of my land."

Fin held his breath, knowing where the conversation was headed.

"Last fall the water in our stream grew vile, forcing several villagers in search for a fresh source. Some didn't return, others did and reported a small band of men abducting the stragglers in their group."

"What do the two things have in common?" Laird MacClain asked.

"The villagers believe the river was poisoned."

"An entire river?" Several men laughed.

"What of ye, MacCoinnich? Yer south of Lancaster, did ye notice a stench in your drinking supply?"

Ian squared his shoulders and replied with careful words. "Nay, yet we did have a flock of crows die a strange death close by. Perhaps victim to the rancid water Lancaster speaks of."

Fin stroked the short beard on his chin and considered his father's words. They hadn't lost men, but some villagers fled because of the magical attacks from Grainna.

Lancaster turned to Ian again. "I remember tales spoken from my grandfather of a plague upon his land. Undrinkable water, animals dying, and villagers disappearing. Some said a witch was responsible."

"A witch?" Brisbane asked. "There is no such thing."

Fin held perfectly still. Duncan's eyes found his.

"Don't laugh or deny what ye have no way of knowing." This warning came from the only man of the cloth in the room. The priest went on. "Does the Bible not speak of witches?"

"Forgive me, Father, but we are not speaking of biblical times. We are discussing what is happening now."

"Where is it written that there are no witches now? Mayhap they are better hidden among us, but there is no reason to believe they are not here."

Several men dismissed the priest's ramblings while others seemed to take in his words a little too close.

"Do not suffer a witch to live. If evil resides inside a person, 'tis our duty to God to remove the spirit." The priest eyed the men in the room daring them to say anything.

Fin noted several reactions, from dismissive to serious. Some lairds in the room started each day in prayer with a man of the cloth. Several didn't have the luxury nor the desire to spend such time in prayer. A few would think nothing of what the man said and think only of how to fix their problems with war and bloodshed. Fin didn't worry about the men of war. 'Twas the others that bothered him. Letting loose those men on Grainna would suit all their needs. But exposing her would most likely expose them. And that simply wouldn't do.

"Witches and spirits," Logan said beside him. "Methinks the man has been spending too much time in his cups."

Fin forced a laugh and a quick agreement, but

said little else.

Before the gathering adjourned, several men from distant clans agreed to scout the area for a cause of the bleeding of Brisbane's men. They would comb the area during the wedding festivities and report back before the lairds and their ladies returned to their own homes.

~~~~

Tara sat holding her son while whispering her warnings to the rest of them. "Duncan says the men are talking about witches and evil spirits. Apparently Lancaster isn't as blind to Grainna's antics as we'd have liked."

"Aye," Lora chimed in. "Ian tells me to forbid the use of the simplest of our gifts while we're here."

"I guess that means I won't be trying to be a wolf anytime soon."

Liz didn't mind that.

"I get the feeling that coming here was a bad idea," Tara said. "If Grainna walked in here right now, we'd be forced to ward her off and be exposed in front of all these people."

Rubbing her nervous stomach, Liz added, "There's got to be something we can do, some way to keep who we are away from everyone out there."

Outside their tent were too many people to count. Granted, Liz and the others had charmed the material covering them in a way to keep their words only for the ears of those inside. No one could lurk outside and overhear anything they said. But they didn't spend all their time inside the tent.

"I wouldn't mind a premonition either." Lora rubbed the back of her neck while she spoke. "I've not had one in months."

"I wish we could summon Elise." Elise was one of the Ancients, the only one who'd manifested for them to see. She appeared preceding their last showdown with Grainna, warning them of their impending battle. Even if she didn't have all the answers, she'd given them enough advice to keep them alive and safe.

Not knowing what to expect weighed on Liz more than she'd like to admit. In her other life, the one back in the twenty-first century, there where very few things left to chance. Her bills were always paid on time, her car's maintenance always up to date. Everything was in control. Completely the opposite of how she lived her life now.

"Even if we could call the Ancients to us, how would we explain a flying ghost in our tent if she were seen?"

Amber was right. Having the Ancients hanging around could be nearly as dangerous as Grainna. The crowd of people would turn into a riot against them if they thought the MacCoinnichs were possessed, or somehow responsible for their problems.

"What if the Ancients approached everyone here and told them to band together in unity?"

"I don't foresee that happening," said Lora. "'Tis never happened in the past."

"Yeah, but if it did, we wouldn't be singled out." At least that's what Liz thought. She really wanted the Ancients to step up to the plate and help a little more than they were. Seemed to her, the Elders screwed up by not making Grainna's curse more difficult to break.

"Careful, Mom," Simon warned, obviously hearing her inner thoughts.

"You know, buddy, peeking inside my head without my permission is going to bring on some serious consequences if you're not careful."

Simon smirked. "What are you going to do, take away video games for the week?"

Liz reached over, grabbed a pillow, and tossed it at her son. "I mean it, Simon."

"Okay," he mumbled.

~~~~

Tatiana hid her shaking hands in the fold of her dress. Her eyes shot to her feet anytime someone glanced her way.

Grainna had sent her there as a test. Her loyalty and usefulness needed to be proven in order for her to survive.

Although Tatiana dressed in a gown befitting the station of one of the guests, she knew she didn't belong. Surely everyone around her could smell out an imposter such as she.

The wedding was two days away according to the conversations she'd overheard when she'd arrived in the makeshift village. Tatiana needed to find one of the youngest MacCoinnichs. Cian, Amber, or even Simon would do. She needed to befriend them and then wait for further instructions.

She knew she'd find one of the MacCoinnichs. That much she had seen in her own future. What frightened her most was her inability to discern what Grainna would ask of her.

The woman's hatred of this particular clan blackened her eyes every time she spoke of them. Would she ask Tatiana to kill for her? More importantly, could she consider doing such a thing?

Tatiana's gaze swept over the crowd searching for her goal. The descriptions Grainna gave her painted a picture in her mind, but she didn't know exactly what the MacCoinnichs looked like. With her jaw clenched in desperation, her eyes searched the people for any familiar sign.

Behind her, a commotion forced her attention. A group of young men boasted over the horde of people.

"My aim is better than any Scot's."

A handsome dark haired young man with

about as many years as she, stepped forward. "Is that a challenge?"

"It is. If you're up for it, Scot."

Tatiana leaned in and listened to the exchange. The Scot wore a kilt, while the blond English lad did not.

"I'm more than ready for the likes of ye."

The blond laughed alongside his friends, and moved in the wake of his peers into a position to make the match. Unable to stop herself, Tatiana followed the crowd. The kilted one glanced around, his gaze landing on hers for only a second. The smile she didn't realize she wore fell quickly as she snatched her gaze away. When she glanced back up, the boy still looked her way. Their eyes locked, and his lips turned up into a slight smile.

Without thinking, Tatiana turned around, ready to flee but found a crush of young people behind her, all pushing in the direction of the contest.

By the time she peered in his direction again, the lad held a crossbow in his hand and stood facing an open field.

Ahead of him, a younger boy ran to place two pieces of fruit upon a nearby stump of a fallen tree. "Is this good?" the boy yelled.

The Scot nodded to his challenger. "Would ye like to go first?"

Instead of answering, the blond lifted his bow, took aim, and fired.

The arrow found the heart of the fruit, and his friends hollered in triumph.

Unaffected, the Scot quickly lifted his bow and split his fruit in two.

A round of boasting commenced, along with a rash of quiet betting behind her.

Both boys stepped several yards back while the younger boy set up two more pieces of fruit.

With each pass, and each arrow aiming true,

Tatiana found herself cheering secretly for the darker haired boy, with an accent matching her own, to win.

Two more rounds and the crowd hushed while the boys laid aim.

She held her breath when the English boy wiped the sweat from his brow. His hand flinched just before he let his arrow fly. Before the arrow reached its destination, Tatiana knew he'd missed his mark.

His friends went silent.

The kilted lad raised a brow and nodded his head. "'Tis a long distance," he said. "One very difficult to make."

Warmth swept over her and a smile fixed to her lips.

The Scot narrowed one eye and peered over his bow. When the arrow whipped through the air, Tatiana saw it reaching toward the heart of the fruit.

The arrow severed the apple and the crowd cheered. The winner quickly found himself surrounded by others.

"Cian. You did it!"

In that second, her smile fell and her heart split in two.

The younger boy who'd placed the fruit rushed to his friend and patted him on his back.

"Did you ever doubt me?"

Tatiana stood frozen in place. The victor had to be Cian MacCoinnich. He used words much like the English, yet he was clearly a Scot. The boy to his side, his friend, held an accent all to his own.

Simon.

She felt suddenly sick. Turning, Tatiana pushed through the crowd until she found a clearing and felt well enough to breathe. The sun overhead heated her skin, adding to her discomfort. This wasn't right. She ran her fingers over the back of her neck and willed her heart to stop racing. The urge to run closed in on her, fast.

"Are ye well, miss?"

A voice startled her into a spin and straight into the face of Cian, the youngest MacCoinnich male.

"Aye, I am," she managed. Yet she wasn't. She was anything but well.

"I noticed ye ran from the crowd. Did my winning the match bring ye such grief?" Cian leaned closer.

If he meant his smile to put her at ease, it worked.

"Nay. Ye are a marvelous marksman. I felt in need of water is all."

Cian reached to his side, pulled up a flask, and offered it to her. "Here."

Hesitant, Tatiana reached for his offering and brought the drink to her lips. It cooled her dry throat. "Much thanks."

Cian plugged the flask. "My name is Cian."

"I'm Tatiana."

Cian reached for her hand and slowly brought the back to his lips.

She had to stop the sob from reaching her throat. No one had ever touched her with such tenderness. She knew her cheeks warmed, but couldn't stop it from showing any more than she could erase the reason she was by his side.

"I've not seen ye in these parts before."

"I've just arrived."

Cian stood taller, and let her hand go. "Mayhap ye'll let me show ye around?"

Her lips fell. She hadn't expected Cian to be so kind. So handsome. Equal parts of her wanted to run away and follow. Instead, she stood, too petrified to move.

Luckily, a girl ran in his direction, her skirt nearly at her knees.

Cain swiveled and caught her in his arms. Concern marred his face.

"Cian, come!"

"What is it, Amber?"

The girl stared up at the sky, not seeing what stood before her, and said, "She's here."

The air rushed from Tatiana's lungs. Her head pivoted toward the trees, searching.

Cian grasped the girl's hand, his smile sunk to the lower depths of the earth.

"Are you sure?"

"Aye."

He glanced toward Tatiana. Sadness filled his eyes. "I need to go."

Tatiana nodded and watched as Cian ran with his sister's hand in his.

Above, a seagull cried.

Tatiana turned toward the sound and walked quietly into the cover of trees.

Chapter Thirteen

Cian and Amber fell into the tent on a full run. Liz shot to her feet. "What is it?"

"Grainna."

"Where?" Myra stood beside Tara and Lora.

Liz franticly searched behind Amber. "Where's Simon?" Her heart leapt in her throat. The three of them were always together. Where was her son? Why wasn't he with them?

"He ran off with Fin and Todd."

Lora placed a calming hand on her shoulder, focusing her. "Where is Grainna?"

Amber shook her head. "I don't know. I felt her."

"Where did you feel her?"

"Everywhere. 'Twas like she hovered over the camp."

Myra slid her arm over her sister's shoulder. "Ye didn't see her?"

"Nay. But she was here."

"Was? She's gone now?" Liz realized she held her shoulders tight, her hands clenched at her side. Get a grip, she told herself.

Liz tuned the talking in the room out and attempted to find her son. *Simon? Can you hear me?*

Nothing.

He'd been out of her head since she'd scolded him for peeking into her thoughts. She started to panic all over again.

Simon?

"Lizzy, what is it?"

"I can't hear him."

"Who?"

127

"Simon," she snapped. "I can't reach him." She tapped her head so the others knew what she meant. "Can you reach Ian?"

Lora paused for a moment, then nodded. "Aye, he's on his way here now with Duncan."

"Simon's not with them?"

Amber stepped forward. "Fin, Todd, and Simon were alone."

Liz smoothed a hand over her hair bound in a snood. *Simon? Dammit, where are you?*

Nothing.

Tears stung the back of her eyes. Flashes of Grainna holding her son to her side and laughing grabbed hold of her head and repeated over and over. *Not again.*

"Fin and Todd wouldn't allow anything to happen to Simon." Myra's smooth voice of reason reached her thoughts.

"We need to find them."

They started toward the doorway and were intercepted by Ian and Duncan.

Lora explained the situation quickly.

Ian lent a reassuring smile. "Calm yourself, lass. Duncan and I'll search for them."

Liz stepped forward. "I'm going with you." There was no way in hell she'd wait behind.

Ian appeared ready to argue, and then nodded once. "Verra well." He turned to his wife. "Let us know if they return here."

She smiled. "Be safe."

Ian winked before the three of them headed out.

The masses of people swam before them, laughing and carrying on as if not having a care in the world. Somewhere, deep inside her, Liz knew they didn't have a clue about Grainna, or the danger she posed.

One of the MacTavish sons smiled as they approached his party.

"Laird Ian, Duncan... ye look to be on a mission."

"Searching for Finlay and Todd. Have ye seen them?" Duncan asked. On any other day, Liz would be annoyed that the men overlooked her. Even her son was omitted from their search.

"Not for some time. Is anything amiss?"

"Nay," Ian added quickly.

Liz seethed quietly. She wanted to correct him and strengthen their search by using all the people there to look.

"If they come this way I'll let them know yer looking for them."

Duncan thanked him.

"Why not let him help search?" Liz asked as soon as they were out of earshot.

"Lass, ye know we can't do that. If..." Ian paused and glanced to the sky. "If *she* is found with them, ye know what we'll be in need of doing."

Oh, God. Her hands shook violently now. Memories of Simon's abduction by Grainna and now dead accomplice Michael, seized her. Simon stood in the circle of stones. Michael held a knife to his throat. The knife pushed into his flesh.

"Elizabeth." Ian sounded like Fin.

"I'm okay." She pushed past him. "Come on."

They found the outskirts of camp and started toward the back of the keep.

Where are you, Simon.

Liz stopped, pivoted. She heard something.

Simon?

"What is it, lass?" Ian asked.

"Shhh!" She closed her eyes and attempted to block out the sound of nearby people. *Simon? Can you hear me?*

Mom?

Her knees gave out. Ian kept her from falling. "Where are you?" she said the words aloud for Ian

129

and Duncan's benefit.

We're... the...

Liz couldn't make out his words. And he sounded strange.

Simon?

The next time he spoke, she heard the words *woods* and *ocean*. Her brief reprieve from hearing his voice gave way to another worry. Why did she have trouble hearing him?

"I'm having a hard time hearing him. He said something about the woods by the ocean."

They turned in that direction and quickened their pace. The crowd thinned out the closer they came to the woods.

Where are you?

You're getting closer, he said, his words clearing in her head.

How did he know where they were? *Can you hear us?*

Not exactly.

Is everything okay? Are Fin and Todd with you? Something wasn't right.

Fin and Todd are right here.

"This way." She pushed through the brush, toward her son's voice. Ian and Duncan kept close.

Movement caught her eye and had her picking up her skirt to move faster.

Todd came into her view first. His face turned toward hers. He acknowledged her with a nod and turned his attention back behind him.

Fin knelt beside a large gray wolf, his hand resting on top of its head.

"Where's Simon?" He wasn't anywhere around. "Simon?" Liz yelled aloud.

Ahh, I'm right here, Mom.

Her eyes widened and her gaze fell to the four-legged animal who sat next to Fin. "Ohmygod." She ran to his side, skidded to a halt, and pushed Fin aside. "What did you let him do?"

"Calm down, Elizabeth," Fin told her, knowing she wasn't going to do well with the new change with her son.

"Calm down? You're telling me to calm down?" she yelled. "We've been looking for you guys for nearly an hour. And didn't Ian tell us to not do this?" She waved her hand toward her son.

"That I did," Ian chimed in, pissed off.

"See? Even Ian's mad."

Fin eyed his father and opened his mouth to explain.

"Stay out of this, Simon," Liz scolded her son who obviously was talking in his head. "No *but Moms*. Change back and let's get you back to camp."

This wasn't going to be good. Fin waited for Lizzy to explode.

"What?" Liz turned her deadly stare Fin's way.

"He's having a hard time shifting back." Which was why they were still in the woods.

Liz's hands flew to her face. "No. Oh, God no."

"Relax." Wrong word. Fin knew it before he even closed his lips.

"Don't tell me to relax." She took Simon's furry head in both her hands and petted the top of his ears. "Are you okay?"

Fin felt the pressure of Simon's inability to shift back start to ease. Without being able to talk with the boy, he didn't exactly know what stopped him from turning back. Now that Lizzy was there, maybe they could figure it out.

"I'm not mad," she told him.

Duncan leaned down. "We didn't know where you were and your mom was frightened."

Fin noticed his father staring his way. He stepped over and let Liz talk with her son.

"It isn't how it looks," Fin told him.

More patient than he would be, Ian crossed his arms over his chest and said nothing. Fin turned to Todd. "Why don't you and Duncan keep an eye out for others?"

"Good idea," said Todd.

By the time Duncan and Todd stepped out of sight, Liz spoke to her son completely inside her head. Every once in a while she'd glare Fin's way and then turn her attention back to her son. After a few minutes, Fin couldn't take any more. "What is he saying?"

"He doesn't know why he can't change back."

"Why did he change in the first place?" Ian's loud baritone voice left little doubt to his anger.

Lizzy quickly waved her hand at Ian behind her back, and she attempted to sooth Simon. "No, honey, he isn't angry. Just try and relax. You can switch back."

Ian stopped asking questions.

Simon closed his wolfish eyes.

Fin held his breath and prayed the boy would change back.

"Remember your legs, your arms. Think of being—" Liz didn't have a chance to finish her sentence. Simon transformed out of the shift in only a few seconds. He stood on the ground, naked and quickly covered his genitals.

Liz gasped and gathered Simon in her arms despite his protest about being naked.

Fin's heart lifted. Relief flooded him.

Ian picked up Simon's clothing at his feet and brought it to him. "Well done, son. Now hurry with these."

"I'm sorry." Simon's voice sounded small.

"It wasn't your fault," Fin reminded him. "You've nothing to be sorry for."

Simon lifted a leg and dressed swiftly.

Lizzy turned her back to them all. Fin heard her sniffle and knew she did her best to hide her tears.

Once Simon was dressed Fin said, "Father,

could you take Simon back to camp? I'd like a word with Elizabeth alone."

Ian clasped Simon around his shoulders. "Come, the rest of the family is anxious to see you."

Simon smiled. "I didn't mean to worry everyone."

"Yer well. 'Tis all that matters."

Simon turned to his mom. "Are you okay, Mom?"

Lizzy pivoted and sent him her most endearing smile. "I love you, sport. We're good."

Fin watched until his father and Simon disappeared from sight. Then he turned and found Lizzy's fist pounding into his chest, nearly throwing him off balance.

Chapter Fourteen

"Why? Why did you let him do that?"

Fin accepted her fists as they hit his chest with each word. The tears streaming down her face brought home how frightened she'd been. With Lizzy, anger always followed scared.

Her accusation didn't surprise Fin. "You said you'd watch over him, keep him safe."

"Is he not safe?"

"He couldn't turn back. God, what would we do if—"

"He did shift back. Everything is fine." The fire spitting from her eyes put the blame squarely on his shoulders.

"Simon told me that he was talking to you about trying a new form."

Which was true. While the three of them were alone, Simon had approached the subject. For a moment, Fin thought it wouldn't do any harm for Simon to try, so long as no one from camp saw. This was surely the reason why he felt guilty when it happened. He hadn't stopped Simon in time.

Then again, the three of them had been distracted.

He tried to reason. "Simon felt Grainna's presence."

Lizzy ran a dry hand over her wet cheeks. "Yeah, well, he wasn't the only one. Why do you think we were frantic to find you guys?"

"Before we knew it, Simon had changed," he explained. "I think his fear caused his reaction."

"You should have stopped him." She swiveled away from him and started pacing.

"I did." He had yelled out for him to stop, but

it was too late. As seconds passed, then minutes, and Simon didn't shift back, Fin knew they had a problem. "You would have fared no better in stopping him than I did."

"That's where you're wrong." She stormed his direction again, stopping only when her chin was a breath away from his chest. "I would have," she said, poking his chest with her finger.

Enough. He grasped her hand in his, halting her assault. "You're scared, worried, and perhaps even mad at yourself for not keeping Simon within arm's reach. I understand that. The boy is fine, Elizabeth. Grainna didn't touch him." *Thank God.*

Her shoulders rose and fell with each heated breath she pulled into her lungs. Her pert little nose flared as her eyes swiveled back and forth between his. Fin knew the moment the ranting fled her body and relief took its place.

She laid her head on the chest she'd stopped poking and gave into the flood of tears.

Fin wrapped his arms around her lithe frame and absorbed her cries.

God she was fragile, delicate, and in need of protection just as Logan had hinted days before.

Fin ran his hand over her cold shoulders and leaned his body into hers. He closed his eyes for a moment and opened his mind to hers. What he saw there wasn't a frightened mother. What he found petrified him. For a brief moment he envisioned Simon lifeless and at the feet of Grainna. His heart lurched in his chest and had him holding Lizzy tighter.

"I'll never let that happen," he pleaded, praying she'd empty her mind of such images. They would surely give her nightmares.

Her sobs echoed in the forest.

When Fin couldn't take her pain any longer, he placed his hands on both side of her head and gently pulled her face from his chest. He stared deep in her sky blue eyes and did the only thing he knew would take her mind off what might have been.

He kissed her.

Salty tears wet her lips and reminded him of how brittle she was. Lizzy's breath caught in her chest and for a moment, she simply accepted his mouth on hers, his touch, his taste. Then her fists that clutched his chest moments before raked behind his shoulders and forced him so close he wasn't sure where his body ended and hers began.

His body responded with an urgency reminding him of his youth. Lizzy swiped her hand down his back and over his ass, inflaming his need of her to a feverish pitch.

Their tongues dueled, each demanding possession. Fin spread his fingers wide and traced the length of her back until he found the curve of her backside. She shuddered in his arms and melted against him. Under her kiss, he felt a slight triumph. She nibbled and sucked his tongue into her mouth until he knew every inch of it.

Lizzy pulled away, forcing his eyes to open. Her chest rose and fell with quick, heated breaths. With sober eyes, she released his body.

He wanted to beg, weep to have more of her.

Liz reached behind her and loosened the laces holding her dress together.

Mesmerized, Fin watched the length of her finger trace a line along her gown until it sat in a pool by her feet. Within seconds, she kicked away her clothing and stood naked before him.

Beautiful. He knew she would be, but to see her against the backdrop of trees and to hear the birds calling above them, Fin thought he'd died and found heaven.

The rosy tips of her breasts tightened with the cool air, and with her hands clutched by her sides, they were the only indicator that she waited for him to stir.

In the seconds it took for Fin to move her way, Liz held a rare moment of self-doubt. His stare penetrated into her mind as he devoured her body with his eyes. He left her moist with wanting.

She needed this, him. Release. Denying it proved useless, and if the past year of her life hadn't reminded her how short life was, nothing would.

Fin's dark eyes swirled as he approached her. Finally, he responded to her invitation and took her in his arms again. His hands smoothed over her body until the cool open air around them disappeared.

His lips possessed hers and heated her completely before moving to the long column of her neck. The soft wisp of his beard sent an erotic shiver down her spine.

Skin, she needed to feel his. Liz found the clasp of his sword and worked it until it fell from his side. The mantle over his kilt followed quickly.

His fingers brushed against her breast and gave her pause.

"Do ye know how long I've wanted this, Elizabeth?"

Yeah, she had a pretty good idea. But she wasn't about to tell him that.

"How long?" she asked while her nimble fingers inched the edge of his kilt higher.

"The first night, when you arrived with Myra..." He gasped when her hand found the curve of his bare ass. Tight. He was so firm absolutely everywhere.

"The first night?" she redirected his words.

"When you *told* me to call you Liz."

She remembered. He'd been such an ass. Forcing his ways down her throat. *"You're Lady Elizabeth,"* he'd said. *"Widow and mother to Simon."* She'd corrected him, but he didn't budge.

He wasn't going to have Simon humiliated by her past indiscretions. In a way, he'd protected her, too. Not that she saw it that way at the time.

"You were such a shithead that night."

"And you, unmoving."

Her free hand wrestled with his kilt and shirt, wanting them off. Fin shrugged his shoulders and released the garments.

Pure, hard muscle met her eager hands. "You pissed me off."

"Your fire made me need."

Need what? she mused. But her eyes traveled down his long torso and followed the ripples of his chest until they met his *need* head on.

"Good God, MacCoinnich, what do you feed that thing?" She licked her lips and prayed he hadn't seen her response.

He didn't answer until her gaze returned to his.

"Blondes."

She gulped, batting down the smile she didn't want him to see.

Before reaching for her, Fin spread his plaid on the mossy surface of the forest floor. It wasn't a bed, not that she needed one. All she had to have was him.

His powerful arms gathered her in, warming her. Soft lips returned to hers. Liz felt her eyes roll back and her head grow faint. Everywhere he touched fluttered with sensation. Desire.

Fin eased his thigh between hers. The friction delighted her deep inside. Her hips buckled and her knees weakened.

"Oh, lass," he moaned as he helped her to their makeshift bed. His thigh pinned her down, the weight a small token of how strong he was.

A callused hand cupped her breast and gave a not so gentle squeeze. She arched into his touch, urging him to explore further. His breath skimmed over her collarbone, his teeth grazed her skin with tiny bites that had her thrusting her mound over his thigh.

His tongue swirled over her nipple, teasing the soft space under her breast until she screamed. "Suck it. Deeper into your mouth. Please."

Her plea brought a teasing chuckle from him, and her desired response soon followed. His lips latched on, shooting flames straight to her core.

The long length of her leg lifted over his hip, his erection hard against her thigh. Liz reached between them until she held his heated length in her hand. Fin stilled. His moan elicited a giggle from her. She stroked the velvety softness to an impossible length.

Fin's breath caught, his forehead came to rest between her breasts. "How I've dreamed of you touching me like this."

Smiling, Liz shifted her weight until Fin lay on his back, his eyes gazing into hers. She ran both hands up his taut chest. "Have you dreamed of this?" she asked before dipping her head and circling his hardened nipples with her tongue. She nipped as he had and awaited his answer.

"Aye," came his guttural cry.

She moved lower, her mound still straddling one of his thighs. She kissed his stomach and ran her tongue along his rib cage. His abdominal muscles tightened, quivered. This was nice, having Fin on his back and at her mercy. Liz allowed her hair to graze over his erection. Her hands skirted his hip until she leaned over to taste his skin there. The heat of his shaft was close to her cheek, the scent of his skin penetrated her mind.

Fin's hand stroked the side of her face. She looked his way, caught his eye, and angled her lips to taste him for the first time.

With the first contact, Fin let loose a long-winded moan. Her tongue lapped up the vein on the underside of his cock and back up to the tip. The size of him stretched her abilities to take him in, but she gave it a try. Salty and warm and oh-so-Fin was his taste.

"Sweet Lord," he said when she pushed him further down her throat. A few more strokes and he reached to pull her away. "Perhaps later ye'll let me come in your mouth, but this time I want to be buried deep inside of you."

Deep? Oh, that sounded so good. He leaned her back and took possession of her mouth in another soul-wrenching kiss. His knee pressed her thighs wider, the cool air around them sending a wave of raw pleasure throughout her body. Had she ever made love outside, in the open, where anyone could come along and catch her? Liz knew she hadn't. For as much as she prided herself on not being a prude, she certainly wasn't *that* experienced.

"I want to taste you," he said between kisses, but his erection pressed closer to her moist center. The fire in the pit of her stomach burned so hot. She simply wanted the *buried deep* part he'd just spoke of.

"Later," she promised. "Please, Fin." Her hips lifted toward his, leaving no doubt as to what she asked for. "I need you now."

He positioned himself above her, his tip slid between the folds of her sex, grazing her. "Ye'll never need to beg me, love."

"I'm not begging." But they both knew that was a lie.

His eyes bore into hers as he pressed his length past her swollen nub and slowly inside.

Her body opened in small degrees, accepting, until her body completely engulfed his shaft.

Once fully seated, Fin said, "Finally."

Yes, this coupling was a long time in coming. Neither of them had been able to deny their attraction. But Liz didn't want to think beyond this act, at least not now.

Fin set the pace, his hips rounding over hers in just the right way to have her seeing stars long before her body started to build toward climax.

"Ye're going to have to get used to me, Elizabeth." His lips met hers again, not giving her time to speak. Not that she knew what to say in response. Except maybe she could get used to this, to giving her body to him to the way his body could make hers sing, just the way he was doing now.

"Oh, Fin," she managed when he nearly drew all the way out and plunged back in. He filled her so completely she wanted to cry. Although he quickened his pace and his body shook with the force of his passion, Fin held fast to her body with such tenderness she felt frail and yet completely protected at the same time.

Months of longing fired deep in her belly with every pass of his sex inside her. Her legs wound around Fin's hips to press him even deeper. Her cries broke the silence of the forest. He leaned down and grasped her nipple between his teeth, shooting her over the edge, and shattering her into sparkling pieces of pleasure. Every muscle tensed as wave after wave of her orgasm washed over her. Her sheath constricted around him with each spasm.

Fin's eager thrusts lasted only seconds longer until she felt his heated seed flow deep inside her. His head fell back and his body trembled.

When he opened his eyes, a smile lit his face before he collapsed on top of her. He moved to the side enough to keep from crushing her. Liz burrowed into his chest with a satisfied sigh.

Chapter Fifteen

Grainna soared above the gathering, her stomach churning with the revelry below her. Merriment presented itself with laughter and raised voices. Children ran and played and even a piper played a tune.

It made her sick.

She flew to distant hill and landed on human feet. Fog meandered in from the sea at a snail's pace.

It was time for chaos. "Time to see some self implosions," she mused.

Grainna tucked her chin deep into her chest and closed her eyes, lifting her palms to her sides and up into the air. "Come this way," she bid the fog. "Flood these people with doubt and fear. Make the first wish of every family come to pass. As wishes are granted, so give the remaining family the knowledge of who extracted these desires. Let friend turn on friend, lover on lover, family on family. Let no one go unscathed."

The earth rumbled and the sky darkened. Winds blew from the west, whipping her hair behind her. Power coursed through her body and slid past her fingers until lightning shot from their tips.

White ghosts of fog billowed toward the keep and the people in its path. Some turned toward the ocean and watched while others ducked into the useless canvas of their dwellings.

"This ought to be fun."

With hands perched on her hips, Grainna rocked back on her heels and watched.

~~~~

Fin refused to move from the haven within her arms. Even though the air around them stirred with a possible storm, he didn't want to break their peace.

Lizzy purred alongside him and shifted deeper against his side.

Thunder cracked over the sea.

Fin groaned.

"No," Liz said when he started to lift himself from the ground. He drew her dress over her frame and wrapped the edge of his kilt beside him. His hand landed on his claymore.

"I don't want to move yet," she said.

He chuckled. "Neither do I, love, but the others will worry."

Lightning lit the sky. The hair on Fin's arm stood on end. Something about the energy around them felt wrong.

Lizzy's hand came to rest on his. "This is a mighty big sword, Fin." But he didn't think his blade was what she spoke of. "God, I wish we were back in my bed at my apartment. Then we could make love all night and not have to worry about bad weather."

The earth beneath them heaved. Lizzy's eyes shot open and dumped her out of her dreamy state. "Did you do that?"

Lightning and thunder burst above them.

"Nay."

The ground shook again and everything swam out of focus.

~~~~

"'Tis time to fetch them, Duncan," Ian told his son, knowing full well what kept Finlay and Elizabeth away.

He'd asked Simon to call his mother in his head some time before. Only to hear the child squeal and see the boy's eyes pinch close. He quickly shook his head and appeared sick. "Oh, that's just gross," he'd said.

"Are they well?" Lora questioned.

"Oh, they're fine. I think I'm going to need therapy though."

Todd burst into laughter.

Tara chuckled. "I guess it's best you stay out of your mom's thoughts from now on."

Simon eyed all the adults in the room before finding a quiet spot in the shelter to hang his head.

Ian wouldn't put him through the ordeal again. Secretly, he smiled at the knowledge of Fin and Elizabeth finding each other. Perhaps now some peace could come between them.

Someone screamed beyond the tent. Ian's head snapped up as his hand reached for his weapon.

Duncan tumbled outside along with him, Todd followed.

A woman's lifeless body lay in a heap beside a young girl. Tears streamed down her face. She shrieked and waved an accusing finger at the man in front of her. "Ye did this. Ye wanted her dead. How could ye, father. Why?" she sobbed.

Swords clashed beyond the woman as two warriors, one half-clothed, the other with blood streaming from a cut in his arm, fought. Both hell-bent on death. A woman held a bed sheet to her naked frame, screaming for them to stop. "'Tisn't what ye see," she cried.

"What the hell is happening?" Todd asked.

Smoke rose from the keep, above the fog that thickened before their eyes.

"Grainna," Ian whispered.

"Oh, God."

Ian swiveled toward the tent to see his wife trembling.

"What, love?"

A single tear drifted down her soft cheek. "Don't ye feel it?"

He started to shake his head when knowledge

flooded his mind. "Fin."

"Mom."

"Oh my God." Tara stepped into her husband's arms. "They're gone."

~~~~

The world ground to a quick halt, jarring Liz so hard her head felt as if it were going to split in two. Her ass on the other hand felt cushioned as if she'd landed on the softest pillow ever made.

Fin grasped her closer, cutting off her air. "Ease up," she said before opening her eyes.

She took one look around the room, her room, where pictures of Simon as a baby hung on the wall, a clock ticked away the hour and a worn-out TV sat on a dusty dresser. Liz opened her mouth and screamed.

Fin clamped a hand over her mouth.

Panic swam up her spine.

The door to her room burst open and a strange, shocked-faced woman stared at them. "Oh my God. It's true. Son of a—"

Fin recovered first, drawing the sheets over their naked bodies.

The woman's voice nearly screamed. "You are real, right?"

Liz nodded.

"Where are we?" Fin asked.

"Elizabeth McAllister's apartment."

"My apartment." The stranger and she spoke at the same time.

"You are her?"

Liz released a breath and willed her heart to slow. "How did we get here?" *And how the hell were they going to get back.*

Fin shook his head. "Grainna."

Of course, it had to be. "But how?"

"Ye wished for this bed, remember?"

With his words came the realization that her wish had been granted.

"Simon! Oh, God, Fin we need to go back." She started to shake.

This couldn't be happening. She wanted to be home, but not without her son.

Not at the expense of their entire family.

"Shhh." Fin wrapped his arm around her in comfort.

The woman at the door approached. Fin found his sword and quickly raised it toward her.

Her hands shot in the air. "Down, cowboy. I'm not the enemy."

Liz pushed his hand aside and helped him lower his weapon. "Who are you?"

The woman's unruly red hair shook when she laughed. "I'm sorry, I'm Selma. Selma Mayfair."

How did she know that name? Liz knew she'd never spoken to this woman before. Then recognition hit her hard. "The book." *Seventh Sense*, her bible on Druids that sat back in the sixteenth century, buried in the wall of her room there.

Selma smiled and shifted her gaze to Fin's naked torso as her cheeks flooded with color. "I guess maybe you two should get dressed."

The door closed behind her, giving Fin and Liz privacy.

"What are we going to do?"

Fin kissed the top of her head. "I don't know, lass."

"I didn't want this. I mean, I did, the bed, the privacy. But not this way."

"I know."

Her heart started to crumble. She reached to Simon with her mind, knowing he couldn't answer her back. As tears stung the back of her eyes, Liz forced them back. "That witch. I swear if I ever get my hands on her, I'll rip her neck from her shoulders with my own hands." Liz pushed out of the bed, grabbed her gown, and struggled into it.

There had to be a way. Some spell to get them back where they needed to be. Hadn't Tara forced Grainna back to this time without the stones? If she could do it, so could Liz. She just needed to focus.

Fin stared at her from the bed.

"What are you waiting for? Get dressed! We can't stay here."

Chapter Sixteen

Fin ducked his head through the door leading to second room of the apartment, making certain it was safe before allowing Lizzy to follow. He'd seen this apartment before, the one night he'd spent in it well over a year prior. His task then was to drop Lizzy and Simon off in this century and go home. Fin ended up staying and defending his sister's honor against Todd.

He smirked at the memory of Todd opening the door of his home and meeting Fin's fist. The man hadn't seen him coming. In the end, Grainna had kidnapped Simon with the intention of returning to the sixteenth-century and regaining her power. All of them ended up traveling through time, and half the stones that gave them the ability to travel through time were now in Grainna's possession. Without them, Fin held no knowledge of how to return home.

Selma paced the main living space of the dwelling but stopped moving once he and Lizzy walked into the room. Her gaze swept over the both of them with a mixture of awe and excitement.

Fin wondered who the lass was, and how she had come about being in Lizzy's apartment.

Lizzy must have been asking herself the same questions because she wasted little time with petty conversation.

"I don't want to sound rude, Ms. Mayfair, but what are you doing here?"

The woman shook her head, her green eyes wide. "Waiting for the two of you."

Lizzy's gaze shot to his, her confusion

palatable. "But we don't know you."

"I know, crazy huh?" She stood and made her way into the kitchen and opened the icebox. "You guys have got to be hungry."

"We've no time to eat. We need to get…home."

Selma removed brightly colored containers from the icebox. "You mean sixteenth-century Scotland."

"How do you know this?"

She blew out a breath with a laugh. "Because you told me."

"Ms. Mayfair, can you stop what you're doing and fill us in on what you know?" Lizzy's raised voice caught the woman's attention.

"Call me Selma. And I'm getting there. You might as well make yourselves comfortable. You're not going anywhere. At least not now."

Fin didn't like the certainty in the woman's tone. It was as if she had knowledge of their future they did not.

Selma stepped out of the kitchen and handed him a bright red metal object. The material seemed to hold some type of liquid but he hadn't a clue as to what.

Liz placed her container on the table and reached for his. She snapped something on the lid and handed it back to him. "It's a soda. You drink it."

Fin brought the strange glass to his mouth and sipped. His nose fizzled as the icy, sweet concoction slid down his throat. He'd never tasted anything of its kind. When he and Duncan had visited the future before, they only spent time at Grainna's Renaissance Faires, and the only beverages available to them there were strikingly similar to what his time offered.

Selma crossed to a satchel and removed a large box. "I think this will explain a lot," she said.

Lizzy sat and pulled him down to her side.

Selma handed the box to Lizzy.

"What is it?"

"My book."

Lizzy's hands carefully removed the lid and set it aside. Inside, the book Fin had witnessed Lizzy reading time and time again at his home sat. Only this book had evidence of age. The edges were tattered and well worn from use and time.

"Oh my God," Lizzy exclaimed while her hands swept over the cover of the book in a light caress.

"Yeah, that's what I thought when I found it."

Lizzy's brows pinched together. "You need to explain."

Selma folded her hair behind her ears while she sat. "Okay, first though, you know I'm a witch, right?"

Fin's back stiffened.

"I think you're a Druid, Selma, but if you'd prefer to be called a witch, fine by me."

"Lass!" Fin shot her a warning. They didn't talk freely of their heritage.

"Oh, give me a break, Fin. She knows more about what's going on than we do at this point."

His jaw clenched.

"Anyway," Selma continued, "I see things others don't. The cops often seek my advice on missing person's cases. After you and your son disappeared, along with Blakely, the police called me."

"Why you? That seems a little too coincidental, don't you think?"

"Not really. Jake, Blakely's partner, traced a lot of his activity back the month before you guys dropped of the face of the earth. You bought a bunch of stuff with your credit card that seemed out of character according to some of your co-workers. At least that's what Jake told me."

"Your book was on the list."

"Yeah. Jake called the police department I

150

worked with occasionally in Ohio, who contacted me on his behalf. He offered to pay my way here so I could poke around, maybe give him a few answers." She spread her hands wide indicating the room in which they sat.

"The first time I set foot in this apartment I knew something bigger than an abduction had taken place." Selma's face paled.

Fin reached to take Lizzy's hand in his. Simon's abduction by Grainna was the last thing that took place in the apartment before they had all been swept back in time.

"What then?"

"I knew someone evil had been here. That you feared for your son."

Fin felt a kinship with the woman speaking. Her gifts were similar to Amber's. He agreed with Lizzy, Selma was kin to them. She was a Druid, not a witch.

"I also knew you'd be back."

That explained why the woman waited for them. But to determine the precise day didn't seem possible.

Liz took to her feet and walked around the room. "Why is everything exactly the way I left it? Why didn't the landlord take possession and sell my stuff for back rent?"

"I haven't gotten there yet. A man from an antique shop called me a few days after I arrived and told me he had something for me. That's when I was given this." She motioned to the book in Lizzy's hand.

"Didn't the dealer question the age of the book?"

"Mr. Harrison handed me a crate with this buried inside a chest. He didn't know what was inside of it."

Fin held up his hand. "Are you saying that our family bequeathed this to you and it's been safe all these years?"

Selma nodded. "You could say that. I was told that a strong family trust shuffled the crate around the world at specified times until it landed here a few weeks after you disappeared. No one was more surprised than I to find my name in the will."

Some of the tension fled Fin's shoulders. "Do you know what this means, lass?" he asked Lizzy.

She sent him a puzzled look.

"We must find our way back in order to set all of this up to happen in the future."

A slow smile spread over Lizzy's features. "Of course. I would have left instructions on how we get back."

"You left me a note, but I'm not sure how much good it's going to do." Selma retrieved the tattered book and fingered through the pages until she found what she searched for.

The paper used was from the supply Myra brought back with her, the ink difficult to decipher. In several places, holes wore into the parchment and it appeared as if some had been burned deliberately.

The script was in Lizzy's hand.

Selma,

You don't know us, but we need your help.

A large space followed with only a few words readable. The letter gave the date and instructions to hold Elizabeth's apartment with the money obtained by the contents in the box. Anything left over was hers to keep. This part was clear and obviously followed by Ms. Mayfair.

Here the letter fell into disrepair and left only a sprinkling of words that held no meaning.

To...home... Observe the stars...only days...use the energy of...all around. Soar above... Ancients...vows...death and sorrow... Redemption.

Liz lifted the paper to the air and tilted it to

the light shining in from the window. "This can't be all."

"That's all there is," Selma told them. "I hope it means something to you, because I couldn't make any sense of it."

Liz's gaze met his as a wave of panic swept up his spine.

"What else was in the crate?" he asked.

"Not a lot. Todd's cell phone, which Jake has. There was a ruby the size of my thumb that I sold to pay for this place like you asked. Some cloth used to preserve the book and a strange rock."

Fin shot to his feet. "Where's the rock?"

Selma retrieved her bag once again. She dug inside, removed aged cloth, and uncovered the stone, one of the six sacred stones that moved them through time. She handed the Ancient's gift to him. Once his fingers touched the surface, a soft pale light glowed from deep inside.

Selma gasped and reached for it again. With her touch, the light pulsed. Liz stood and added her hand. Waves of blue hummed and pulsed along with the beat of their hearts.

Hope spread inside Fin's chest.

All was not lost.

~~~~

They had tons to do, but Liz would be damned if she wasn't going to take advantage of the indoor plumbing with a hot shower and a working toilet. As the steaming water cascaded off her skin and the strawberry scent of the shampoo penetrated into her scalp, Liz wondered about the words left in her own handwriting to a person she didn't even know.

The entire passage started with the word *home*, which obviously meant the sixteenth century keep. Because in truth, the place her feet were planted now might have been familiar, but it no longer felt right. Simon wasn't going to barge in the door. Myra wasn't hiding her laugh behind her hand and Tara wasn't stand beside her husband holding her son. Where was Amber holding one of the keep's cats or Cian teaching Simon how to ride a horse at breakneck speed? Not here! No, this no longer felt like home. Home, at least while the threat of Grainna hung over all of them, was in the sixteenth century. Home was where Liz was needed, where she belonged to a gaggle of family destined to destroy the wicked witch of Scotland.

Observe the stars.

What the hell did that mean? Why on earth would she have been so cryptic in a note to herself? Then again, half the message was unreadable. Maybe she hadn't been such a putz in the past, or future? Or whatever the hell she was going to be.

Liz's head started to pound.

The water grew cold causing a shiver to run down her spine. Slipping from the shower, Liz toweled herself off and dripped dry on the mat covering the linoleum floor. The room felt chilled. She lifted her hand to bring the flame of the fireplace higher and stopped. She wasn't in her room in the MacCoinnich keep. There wasn't a fireplace keeping her room warm.

Liz studied her hand and realized how much she'd changed since the last time she'd emerged from the plastic curtain surrounding the porcelain tub.

Soar above.

The words haunted her. She'd thought them endlessly since the day Simon shifted into a bird and took to the sky.

She'd elevated from the ground without the aid of wings. Deep down, she knew she was the reason she and the sisters hovered above the earth each time they cast a circle and attempted a spell.

She couldn't control it. Then again, she hadn't tried.

Shaking the thoughts from her mind, Liz wrapped a towel over her wet hair and secured another towel around her bare body.

Voices met her ears as she slipped into her room and opened the chest by her bed. She reached inside and found a bra and panties.

"I took the liberty of washing a few things last week, just in case you two actually showed up." Selma spoke from the doorway. An easy smile played on her lips.

"Thank you." Liz ran her fingers over her underwear. "You have no idea what it's like to live without the simplest of clothing." Liz could hear the longing in her own voice.

"No, no I don't. I hope to hear more about it, though."

Liz pulled on a pair of panties under the terry cloth towel and turned away from the door to put on a bra. "I'm not sure how much time we'll have, but I'll fill you in as much as I can. Seems only fair. I can't believe you're here. I don't know if I would have been, if I were in your shoes."

Selma laughed. "And pass over the opportunity to meet a real life time traveler? I'm the one who's lucky. Lucky you found my book and believed what I'd written."

"Your book, your knowledge, has helped us more than once."

Selma turned away, her voice grew dim. "I'm glad it helped you. It didn't sell, and I'll never publish another book again."

Liz wiggled into a fitted T-shirt and zipped up her capris. "Your book, no, *you* have already saved many lives. Don't sell yourself short, Selma." Liz stepped into the other woman's personal space and placed a hand on her arm. "You and I, Fin, we're all family, in a way. Druids. We have a connection, goals that are bigger than any number of books sold in a bookstore. You help people with your gift, right?"

"Yes," she said, green eyes staring into hers.

"Then that's all that matters. Because this—" Liz tossed her hands in the air. "This is only stuff. Helping others, keeping witches like Grainna from taking control, that's more important than stuff."

The sound of a door bouncing off its frame rattled every nerve ending in Liz's body.

"Don't move or I'll shoot." The male voice boomed in the room and brought a second wave of alarm over her.

In the time it took to leap into the living room, the walls started to rattle and the floor shook. The frame of Todd's ex-partner Jake filled the entrance to the apartment. The cold, black steel of a gun was aimed at Fin's chest.

Fin's jaw went taut under the strain of his teeth, his expression deadly.

Jake's gaze wavered as the tremor beneath their feet grew.

With his hand in the air, Fin brought a golf ball-size orb of flame to light. With a toss of his fingers, the ball soared through the air, knocking the gun from Jake's hand. The flame burned out with a small trail of smoke.

"Holy cow," Selma exclaimed.

Jake recovered and lunged for his weapon.

Fin cut off the cop's path and laid the tip of his claymore to his throat.

Pictures on the wall started to fall.

"Finlay?"

"Not now, lass." Fin stared into Jake's eyes, daring him to move.

"Fin! Can you stop the earthquake before the walls crumble and take us all out?"

In a heartbeat, the earth stilled and the room grew quiet.

"Wow!" Selma breathed the word with excitement.

Jake wasn't impressed.

"Elizabeth, remove the second weapon on his leg."

Liz fell to her knees, searching for Jake's backup gun. She and Fin both saw Todd arm himself anytime he left the keep. For good measure, Liz patted down the cop, found a taser tucked at the small of his back, and removed it.

"Until you realize we're aren't here to hurt you, and we haven't done anything wrong, I'll hold on to these." Liz picked up the small arsenal and dumped them in her room.

Fin still held the sword to Jake's neck, neither of them moved.

"Where's Todd?"

Selma shoved herself between Fin and Jake, her hands met her hips, her voice edged on pissed. "Where the hell do you think he is, Jake? He's in the past. Five hundred years in the past. Or haven't you been listening to anything I've said?"

Fin fastened his sword to his side but didn't move far behind the two arguing.

"I don't believe in time travel."

"Did you believe in the fireball that just whizzed by your head?"

Jake shifted his eyes to Liz.

"What about the earthquake? Did you feel that?"

Liz heard his words in her head before they left his mouth.

"We live in Southern California. Earthquakes happen."

Rolling her eyes, she motioned to Fin. "Help him believe."

The smirk flirted across his face sending a strange level of excitement through her. Most of the time his smartassness annoyed the hell out of her. Not this time.

Fin backed up four steps. "Walk toward me,

Jake."

Instead of moving, he glared.

A jolt from beneath his feet urged Jake forward. Each time the man picked up a foot, Fin shook the earth. With each step, Jake's expression shifted from its early hard edge to one of indecisiveness.

"I told you." Selma stood before the cop, placed both hands on his shoulders, and pushed him down into the nearest chair.

Liz could still see the worry and hurt expression on the man's face. Not knowing what happened to his friend obviously ate at him. She knew the look well. She'd worn one herself for half a year when Tara disappeared.

"Todd is alive, well, and happy, Jake."

"Five hundred years in the past?"

Fin positioned himself by her side, his hand rested on his sword.

"Yes. He wouldn't want you to mourn him. And he'd appreciate any help you can lend us."

"You—" he pointed a finger at Finlay "—are wanted for the disappearance of Tara. And you—" he said, waving his hand at her "—are wanted for questioning in regards to a missing police officer. I could have you both in jail within the hour."

Fin edged closer. Liz placed a hand on his thigh, hoping to keep him seated. She said, "Yes, you could. But if you hear us out, I don't think you'll do that. Todd is fine, living happily, back in Fin's time, but that could change if we don't make our way back there."

"What do you mean?"

"Remember the woman you both interviewed in the hospital shortly before we left?"

Jake nodded.

"She makes Osama look like a choir boy. She's why we ended up here now, and the reason we need to hurry back. We need your help, Jake. Todd needs your help. Selma tells me you retrieved his cell phone, the one he locked in a trunk dating back five hundred years. Todd put it there to prove he had traveled back in time, and he wanted you to know he was okay."

"I don't know." Jake ran his fingers over his jean-clad thighs.

"I didn't either, at first. We need you to take a leap of faith. You haven't found bodies because no one is dead."

"We found blood in this apartment."

"Yes." Liz cringed, remembering. "My son's. Not Todd's. Simon survived because of Todd. He wouldn't want to see him hurt now because we can't get back to where we need to be. If we're forced to spend time in jail or answering questions no one will believe, we may get back too late."

Jake settled back in his chair and listened.

Chapter Seventeen

Tatiana stood on the edge of the ridge and witnessed the chaos unfolding before her eyes.

Clans separated from the others, each claiming a patch of land as their own. Knights stood guard, ready for battle. Where was the quiet harmony that met her only hours before?

The wedding that brought all the people together was called off because the bride "wished" she'd never heard of Lord Brisbane. And as a result, didn't.

Grainna held her hands in her lap. A small lift in her eyelids was the only indication of her pleasure at the pain of those who scrambled below them.

"What have ye done?"

"I've done nothing. This is of their making, their desires, their wants. I simply gave it to them."

Something cold and dreadful filled the bottom half of Tatiana's heart. An image flashed in her mind and brought with it a glimmer of hope. A premonition? Desire?

Cian.

A child cried in the distance. The sound scratched her soul.

"Go. Go find the young MacCoinnich. Console him." Grainna's view never faltered. Her eyes stayed on the destruction before her.

"Why?"

With a slow thoughtful movement, Grainna tilted her head in Tatiana's direction, her eyes black with evil. "Is that not your desire? I'll allow your heart to have this." She turned back to the field. "Go."

Without turning her back on Grainna, Tatiana stepped away, forcing her body to keep from running. She tripped on a fallen branch, righted herself, and continued her backward walk.

Only when Grainna was well out of sight did she turn on her heel, lift her skirts, and run.

Laughter followed her.

Night started to fall on the encampment but none inside were seeking their rest.

The MacCoinnichs had pulled their tents to the west, their men sat in arms, waiting to take on any threat.

Tatiana stood beyond their perimeter and watched the movement of the MacCoinnichs and their men.

The masses of people around them thinned. At least two traveling parties had already departed. Tatiana didn't think Grainna would allow them to get far. Grainna didn't allow anything to happen that she didn't have power or gain over.

The thought stalled her.

She was a pawn in Grainna's game. Expendable.

Tatiana pivoted toward the west and inched her way toward the sea cliffs. The ocean crashed upon the shore below, the noise rose above the sound of her breathing, her heart.

Tatiana had suffered her entire life. Her recent visions gave her little hope of any change. She'd had one glimmer of brightness, but the flame quickly faded, leaving her to wonder what the vision meant.

She found a large rock and sat down before crossing her hands over her arms in an attempt to keep some of her warmth. Below her, the image of two people walking caught her eye. Peering closer, she recognized the boy Simon alongside an older woman. His mother, perhaps? Maybe his aunt.

A sound behind her forced her to her feet. Her breath caught in her chest.

"I didn't mean to startle you."

Cian stood within feet of her. His kind face brightened when he recognized her.

"I-I'm... I shouldn't be here."

Cian glanced around. "Where is your kin?"

"My family is..." What could she say to avoid suspicion? Grainna was her only family now. And not one she truly wanted to claim. "They aren't acting normal. I don't know where to turn."

His strong jaw snapped shut and his gaze shifted to the ground. "Seems the entire camp is under some..."

"Spell?"

"Aye, spell."

He stepped closer. On instinct, Tatiana retreated.

"I'll not hurt ye."

She forced herself to smile, relax. "Do ye mind if I sit here a while?"

"I don't own the rock," he said, laughing.

Shifting her skirts, Tatiana seated herself again. The clouds hid the sunset but the sky turned to a deep amber haze.

"Might I sit with ye?"

"I don't own the rock, either."

Cian chuckled before sitting beside her. The warmth of his body caught her by surprise. In years past, the closeness of a man only sent a chill down her spine. Not with him. The coolness of the night drifted away like the sea birds above.

"Is that yer friend from earlier?" Tatiana motioned toward Simon, knowing exactly who he was, but hoping to learn more about the woman with him, and to avoid any uneasy feeling between the two of them.

"Aye. 'Tis his aunt by his side."

"Oh."

"Seems his mother…" Cian abruptly stopped his words. "With all the chaos, he's finding it difficult to locate his mother."

"Oh, how horrible."

"We'll find her."

Tatiana glanced his way. His dark hair brushed the edges of his shoulders, his skin the color of honey. His chocolate brown eyes found hers. Heat rose in her cheeks.

"I hope ye do."

"Do what?"

"Find his mother."

"Oh," he managed, distracted by something. "We'll find her."

Tatiana's mouth grew dry. "'Tis nice to have such confidence."

"Confidence?" Cian shook his head, his gaze left hers briefly. "I'm sorry. I seem to be distracted."

"I understand. With all the strange happenings 'tis hard to focus."

Cian reached his hand out and smoothed a fallen lock of her hair from her face. His hand lingered on her cheek. "'Tis yer face that drives me to distraction. Yer beauty."

Something inside her started to melt. She knew she wasn't beautiful, but to hear the words so clearly and with such conviction nearly drove her to believe them.

"I'm not a bonny lass."

"Yer wrong, Tatiana."

The way he voiced her name made her heart beat faster.

"I-I…" She what? Needed air? The world was filled with air, and yet none seemed to be reaching her lungs.

Cian inched closer. His hand had never left her cheek, and suddenly it seemed to find its way behind her head. He slid closer to her, his eyes searching hers.

She licked her dry lips.

She should run. Hide. But when his lips met hers, it was too late. His warm touch was both tender and frightening, but oh so wonderful.

He pulled her close, and she noticed the sizzle his hand left in its wake as it slide down her neck.

Tatiana was lost in his arms. Damned in her own mind.

~~~~

"There has to be more!"

"There isn't." Selma stretched her hands over her head before checking the time on her watch. Two empty pizza boxes held discarded bits of crust. Empty soda and beer bottles made the apartment look like they'd had a college party instead of plotting a trip through time.

"It's after midnight," Selma informed them.

Liz couldn't stop her thoughts from shifting to her son. Was he worried that she'd gone and left him? Did he think she was gone from his life forever?

And Grainna, what was she doing to the family?

Liz dropped her head in her hands, suddenly all the weariness of the day catching up with her. Fin's hand kneaded the taut muscles of her back. Her eyes drifted close as she relaxed into his touch.

"'Tis time to find our rest. Perhaps tomorrow things will become clearer."

Her head shot up and her gaze met his. "No, we need to get back."

"We've no idea how, Elizabeth. Sleep will regenerate our minds," Fin argued, fatigued laced his words.

Shaking her head resulted in Fin pulling her closer to his side. "Stop. I'm anxious to return as well—"

She moaned, "Simon—" The mention of her

164

son's name from her lips ripped a hole in her heart.

"Simon is safe with our family. No one would allow Grainna to disturb a hair on his head, lass."

Fin was right.

Jake kicked off his shoes and folded his arms over his chest.

"I take it you're not leaving?" Selma glared at the cop. The two of them hadn't stopped arguing. They'd continually disagreed throughout the night, setting the tension higher.

"You've got that right."

At least he hadn't forced them to the police station. Liz had to give him credit for that. Yet, no matter how many times Fin proved his gifts to the man, Jake refused to believe in time travel.

Selma rolled her eyes and mumbled something under her breath. "I'll crash in Simon's room."

Liz nodded and reached for Fin's hand as they stood and headed for her room. Once alone, Fin removed his sword and allowed it to lie beside her bed.

He cocked his head to the side and studied the lamp. His kilt brushed below his knees, his muscular arm reached out to touch the hot glass. Before she could shoot out a warning about the light being hot, Fin drew his fingers back.

Liz wondered what his thoughts were. Did he wonder about everything in the room? The digital clock on the nightstand blinked, the time completely wrong. There must have been a power outage. Or maybe the landlord cut it off at some point.

At one time she'd thought this room was big, but with Fin standing in it, she realized how small it really was. She was used to seeing the man surrounded by twenty-foot tall ceilings, rooms a horse could ride into, and fireplaces a small person could stand upright inside. Liz realized just how out of place he was in this time. He was all things

Scottish, all things Highlander. He didn't belong in L.A.

Fin must have felt her eyes boring into him because when he turned, a small smile sat firmly on his lips.

Pivoting, Liz scrambled to find a nightgown. Heat flushed in her face. *What will he wear to bed?* Where the hell did the shyness come from? It wasn't at all like her.

"I'll go change," she managed, before slipping through the door and making her way to the bathroom down the hall.

Liz turned the water on cold and splashed her warm face. She hadn't had time to process her and Fin's intimacy before everything blew up in their faces. How was she supposed to act? What did he expect? Never for a moment did she think they wouldn't share her bed. The thought of him sleeping on the couch made her chuckle. He simply wouldn't fit. Not to mention how empty she'd feel without him by her side right now.

Fin was her connection to the past, to where Simon was alive and well. Somewhere deep in the far reaches of her mind, Liz knew if she couldn't see or touch Fin, she'd wonder if everything that had happened was a nothing more than a bad dream. She'd awake in the morning and expect Simon to be bouncing around in the kitchen and getting ready for school. Okay, maybe not school since it was summer, but still...

Liz opened the medicine cabinet and found a toothbrush. The toothpaste was hard at the cap, but with a little influence, Liz managed to bead a strip of minty fluoride on the brush and gave into a decent cleaning of her teeth.

After wiggling into a soft satin nightgown, she made her way back to her room. Light from the kitchen tossed a shadow on Jake's frame. He'd positioned himself on the couch and had moved the chair in front of the door. Like they'd leave. The man didn't get it. They had nowhere to go.

Inside their room, Fin's sword was within arm's reach. The broad expanse of his naked chest brought a ripple of pleasure down her neck. She remembered how good it felt to touch, to smell, to taste. His kilt sat on the dresser. She shivered.

"What is that you're wearing, love?" His husky voice rumbled in the room.

"It's a nightgown." Why was her mouth so dry?

"Gown? It doesn't reach your knees."

Liz glanced down at her nightclothes. "We still call them nightgowns, even if they don't reach the floor."

Liz forced her eyes to his. His brow lifted in amusement. But it disappeared quickly. "Did you walk by that man wearing only that?"

"What man?"

"Jake?"

"He's in the living room."

"But he could have seen you."

Liz felt her shoulders start to shake. This was rich. Fin was worried about another man's eyes on her body. "I don't think he noticed."

"The hell he wouldn't. You need to cover yourself when you exit this room."

Her head fell back with a full-blown laugh. "Right."

"I mean it, Elizabeth. I'll not have any man feast his eyes on what is mine."

"Yours?"

"Aye. Mine."

Oh, the gall. "Listen, just because we've...slept together, *once* I might add, doesn't make me yours." Her laughter was gone, and her mouth no longer felt like the Sahara desert.

Fin's eyes turned to stone. He flipped off the covers and revealed every asset the good Lord had given him. His cock stood erect, reaching toward his chest.

Liz blinked, forcing her eyes away from him. She placed a hand on her dresser and caught his reflection in the mirror. He reached her in two strides but didn't touch her. His breath reached out and stroked her skin. "Shall I prove it?" he whispered close to her ear.

"I don't belong to anyone." And never had. What she and Fin shared was chemistry. Hot, fiery chemistry.

Fin stalked behind her, his body so close his heat tickled her nipples into an erect state. "You are mine," he said before his lips found the top of her shoulder.

Her head tilted to the side by only an inch. His tongue caressed her skin before giving her a quick nip with his teeth.

The inner folds of her sex liquefied instantly. His hands hadn't even touched her yet, and she was ready to fall on her back and open up for him to sink into.

God, she was pathetic. "I'm not yours, Finlay." Her words held no conviction. They fluttered out, weak, meaning nothing.

She watched him through the mirror. His fingers feathered up her bare arms until they found the thin strips of her nightgown and eased them over her shoulders. It fell to the floor and left her completely bare. Liz closed her eyes and held her breath.

With only his fingertips, Fin guided his touch over her back and down her hips. Heat built and trickled down her spine, settling between her legs. As if sensing her need, his palm reached around her body and flattened against her quivering stomach. She held perfectly still, desperate to convince him she wasn't affected. Her hand gripped the dresser painfully.

"Are you still denying you're mine, love?"

She swallowed hard and gave a quick nod. She didn't trust herself to speak. Only his arm around her waist, and his hand tempting the tender flesh of her abdomen, touched her, but she burned from the heat of his body. She knew if she inched back, even a little, she'd feel his erection press against her skin.

Fin's hand slipped lower, brushed against the hair nestled between her legs. She squeezed her eyes shut, waiting. One long finger sank into her wet flesh, her mouth dropped open.

"You can pretend all you want, Elizabeth, but your body does not lie." His fingers slid over her swollen clit, forcing a groan from her lips.

Fin moaned and pressed his body to hers.

She couldn't take it. Her hips bucked forward, reaching into his touch, her head fell back on his shoulder. Her body swelled and tingled with each touch, each caress. His other hand came up and cupped her breast. She wanted to cry out but remembered the other people in the apartment.

"Open your eyes," he demanded.

She couldn't. She knew he'd be watching them in the mirror. He'd force her to see just how much control he had over her. "No."

His fingers sliding in and out of her sex, forcing her desire to build, stopped. She wanted to weep and beg him to continue.

"Open your eyes, love." This time his words sounded more like a plea than a demand.

Her lids fluttered open. She noticed both her hands grasping the top of the dresser, her knuckles white with strain.

Fin flicked her sex with his hand and pulled her back into his arms. When she met his gaze, she didn't see the triumph she expected. Instead, his eyes melted in a pool of softness. Something she couldn't identify. Something she'd never seen from him before.

He bent his knees and allowed his erection to slip between their bodies.

She started to turn toward him, wanting to feel him inside her. He refused and kept her facing the mirror. He reached down, opened one of the drawers, and lifted her knee up until her foot rested on the wood.

Fin wanted to watch. Damn if that didn't turn what wasn't already lava in her blood into a fiery mass of liquid heat.

Liz released her death-grip on the dresser and reached around to stroke Fin's steel-like thigh. He ground his teeth when her fingers brushed his erection.

Liz found the pearly drop of moisture at the tip of his cock and ran her thumb over it. Fin cursed and thrust his hips into her hand and closed his eyes.

She stroked his heat once, twice and then leaned forward on the dresser. Opening his eyes, Fin bent his knees until she felt the length of him sliding up behind her. He wrapped his hand, wet with her moisture, around his erection, and slid it down the cleft of her ass.

His hand gripped her hips and spread her wider for him. His eyes kept hers in the mirror as his thumb caressed her from behind. A flicker of challenge crossed over his face.

Pleasure ricocheted over her skin.

He positioned the large bolus of his erection between her folds. "This is where I always want to be." One swift thrust and he penetrated her completely.

Liz bit her lip to keep from moaning too loud. "Yes," she whimpered. This was what she wanted, what she needed. Fin held her hips and set the pace of forceful, well-placed thrusts. The long hard length of him filled her completely. Each time he retreated, he rubbed against her at the perfect spot. Tension raced through her and kept her hovering over bliss. Her eyes lost focus and started to close.

"Please, Elizabeth. Open your eyes."

She did. His hungry body melted into hers. Her eyes shifted in the mirror and saw them joined. Her orgasm hovered, just out of reach. Then she saw, before she felt, Fin reaching around to stroke her swollen flesh. Her eyes met his when pleasure shifted and her release collided with his. They rode the waves of ecstasy together. His mouth gaped and his arms held her close as his seed filled her.

Chapter Eighteen

Coffee dripped from the pot at a slow, painful rate. Selma sat at the counter with a cup of tea, Jake watched the news on the TV. The pipes in the apartment hummed since Fin was taking a shower. He'd been in there a long time. But who could blame him. Showers were a taste of heaven!

Unable to wait any longer, Liz removed the carafe and poured herself a cup of java. As the first sip rolled down her tongue, Liz savored the taste. There was very little left of the stash of coffee Myra had brought back with her. They didn't indulge in it often, which made this taste all that much better.

"So are you and Fin married?"

Liz coughed up the coffee and sent a spray over her new friend's shirt.

"W-what?"

Selma chuckled. "I guess not."

"No. We're not married." Liz mopped up the mess she'd made.

"But you're close."

Oh, God, how loud had they been last night? But then, Selma had walked in with the two of them buck naked the day before.

Yesterday already felt like a lifetime ago.

"We're close."

Selma rubbed her chin. "Isn't *that* frowned upon in the sixteenth century?"

Probably. "Would you like some more tea?" Liz changed the subject.

"You don't strike me as shy, Liz. Unless..."

"Unless what?" She didn't know if she wanted in on Selma's thoughts.

"Your closeness is new, isn't it?"

Liz shifted to the cupboard, found it bare. "Uh, you could say that."

Selma lowered her voice. "How long have you two been lovers? If you don't mind me asking."

"What time is it?" Liz wasn't shy, so what was up with her hesitation?

"Eight, and you're changing the subject again."

"No, I'm not. Let's see. Seventeen hours, give or take..."

Selma plopped her tea on the counter. Her mouth opened.

Liz waited for a barrage of questions, but was saved by the sound of pounding.

Jake jumped to his feet as Liz and Selma rounded the corner of the hall. The sound emanated from the bathroom.

"Fin, is everything okay?" Liz called through the door.

"Aye," he grunted. Another crash came. It sounded as if something hard fell against the bathtub. Was Fin showering with his sword?

"What's going on?"

Another grunt, another crash. Liz turned the handle, found it unlocked, and opened the door.

Fin stood in only a towel and was pulling chunks of drywall off the wall, along with the tile from the shower.

"What in the hell are you doing?"

Wiping dust from his hands, Fin peered into the wall. His hand slipped into the dark space and came back with a handful of insulation. Before long, he exposed the pipes, reached in, and grasped the copper. He started to pull.

Liz placed a hand on his arm, stopping him.

"Leave me be. I need to see what holds the water inside."

"Son of a—" This came from Jake. "You really are from the past."

173

Liz started to laugh. Of course, Fin had struggled with the commission of a modern day bathroom ever since Tara returned to the sixteenth century. Until now, he'd only seen diagrams in books and hadn't any idea how the plumbing really worked. Of course, he was destroying her apartment and stopping their ability to use the shower while they were there. He had to be stopped.

"Fin, stop. If we have time, I'll take you to a plumbing store for a demonstration. Right now isn't the time." Although the determined expression on his face did bring a smile to hers.

"I just need this part here I think."

"If you rip that out, the room will fill with water and our presence will be discovered."

Fin glanced at her and stopped his mutilation of the bathroom wall.

"Why don't you get dressed?"

Jake and Selma turned to leave.

"He's going to need something other than his kilt to wear," Liz said. "Can you go get something, Jake?"

"And leave you two? I don't think so."

"What is up with you?" Selma yelled at him.

In the end, Selma left with a few measurements and returned within the hour with jeans, a T-shirt, and a pair of sneakers.

When Fin walked out of the bedroom, his shirt snug over his chest with muscles rippling underneath, Liz's heart lifted with pride.

"Nice! I kinda liked the kilt, but this isn't bad, either," Selma said, her tone teasing.

Jake grunted.

Liz didn't have the patience for small talk. They needed to find a way home. According to her note from the past, they only had days to do it.

An idea formed from the information Selma gave them, or at the very least, clued Liz into a starting place.

"Okay, let's go."

"Go where?"

Liz glanced at Fin. "Selma, you said the trunk came to you from Graystones."

"That's right."

"Well, the name didn't just appear out of thin air. That's the auction house Myra used to sell the candlesticks when she traveled here. I remember Mr. Harrison asking if we'd met before? He acted like he'd seen me and Myra, but I know we hadn't."

"You think he may have some information, lass?"

"I think we need to look, find out what he knows about that trunk. Maybe it's been hidden somewhere, and whoever had it, could give us clues about what to do. It's a long shot, but we need to try."

"Sounds like a plan to me." Selma picked up her purse.

Liz reached over and picked up the remote from the coffee table. She glanced at the news. "Michael Jackson died?"

"Yeah," Selma said.

"Who is Michael Jackson?" asked Fin.

The news switched over to a story taking place at the observatory. Liz turned off the set. "He's a singer."

Fin tilted his head to the side in question.

"Never mind, I'll explain later."

After a quick discussion about how Fin couldn't walk around the streets of the city with a sword strapped to his hip, they left the apartment with the sacred stone and the ancient note Liz hadn't yet written from five hundred years in the past. Talk about an oxymoron.

~~~~

Oversized sunglasses shaded Liz's eyes as they moved from the car to the entrance of Graystones.

As much as she wouldn't mind seeing an old friend or two, she didn't have time for explanations and didn't need the complications that would arise from her sudden appearance.

Selma stepped inside first, followed by Liz and Fin, with Jake trailing behind. Liz never forgot for a moment that Jake now carried his guns and didn't trust them an inch.

It didn't take long for Mr. Harrison to make his way to Selma's side.

"Ms. Mayfair, how good it is to see you again. I've thought of you often over the last year."

Selma shook the man's hand, sent him a smile. "I do hope all your thoughts were good."

The man's belly shook when he laughed. "Of course. I'd hoped you'd come back this way."

"Really, why?"

Liz wondered briefly if the man had something else for her from the past. Something to help them.

"I've wondered endlessly what was in that crate." The wishful gleam in the man's eye matched the tilt of his head.

Selma glanced their way. Mr. Harrison noted them for the first time.

"Where are my manners?" He recovered quickly and stepped forward for introductions. "We've met, haven't we?" he asked Liz.

"Yes, over a year ago. Winter."

His eyes peered over his glasses, obviously trying to place her before shifting to Fin and then Jake.

Mr. Harrison lifted his plump finger in the air. "Candlesticks. Twelfth century."

"Aye," Fin murmured by her side.

The man's brows drew together, his brain obviously trying to recall something. "I've not met you, but I've seen you before."

This was good. Some indication that Mr. Harrison knew something they did not.

"I remember. Your picture was all over the news when you—" he pointed to Liz "—disappeared."

Shit.

Liz swallowed, smiled and flipped her hair behind her shoulders. "Oh, God, that was ages ago. You must have missed the follow-up story."

Selma laughed and placed an arm around Liz. "I'll bet you get that all the time."

Fin appeared in shock, and Jake lowered his gaze to the floor. Thank God, Selma could play along.

"Only when I go to places I haven't been in a while. You should have seen my high school reunion."

Selma went on to talk about pictures on milk cartons. Their banter turned Mr. Harrison's confused expression to one of complacency.

"Well, I'm glad to see you're all right."

"Couldn't be better."

"Well then, what can I help you with?" Mr. Harrison directed them to a large conference table toward the back of the shop.

Selma started talking the minute they were all comfortable. "I was hoping you could give me some more information about the trunk."

"I told you most of what I know. The trunk was bequeathed to you from an old estate. The auction house in London that held it for quite some time sent it to us only days before we contacted you. I've often wondered how it is that you've been given something so old without any knowledge of its origins."

Selma skirted a sly look to Liz.

"Selma discovered a family link," Liz said.

Mr. Harrison scratched his double chin, his eyes narrowed. "I'd assumed as much, but the trunk dates back centuries and the letter requested you—" he pointed a finger toward

177

Selma— "by name. How on earth is it possible for your name to be written in a document so many years in the past?"

Selma opened her eyes wide.

"'Tis something we've all wondered about," Fin chimed in.

Liz's spine shivered. She didn't think Mr. Harrison would believe in time travel or ever connect the dots, but to be talking about the trunk as they were opened the possibilities of discovery.

"There have been a lot of Selmas in my family genealogy."

"Well, that may explain some. Surnames change, however."

"True."

"If it's information about the auction house in London you'd like, I can give you their address and the proprietor's name."

"That would be helpful," Liz told him. She'd have to have the name now to send the trunk in the future... or past... or whatever the hell she was going to do. Auction houses didn't exist in Fin's time. Damn all this paradoxical time travel mumbo-jumbo was resulting in a headache.

Mr. Harrison perched his reading glasses on his nose and turned to his computer. He clicked a few times and sent a file to his printer. Liz leaned over to Fin and whispered under her breath, "He's printing out the address from his computer." She'd talked with him and all the MacCoinnichs about computers and the Internet several times.

Fin sat forward in his chair, fascinated with the screen and images on the monitor.

"Is that the store in London?"

"Auction house. But yes." Mr. Harrison removed the paper from the printer tray and handed it to Selma.

"Is there a way to see what is inside that store from this?"

"They have a virtual monitor twenty-four-seven that can be viewed any time," he said with pride. "Here." Mr. Harrison switched the monitor so they could view the inside of the London store.

Light from the windows indicated the setting sun in London, but enough light shone through to give clear images of the inside of the auction house.

"We have the same system here. It enables both security and the ability for customers to view items before stepping into our establishment."

Fin sat closer. "Could you move the camera to the left?"

Liz studied Fin's face. Fascination and acute attention covered his features.

"It's a wonderful technology, don't you think?"

"Aye." He shook his head, inched closer. "There." He pointed toward the left side of the screen.

"See something you like?" Mr. Harrison asked.

"Can you get a closer look?"

"I can zoom in."

Fin rolled his hand, hurrying the man up.

As the image came into view, Liz felt her throat constrict and her eyes narrow. She reached over and grasped Fin's hand. He squeezed hers back. A massive tapestry flanked one wall of the London auction house. It was Lora's. The one she worked on daily. Only this one was complete. The small square that sat blank back at the keep was now filled in with images of the MacCoinnich's life.

Images of their future.

"Are you interested in the tapestry?"

"Very."

Mr. Harrison swiveled the screen toward him, tapped on his keyboard, and started printing out information. "I'm not sure this piece is for sale. It's been hanging on that wall for as long as I remember. But I can put in a query for you."

179

"Can you print up a copy of the tapestry for us to look closer at?"

"I'm one step ahead of you, Miss McAllister. You'd also be able to research this piece and see better images on your own by using this link here." He circled a website on the paper he'd printed out.

After removing the color copy from the printer, Mr. Harrison scrutinized the image. The flesh between his eyes pinched and he peered closer. His eyes shot from the paper to her and Fin, then back to the paper.

"Now I know why you look so familiar. What an uncanny resemblance."

"I don't know what you mean."

But she did.

It was hard to miss. Her image, along with Myra, Tara, and Amber stood in a circle. Other scenes played out a fight, with Fin's image scattered all over the piece of history.

Luckily, the images were made of thread and not pictures.

"This woman here looks just like you."

Liz lifted her lips into a soft smile. "She's much prettier than me."

The image of Myra was near perfect. It was a good thing she wasn't sitting with them.

"Still, uncanny."

"I noticed the resemblance. 'Tis why I'd like to learn more about it." Fin sat back and crossed his massive arms over his chest.

"Here you go." Mr. Harrison handed Fin several papers after clipping them all together. His gaze shot behind them. "Is he with you?"

Liz turned, noticed Jake hanging back in the store. His eyes glanced their way and then back to the object in front of him.

Selma sighed and stood. "Yeah, we had to drag him in here. He hates antiques."

Chapter Nineteen

With bulky arms crossed over his chest, Ian stared over the hill down to the makeshift village they'd broken away from only a day before. His men surrounded their personal encampment with claymores in hand. The stronger families did as he had, the weak boiled in the mess below.

Inside, he raged. His son was gone with no clear vision to believe he could return. Part of his very soul shattered the moment he felt Fin and Liz's absence.

He knew Grainna watched. She must be laughing at the pain and destruction she'd caused.

With their numbers down by two, winning the war against the witch became even more impossible.

Soft footsteps interrupted his thoughts. He turned to see Amber walking his way. She cocked her head to the side and sent him a timid smile. Ian unfolded his arms and opened them to her. Her small frame trembled in his. Quiet sobs echoed his feelings.

"Shh, lass. There is no reason to weep."

Amber held him tighter. "I weep for you, father. Because you can't."

Ian's throat constricted, and he blinked hard several times. "I don't weep because we've nothing to mourn. Fin is strong."

"I know," she murmured, tears soaking his shirt.

"And Elizabeth." He laughed. "Elizabeth will berate Finlay until he has no choice but to spin the wheels of time to bring her back to her son. I'd bet the Ancients themselves would take pity on the lad and grant them safe passage."

This produced a tiny laugh from his daughter. He wished he could give her more, something solid to hold onto. Hope seemed to be fading by the hour.

Ian pulled away and ran his thumb over Amber's flushed cheek. He opened his mouth to tell her that everything would fare well, but then closed it. He could not guarantee any outcome. With Amber's gift, she'd know if he lied. Her gift robbed her of her youth, and her innocence. If it were his choice, he'd have withheld her gift from her until she was of age. When she said she cried because he couldn't, he knew she'd felt his pain.

For Amber's benefit, Ian pushed away his doubt and willed his heart to mend. They had to find and destroy Grainna.

With or without Fin and Lizzy.

~~~~

"Are you just going to sit there and do nothing?"

Fin lifted his gaze to hers. "I'm thinking."

"Well, do it faster. You've watched your mom working on that thing for years. I can't believe you've never asked her about it. I can't imagine how many countless hours and bloody fingers she's endured over it. The least you could have done was show some interest."

Lizzy paced the room like a caged animal. Jake finally gave up on his constant surveillance and went home to get more clothes. Selma retreated to Simon's room to rest, not that Fin thought she could with Liz shouting as she was.

"I showed interest."

"Yeah, right. Like I believe that."

"I did," he lied. Why on earth would he have paid any attention to women's work? He was the one in the tapestry inflicting mortal wounds to their enemies, not the woman chatting over tea. He had no time for such drivel.

He was a Highlander for God's sake. Even Lizzy, with her thick skull could see that. Couldn't she? Fin slid a glance her way. Her hands perched on her hips, her mouth firm in a straight line, her accusing eyes glared at him.

Damn. Maybe he should have given his mother a few more minutes of his time over the years. Perhaps then, he'd be able to decipher the meaning behind the pictures yet to be woven onto the canvas.

Fin studied the paper picture of the tapestry before him. A battle scene was easy to make out. Swords, blood, and the fallen scattered one corner. Whose blood? Not his mother's, for she must have lived to finish the piece. His father would then survive as well since their Druid wedding vows would take them both from this world at near the same time. Fin held some comfort knowing they both survived.

"Hurry up."

"I'm working on it." Fin refused to meet Lizzy's accusatory eyes. If they were back at the keep, he would have retreated to his father's study to find some peace. Lizzy's small dwelling, surrounded by the noise of the city, clouded his brain. And the air wasn't right, artificially cold and dry. Selma had called it air conditioning, not that he knew why air needed to be conditioned. He didn't ask.

Fin's mind wandered to the trip in time when he and Duncan had traveled and found Tara. He remembered wishing for the ability to ride in a car. Now that he'd done so several times, he wished for the simplicity of his horse. That he could control. That he understood.

This world, Lizzy's world, suffocated him. Some of the pleasantries fascinated him, and, in truth, the food was far superior, but for everything he enjoyed, there was something bigger missing.

"Well?"

"Shh!" Fin snapped his thoughts back to his task. Daydreaming wouldn't aide him now.

Lizzy made small huffing noises as she paced. The louder she huffed, the closer she came to the boiling point.

Perhaps he could find an occupation to keep her busy so he could think.

"Finlay?"

"Dammit, lass, stop badgering me."

"Ahh, Finlay?"

"What?" He tore his face away and over toward her. Only she wasn't standing where he thought she ought to be.

She squeaked.

Fin tilted his head back and followed the sound. Liz hovered above his head, her body flush with the ceiling, her hair cascading down.

"God's teeth!"

"Get me down."

Fin jumped to his feet. He reached both hands toward her, but the eleven-foot ceilings were higher than he could manage.

"How did you get up there?"

"How the hell am I supposed to know?"

Unable to touch anything but the edges of her hair, Fin settled with standing below her so he could catch her should she fall.

"'Tis safe to say we now know what your gift is."

Liz shook her head from side to side. "Get me down."

"Settle, lass—"

"Don't tell me to settle. I don't see you flying above ground."

Fin planted his feet directly below her and kept his arms stretched out. "You're the one keeping your body in the air. 'Tis you who need to relax and focus." *'Tis a good thing we aren't outside.* Fin thought twice about voicing his concerns.

"Focus on what? Being the next Superman?"

"You're still a lass, love."

"You're not funny," she spat.

"Sett—slow your breathing and close your eyes."

Liz set her jaw even tighter. "What the hell is that going to do? I'm not in a yoga class here," she yelled.

He had no idea what a yoga class was, but he could tell Liz would be plastered on the ceiling for a long while if she didn't calm down. For one brief moment, he considered stepping into her room or maybe out of the apartment all together to achieve some peace.

He sighed. With their luck of late, she'd likely fall and break a limb.

"Remember how Simon couldn't shift back into his form the other day?"

"Yeah. What about it? I'm not a wolf, I'm flying."

"'Tis the same thing. If you focus you'll be able to control what's happening."

"What's all the yelling about?" Selma walked into the room talking. Her words barely left her mouth before she gave one short, startled scream.

Fin felt his heart kick faster in his chest. They really didn't need this right now. Selma ran toward them, her arms extended like his. "Jesus, how..."

"I don't know how."

"Fetch a chair," Fin ordered. Selma hurried toward the kitchen. She returned and sat the sturdy chair within his reach. Fin tested his weight and lifted close enough to touch Liz with the tips of his fingers.

"Can you move your arms?"

Her head pivoted toward her right arm, her fingers twitched. "They feel like lead weight. Good

185

God, how can I be flying if I feel like a ball of steel?"

"Does it feel anything at all like when you and the others are bound in the circle?"

"No. Wait. A little, I guess."

He brushed her face with his hand. Under her anger, her hysteria, he noticed her fear. "All right. Concentrate."

Her eyes met his briefly, before they closed. She took a few deep breaths.

"Think of the weightlessness you achieve when you're with Myra, Tara, and Amber. In their presence, you've always been free. Free to express your gifts, show your power."

Her chest shuddered, and she willed herself to relax.

"Good girl. You clasp hands with the others, you light the circle, and you all see as one."

Selma gasped. Fin glanced to see a shimmer of flame hovering above the floor. The flame grew and circled the three of them. Selma shifted from foot to foot. He motioned her to remain silent. He was getting somewhere with Liz, he didn't need her concentration wavering now.

Liz fisted her hands, her wrists started to move.

"In this day," she whispered.

"In this hour," Fin said along with her.

Her hand moved toward his, he clasped onto it.

"I ask the Ancients for my power."

Fin moved closer to her. Her face softened. Her pink lips moved and caressed each word as it left her mouth. "Guide me now so I may see, what will be my destiny."

Her hips floated from their anchor until Fin could reach around her frame. Her body pressed against his brought relief to his mind. She'd done it.

"Ah, guys?"

Selma glanced around at the dancing flames then back up at them.

Shit. Fin hovered with Liz. Only now, they were both hovering and in an upright position. Liz opened her eyes.

"This is an improvement anyway."

He wasn't as sure. "If we were to let go, do you think we'd fall to the ground?"

"Only one way to find out." She sent him a timid smile.

Fin closed his hands around her waist and eased his frame from hers. He let one hand drop to his side and felt a shift of weight lurch from beneath him. His fingers gripped her stable hip. Her hands reached out and grabbed hold of him. He floated higher. Without a doubt, he'd fall to the floor without her hold.

"Are you ready?" he asked.

She drew in a deep breath and nodded once. Her hands lifted away from his forearms.

Fin braced for impact and let go.

He crashed to the ground, his arms ready to catch Liz. She leaned forward as if to catch him and slowly floated down. When her feet touched the carpet, the flames dwindled into nothingness.

After scrambling to his feet, Fin clasped onto her hand.

"Wow. Talk about intense," Selma exclaimed. "Is it always like this with you two?"

"No," Fin said.

"Yes," Liz contradicted at the same time. "Come on, Fin, everyday is another crazy series of events with this family."

"Maybe of late."

"Yeah, well, all I can go on is what I've seen. Of late, nothing is normal. Nothing is easy." Liz collapsed onto the sofa taking Fin with her.

"You can let go, love."

"And sail to the ceiling again? I don't think so. What is happening with me? I'm going to have to wear a lead vest before going outside."

He wasn't going to point out that she'd kept his weight in the air as well. A heavy object wasn't likely to keep her grounded.

"You need to channel your gift, Liz," Selma told her. "Pretending it isn't there or denying it will result in what just happened."

"Floating without cause?"

"Or worse."

The palm of Liz's hand grew damp. Fin patted her fingers with his free hand. "You should spend some time trying to control this new power."

"We don't have time right now, Fin. We have to get back."

He felt her panic and added his own. "I'm working on the how, now. Why don't you and Selma work together to force your power into submission."

She opened her mouth to argue.

He cut her off. "I'll work on this." He picked up the paper and waved it at her. "You work on that. Flying above the heads of people here or back home would be difficult to explain. 'Tis best you master things soon."

She ran a shaky hand through her hair. "You're right."

Fin smiled. "Would you mind saying that again, love?"

Liz snatched her hand away from his, the fire returned to her eyes. "Don't press your luck."

He chuckled at the retreating backs of the women as they left the room.

Chapter Twenty

The large metal cylinder held enough wood to keep the fire going for several hours. They'd watched the amber glow of the horizon fade into a deep blue over the ocean. The only people left on the beach were those surrounding bonfires and enjoying a few adult beverages.

Selma sat beside Jake and Fin held Liz between his legs, her back against his strong chest. He drew lazy circles on her jean-clad thigh and listened to Selma talk of her life.

They were running out of time, Lizzy knew it. She'd worked with Selma for hours with her new gift. The more frustrated she became, the quicker Liz was to find her ass floating above the ground. Luckily, with a little focus she could manage to plant her feet back to earth. If everything didn't feel so dire, Liz would be happy to explore her new power. How high could she go? How fast?

They'd exhausted their theories on how to get back. The tapestry had to hold some answers, but the answers eluded them. Maybe after a good night's rest the answers would come.

The waves crashed on the beach. The nearly full moon cascaded light on the white-capped water giving it a silver glow. Something inside Liz's mind clicked. She stilled and sat forward.

"What is it?" Fin asked sitting up along with her.

She wasn't sure. Like a word sitting on the tip of your tongue, Liz reached for awareness. "Something about the water, the glow of the moon."

"There's a lot to be said about the lunar pull.

189

Legends have been built on full moons for centuries," Selma pointed over to a group of people who'd set up a telescope nearby. "I wonder if anything is happening in the sky that may give us a clue."

"Oh, man. Next you're going to ask everyone their sign." Jake rolled his eyes.

"You're a real killjoy, Jake. Has anyone ever told you that?"

"Yeah, my ex-wife. Right before the divorce."

"She and I would get along great."

Liz blocked out their squabbling and stared at the moon. The answer was there, she could taste it.

"Sometimes when I'm trying to solve a problem, focusing on another one allows my brain to rest enough to see the solution for the first." Selma stood and placed her back to the fire searching for warmth. "Has your family considered what to do to destroy Grainna?"

"We're in constant debate on the subject," Fin told her.

"How can you kill someone who's immortal?"

Jake chuckled. "For someone who claims to be up on legends, you don't pay much attention to pop culture."

"Meaning?"

"All the vampire flicks on TV right now."

"I don't think a stake through Grainna's black heart is going to destroy her. Besides, she'd be impossible to get that close to."

Fin agreed. "Still, the Ancients said to consider this time when finding a way to destroy her."

Liz remembered the visit from Elise well. She appeared like a goddess in gold light, her voice was like a thousand voices of a choir. She'd told them they were the chosen, the only ones who could destroy Grainna. Her cryptic riddle didn't give them a lot to go on and frustrated them more than helped.

"If a stake isn't going to do it, then cremation or beheading should do the trick."

"It's a good thing you're talking about someone who doesn't exist in this time, or I'd have to haul you all in," Jake took a swig from his beer and wiped his mouth with the back of his hand.

"You're all talk, Jake."

Liz leaned back into Fin's arms. "We'd have to hold Grainna down to set her on fire. She would just shift into a raven and fly away."

Fin's breath fanned her ear when he spoke. "Maybe now that you've found your gift, you could catch her."

She shivered. Fin held her closer.

"I'd love to get my hands on her neck, but at the same time, I'd be petrified." Considering the amount of power the woman had, touching her might be like staring into the eyes of Medusa. Although Grainna may be in the body of a goddess, she had the soul of a snake-haired demon.

"You'd have to have some mighty powerful protection, that's for sure."

"Do you have any idea how to conjure that kind of protection?"

"Didn't you say Grainna holds the power of hundreds of Druids that she's killed?"

"Yeah."

Selma swatted a bug on her bare arm. "Then it would take the strength of hundreds to combat her."

"Hundreds of Druids?" Fin asked.

"That would be impossible," Liz sighed.

"Maybe not Druids, but souls. Decent, spiritual people working toward the same goal."

"How would we obtain that without exposing who we are?"

Selma shook her head. "I don't know. Maybe if

this Ancient came down like an angel and guided the masses to listen to you to defeat her, the people would listen."

"Like that's gonna happen. Elise hasn't even appeared to us since before the last showdown."

Fin ran his hand down her arm, instantly calming her. Feeling helpless never weighed on her like it did now.

"We must find a way to render her powerless in order to destroy her." Fin mused, his voice distant.

"We need to find our way back first."

"I know, lass. We will."

Liz wanted to be more confident, but as the hours ticked on, hope faded.

Selma let out a deep sigh and pushed herself away from the heat of the fire. "I'm going to see what our celestial friends over there are looking at."

Jake snorted and tipped his beer back for another long pull as Selma sauntered away. Her hips swung in step with her hands attracting Jake's eye.

Liz let a smile slip past her lips.

Jake caught her grin and stuck out a defiant chin. "So, my buddy Todd finally settled down?"

Liz shivered as a gust of cold air blew off the ocean. Fin held her closer. When had she grown so comfortable being surrounded by his arms? His scent?

"He and Myra are very happy," Liz told him.

"Does he wear a kilt like you do?" he asked Fin.

"No. He refuses. I think his exact words were, 'There's no way in hell I'm going to wear a skirt.'"

Jake choked on his beer. "Now that sounds like Todd."

"'Tisn't a skirt," Fin defended the garment he'd grown up wearing.

"The hell it isn't."

Fin snorted, the roped muscles on his arm flexed with irritation. "Women wear skirts."

Jake opened his mouth to air his retort, and Liz cut him off. Fin had already voiced his concern about Jake's lack of trust in them. The cop's continual threat to turn them in hung in the air like thick fog. Although he'd seemed to ease into believing their stories, Liz knew firsthand that blindly accepting time travel, Druids, and witches was impossible without proof. When Myra had come to her with the tale of Tara's disappearance and subsequent travel through time, she didn't believe her at all. Or at least not much anyway. Even when Myra proved she held the power to move objects with her mind, Liz really didn't believe she traveled through time. Not until she stood on the snow-dusted hills of Scotland did she truly believe.

"It's a kilt. And it's sexy as hell." Liz hoped her comment would disperse Fin's temper. She didn't want to see him and Jake come to blows.

Lifting a brow in her direction, the hard lines on Fin's face softened. "Sexy, is it?"

Sometimes men were so easy. "Easy access, too."

Fin's hand stroked her waist under her arms and allowed his thumb to trace the outline of her breast, his touch hidden from Jake by the sweater she wore. Chills of pleasure and something else drifted in her mind.

A soft moan rumbled low in his chest as his lips descended on hers. She reached for him just as Selma strode up to the campfire chatting. "I think I know the date that you two are going home."

Her words registered to both her and Fin at the same time. Their kiss forgotten, they snapped their attention to her.

"When?"

"There's a full moon in two days."

"So?"

"There's also going to be a total eclipse of the moon starting at eleven-fifteen."

"That has to be it." Liz turned in Fin's arms and looked him in the eye. "On the tapestry, there's a spot with a dark circle surrounded by a thin line. It has to be what Lora wanted to portray."

"What are you saying, Selma? The stars are going to align and throw these two back in time?" Jake's sarcasm grew thicker with each word.

"Your skepticism is getting old, Jake."

"So is all this mystical, magical bullshit." He stood and crossed his arms over his chest.

"Why are you here, again?"

"To keep an eye on all of you."

"Oh, yeah, so you can what? Turn them in, keep them from going back, and help their family survive. Help Todd survive? Nice way to show your friend you care."

"Todd knew I would do anything for him. He was like a brother to me."

"Is. Is like a brother. Todd isn't dead," Liz spoke up, trying in vain to remind Jake that no harm had come to Todd.

"Was," he corrected. "If you want me to believe your story, then Todd is long since dead."

"Not where we've come from. But there's no guarantee he'll stay whole and healthy if we don't get back there." Their shouts were drawing attention to them from the other people on the beach. Liz pushed herself out of Fin's lap and lowered her voice. "Todd would want you to help. We've already gone over this."

Jake turned his back to them and took a few steps toward the water's edge. He ran a hand through his hair; the dew from the ocean spray had the short strands standing on end. "I don't know what the hell to believe with you guys. About the time I started to move on, get used to the fact that Todd wasn't coming home, you guys show up and offer some hope he's alive."

The hurt in his voice rang strong in Lizzy's heart. She understood his pain more than most. Six months of not knowing if Tara was dead or alive stretched into eternity for her and Simon.

Selma slowly advanced on Jake until she placed her fingers on his shoulders. He flinched, but didn't move away. "At one time, you believed in me on some level. You called me, remember?"

He graced her with a nod.

"Believe in me again. Who knows? Maybe Todd will find a way to leave a personal note or word for you to read so you'll know the truth."

"If he did, wouldn't there be something from him in that trunk?"

"He left his cell phone in there."

"With no way to power it up after centuries of decay."

"Centuries of decay. Listen to yourself. If Todd didn't travel back in time, how could the phone have been placed in that trunk?"

The doubt in Jake's eyes started to fade, but shadows flickered in the back of his eyes. *If only we could open a window and glimpse back into time for him to see.*

"Wait," Liz said a little too loud, making all of them jump at her voice. An idea formed in her head and reminded her of all she'd accomplished with Tara, Mayra and Amber before being whisked away. She may have stumbled upon the power of defying gravity, but she'd been practicing harvesting power and energy for the use of spells for well over a year.

Liz glanced over to the spot the star gazers had been. They'd retreated from their fire when they ran out of wood. Only a few other parties gathered on the beach but they were far enough away to afford Liz's party some privacy.

"I have an idea." She summoned Selma to her side.

"Fin I need you to make a ball of flame. Make it about this big." She circled her hands to indicate the size of a basketball.

"What are ye going to do?"

"I'm going to try and see what's going on back home."

"How do you plan to do that?"

Liz reached over and picked up the backpack that held the sacred stone and removed it. "With a little help from this and the Ancients."

After setting the stone to the side of the fire pit, she motioned to Fin. "Place the ball of flame over the stone and come and take mine and Selma's hand."

"Should we sit?"

"No, if we start to levitate, it won't be as obvious to anyone watching if we're standing."

"Levitate?" Selma sent her a worried frown.

"Side effect," Liz said as if she'd answered the woman's question. "Don't worry, we won't fly south for the winter."

Fin motioned with his hand and gathered a flame from the existing fire until it wrapped around itself in a neat wispy ball. The flame hovered in the air until it sat over the stone, only inches above it.

Liz reached for Fin and Selma's hands and waited for their connection to complete. "Here goes nothing."

Her lungs filled with salt air and blew out in a slow breath. "In this day and in this hour, I ask the Ancients for some power. Give us a window to see the past, make it solid and make it last. Guide our minds to the Scotland sea, as we ask this, make it be."

"Jesus you've got to be kidding me. You sound like a fucking television show." Jake started to walk away.

The wind picked up around the three of them and the ball of flame started turning blue with white-hot heat.

Liz caught Jake out of the corner of her eye as he stepped toward their small circle and glanced at the flame.

The fire reached toward the sacred stone until the entire piece was engulfed inside.

"Did you do that?" Liz asked Fin.

"No."

"Ah, Lizzy..." Selma screeched when their feet left the ground.

Stay low. Liz willed them to stay close to the sand. They rose nearly a foot then leveled down to four or five inches. Before Liz could congratulate herself on directing her new power, the three of them turned clockwise until Liz faced the nearly full moon. "That's new," she mumbled.

"Look," Fin stared into the blaze that now turned white, iridescent.

It's working. Thank God. Liz hissed at Jake, "Watch. Concentrate on Todd and anything you see. Fin, watch the men. I'll look for Simon and the women." She didn't know how long their connection would last and didn't want them all looking at the same thing.

"What should I look for?" Selma called out.

"You're empathic. Hone your gift."

The words barely left her lips and the white heat swirled into a window of the past.

Images swam at them. The sea rushed on the shore and broke against a camp that resembled their small party while they traveled. Brisbane's home sat in the distance, the harmony of the people obviously disheveled with the distance between the camps.

"Jesus Christ," Jake swore behind them.

Liz's heart surged simply seeing the picture. Her eyes searched the sphere for Simon or Tara. Where were they? She noticed Ian and relief washed over her. They were still there. People rushed past, the white flame distorted her view.

"No," she whimpered, fearful the window would close before she saw her son.

Fin drew in a loud breath while Selma held hers tight.

Cian stood still among the trees. Next to him, a gray, dark cloud swirled. The cloud wasn't right. Something watched him, reached for him. Liz screeched out a warning, at the same time a hand pulled Cian's arm away from the cold swirl of despair.

Simon stood at Cian's side.

Tears stung Liz's eyes. Her hand gripped Fin and Selma's.

The image faded in streaks of blue and orange.

For a brief moment, Liz thought she saw her son turn his gaze on her. *I love you.*

Then he was gone.

The flame shattered into thousands of tiny pieces until only the stone remained.

In slow motion, Liz lifted her eyes to Fin who watched her with an intensity that bordered on frightening. "We have to get home."

"They're waiting for our return."

Liz nodded, knowing he was right.

Selma glanced to the ground. They'd elevated over a foot and a half.

Closing her eyes, Liz chanted inside her mind. *I'm grounded, heavy, my feet meet with the earth.*

When her body touched the ground, Liz felt the weight of their troubles fall on her shoulders.

Selma squeezed her hand. "Can we let go now?"

Liz sent a silent prayer of thanks and let

Selma's hand go.

Fin held on and quickly pulled her into his arms. The tears that threatened before welled and trickled down her cheeks. She needed her son. Had to get back to him.

"Lora is waiting for you both."

Selma's words registered. Liz twisted out of Fin's embrace. "W-what?"

"Lora is waiting."

Chapter Twenty-One

"I've had a vision."

Simon shot up from his reclined position next to Tara and shouted out, "Was it about my mom and Fin?"

Lora's dark eyes leveled to him and filled with sorrow. "No, Simon."

"Are you sure—?"

Ian waved a large hand his way and halted his questions. "What did you see?" he asked his wife.

Simon sat back, but listened to every word. The days started to bleed together, and he felt as if he was falling into a pit of hell. His mother and Fin were gone because of him. If he'd not shifted into a wolf and caused his mother to be so angry at him, she and Fin wouldn't have been isolated when they disappeared, and maybe they wouldn't have left at all.

"We need to restore calm among the people here."

"To do that, we need to stay."

Simon had overheard several conversations and debate over the family leaving and returning to the safety of their home. The only reason they'd stayed as long as they had was in hope that his mom and Fin would somehow return. Hearing the Ancients' desire to keep the MacCoinnichs where they were gave him some measure of relief.

"We must stay."

Myra spoke up. "How are we to restore calm? The people are at arms over the atrocities Grainna spread among them."

"The poison of her magic has touched everyone here," Duncan added.

"If we hold any hope in defeating Grainna, we will do so here, with these people. Alone we will fail." Lora's words hung in the air.

"Since Grainna's black magic penetrated the people, maybe we could counter that with spell of our own," Amber offered. Simon caught her gaze but shifted it quickly to Lora.

"Did you speak to one of the Ancients?" he asked.

"I only listen to the Ancients, Simon."

"Why? When Elise came to us before we spoke to her, asked her questions." Simon's heart fluttered in his chest. He could have sworn he'd felt him mother earlier in the day. He searched their small camp for her after that, hoping to find her.

"I listen to their guidance and seek to understand their messages."

"Why not ask where my mom is? Why not find out if she's coming back?" He hated the tears stinging his eyes and wished he could fight them off before any of the men in the room saw them.

"You can't question the Ancients," Cian clipped.

"Why not?" He dragged his hand over his eyes to brush away the tears.

"It isn't done."

"I would have asked, if the Ancients came to me."

Cian rolled his eyes. "You need to grow up, Simon."

Cian's harsh words didn't completely surprise him.

"Cian," Lora scolded him. "Simon wants answers, we all do."

"Crying about Liz and Fin being gone won't bring them back."

A hush went over the room and all eyes sprung between Cian and Simon.

"You're just mad at me because I interrupted you and Tatiana earlier."

Cian's jaw tightened, his eyes turned to hard stones. Simon scrambled to his feet and forced any more tears away.

"Who is this?" Ian asked.

Simon's need to get back at Cian forced the next words out of his mouth. "Cian's girlfriend."

"Is there a girl you've met?"

When the youngest MacCoinnich son didn't offer any explanation, Simon went on. "Yes, he has. And something isn't right about her."

Cian fisted his palm and stepped toward him.

Simon knew he was going to be hit. A part of him wanted to hide behind his aunt, but another part made him step toward Cian and stick out his chin.

Todd stepped between the two of them before any arm was raised to strike. "Okay you two, knock it off."

"You're jealous," Cian told him.

"Of what? She isn't even all that pretty, and something about her isn't right," he taunted.

Cian pushed his way around Todd and managed to shove Simon back two feet. Duncan restrained Cian's arms while Todd placed a calming hand on Simon's chest.

"You're a child. What do you know about anything?"

"More than you."

"You don't belong—"

"Enough!" Ian shouted, stopping them both. "We have real enemies to defeat. We do not need the two of you at arms with each other."

When Simon looked beyond Cian's hateful glare, he realized that everyone stared at Cian. Even Tara's sorrowful expression didn't shift to his. Lora placed a hand on Cian's shoulder, and Duncan patted his back.

He didn't belong. Not really. Without his mother or Fin around, Simon didn't feel connected as he once did. Now that Cian divided his attention with his girlfriend, Simon often felt alone.

"I think you should apologize to Cian, Simon." Tara told him. "We are all missing Lizzy and Fin, but it isn't right for you to take your hurt out on him."

The heat in the tent crushed in on him with the weight of everyone's stare. He wasn't sorry. Didn't want to apologize for anything.

He caught Amber's eye before she turned away.

He couldn't do it.

Simon rushed from the tent and didn't stop running until he met Logan who stood guard by the mouth of the forest.

"Where are ye going this late, lad?"

Simon didn't care. He just didn't want to be anywhere near anyone.

"I've got to pee," he said the first thing he thought of.

Logan laughed. "Well then, be quick about it and don't go in far."

Simon sprinted toward the darkness of the forest until he heard Logan call out to him. "'Tis far enough."

Turning to the other man's voice, Simon stared past him to the torch that lit up the space beside the MacCoinnich's tent. Amber was the only one walking toward him.

"Hurry up, lad."

Simon turned in a full circle, knowing he had nowhere to run. He'd be hungry and cold if he stayed away from the MacCoinnichs for long.

Then again...maybe not.

Before he lost his nerve, Simon turned his thoughts inside his head and knelt to the ground.

"Don't, Simon," Amber yelled.

The bones in Simon's neck stretched, his hands shifted, and fur covered his body as his clothes ripped and fell to the ground. Within seconds, he bounded forward on four legs and met Amber's frightened stare.

Logan noticed him, pulled Amber away, and drew his sword. "Get back, lass."

Simon pivoted and ran into the thick of the forest, ignoring Amber's plea for him to return.

~~~~

Grainna swiveled her fingers over the crystal. Slivers of gray and silver sparks exploded in the glass until images emerged and took the form of people.

Tara held her son with Myra and Amber at her side. Ian bellowed orders Grainna could not hear. Duncan and Todd mounted horses and led several men into the forest.

As much as her black heart soared at the obvious turmoil in the MacCoinnich's life, she loathed the fact that she couldn't see what caused their agitation. What motivated the Druids to scramble as they were?

She searched further and peered deeper into the glass, and summoned her power to hear something, anything.

The women gathered in a circle and clasped hands, but she couldn't see into their minds.

Somewhere a wolf howled, breaking Grainna's vision of the women. "Damn."

Fog covered the glass until swirls of darkness engulfed the entire piece.

Pushing herself away from the table, Grainna screamed and started to pace. Her palms itched and her head ached. She stepped from her shelter and turned her gaze to the nearly full moon. The closer she examined the deep crevasse of the dead rock floating in the sky, the clearer the image of

Liz stared back at her. Just like the crystal ball, black clouds covered the moon as a gust of wind blew from the west and distorted her vision.

"Something is coming," she whispered to herself. A chill ran down her spine and the hair on her arms stood on end.

Grainna swiveled in a full circle and extended her arms to the sky, allowing her shape to change in the space of one breath. As her black wings took flight, she studied the specks of trees below until she landed on a highest tree staring down on the MacCoinnich's camp.

She dipped her head and followed the sounds until she hovered over the large tent.

"He's running," one of the women inside said.

"He's angry, hurt."

Grainna perched on a nearby fallen log.

"Let's try and get into his head and tell him to come back."

Grainna tucked her wings into her sides and listened. Who did they speak of?

"Shhh! Do you feel that?"

The voices inside the tent faded until Grainna couldn't hear anything but the sound of men shouting around her and horses hooves hitting the dirt. Before she could turn her head, a buzz of wind raced toward her wing, catching the tip she'd just stretched out.

Pain burst inside her morphed state, nearly forcing her body to shift into her human form. Forcing her raven-body to the air, she found the wind and ducked another arrow as blood dripped from her wing. She dipped and nearly plunged to the ground. No simple bird would have continued their flight.

Trees hid her escape until the voices behind her drifted away. The strength in her wing wavered until it couldn't hold her weight any longer. She needed to change back quickly, she could feel something rushing into her bloodstream and causing the earth to pitch.

Poison.

In the shape of a bird, she didn't hold the power to overrule the effect of the drug. As her body dove to the ground, Grainna willed the morph to roll through her frame.

She hit the earth with more force than expected and felt the impact travel in waves over her skin.

Naked and panting, Grainna lay on the forest floor until the pain of the fall ebbed. She closed her eyes for a moment and allowed her mind to rest.

Heat fanned her chin and sprung her eyes open. She blinked several times before hearing something running along the forest floor. She'd fallen asleep. She was sure of it. Although it was still dark, the feeling that time had passed was unmistakable.

Unconscious. She'd been vulnerable and exposed. For the first time in centuries, a shiver of fright overwhelmed her.

Shooting to her feet, Grainna studied her surroundings and searched for hidden danger.

As Grainna lifted her arms, intending to shift and travel back to the safety of her camp, her gaze landed on her right arm. There, among a piercing wound that oozed blood, were several feathers left over from her bird-like state.

She touched her wound with timid fingers. The sting of the poison fought inside her.

As her back teeth ground together, the blackness of her heart dripped oil into her soul.

Chapter Twenty-Two

Fin rolled the copper ring in his fingers before loosely connecting it to its mate. "How do they hold together?" he asked the gray haired man with the bright orange vest who'd answered all his questions.

"With this." He held up a small round can. "It's called red hot blue glue. You place a generous amount along this ring and slip these together. The glue sets in minutes and is guaranteed not to leak."

Fin knew he wouldn't be able to match the chemicals that adhered the pipes together once he returned to his time. "What was used in the past, before this red hot glue?"

"I'm not really sure. I think they welded the pieces together. Over time that would rust at the weakest joint."

Fin nodded.

"Are we done now?" Lizzy shifted on the balls of her feet beside him, anxious to leave the giant store full of customers.

"Looks like the missus is bored. Women always want their pipes to work, but don't care how they're put together."

Lizzy huffed out a heated breath. "We can buy a book, Fin. I'm sure this man has better things to do."

"Ms. McAllister, is that you?"

Lizzy turned in the direction of the small voice while Fin froze.

"Ah, hi Eddie," Lizzy said, glancing back at him, Fin could see the concern in her face.

Eddie couldn't be more than six years old,

probably one of the children Liz had watched when she lived in this time.

The child's gaze swept up Lizzy's frame as he tugged on a woman's arm. "Look Mom, Ms. McAllister."

"Oh my God, Liz."

Liz stepped back and reached her hand toward Fin's arm.

"Hello, Mrs. Aaron."

With wide eyes, Mrs. Aaron shifted around the cart until she stood next to Liz. "I thought you were dead."

"Those rumors were highly overrated." Liz squeezed Fin's upper arm. Her nails dug into his skin.

"Does anyone know you're back? Where have you been?"

Lizzy's hand trembled. "Well..."

Fin circled her waist with his free arm. "We should get going."

Lizzy's shoulders fell slightly, her mouth twisted into a grin. "Right—"

"Wait a minute. I was at the station yesterday and your picture was still up on the missing person's board."

Fin wasn't sure what station the woman spoke of, but identifying Liz as someone the police were looking for wouldn't be good for either of them.

As if sensing Fin's concern, Liz spoke over her shoulder to him. "Mrs. Aaron's husband is a police officer."

"He'd be very interested in speaking with you, I'm sure."

As the woman dug into her bag and removed a cell phone, Fin realized how quickly they were losing their freedom. Before he could fully grasp Liz's frantic expression, Fin did the only thing he could.

The first tremor rolled out of his mind and hit

the earth with a punch. The massive shelves surrounding them shook with a noise that surprised him. Several pieces of pipe crashed to the floor. The clerk held perfectly still, and Eddie grabbed hold of his mother's leg and screamed. Fin expected the people around him to run, but instead they seemed frozen. Liz tugged his hand and nodded twice.

The next shake of the earth Fin forced to last longer, and everyone around them sprang into action and ran. Fin grasped Lizzy's hand and dodged the debris that fell to his feet. People screamed and sprinted toward the huge doors of the building. While others stopped once outside, Fin and Liz kept running until they reached the car Selma had rented for them. Liz jumped behind the wheel and quickly started the engine. Only after they cleared the parking lot did Fin let out a long breath.

"Shit and double shit," Lizzy cursed. She forced the car around another and swerved in the lane. Fin held onto the door handle with white knuckles. "We don't need this."

No, they didn't. The full moon and eclipse was still a full night and day away.

"She's going to call her husband and tell him she saw me."

Fin gripped his seat as she skidded around the corner. "Elizabeth, slow down."

Liz glanced at him, then down at the gauge in front of her. Her foot eased off the pedal and the car instantly lost some measure of speed. "What are we going to do?"

"We must warn the others."

"We can't return to my apartment."

"That would be the first place they would look."

Liz stopped at a red light and opened a compartment in the car. She grabbed the cell phone and tossed it into his lap. "Call Selma, tell her what happened."

The metallic device seemed harmless enough. Fin opened it as he'd seen Selma do in the past. Then he was lost. "What do I press?"

"Go to contacts."

Fin found the button and pressed it once. Selma's name appeared next to Jake's. He tried touching Selma's name, but nothing happened.

"Scroll down with the arrow button until her name is highlighted." Liz maneuvered the car until they were on the freeway.

Once Selma's name was brighter than the others, Fin said, "Got it. Now what?"

"Press call or send."

The minute the call went through, the phone made a ringing noise. Fin pressed the phone to his ear.

"Hello?"

Selma's voice made him smile. The device was truly magnificent. How easy it would be to communicate in his time with such an invention.

"Hello?" Selma repeated.

"Selma?"

"Fin, is that you?"

"Aye, lass," he said, excited to be speaking with someone miles away.

"What's up?"

"Jesus, Fin. Stop smiling like you don't know any better and tell her what's going on," Liz yelled.

"Right. We've had some trouble," he began. Within minutes, Selma knew the story and offered her own advice.

"I'm picking up my sister at the airport now. I'll call you once the others come in. Where are you going to be?"

Fin moved the phone from his ear. "Where are we going?"

"I don't know."

Selma must have heard Lizzy. "Never mind. It's probably better if you don't tell me anyway. Have you called Jake yet?"

"Nay."

"I'll do it. If he calls you, don't tell him where you are, either. My guess is he'll be under suspicion before the day is done. We don't want him in any trouble if we can avoid it."

Fin admired how the woman's mind worked.

"I'll be in touch later. Don't go too far. I think I may have an idea of how to get you guys back home."

"What is it?"

"You'll see. Tell Lizzy to hang in there. Later, Fin."

Before he could reply, the connection went dead.

"What did she say?" Liz questioned.

"She told me she believes she has thought of a plan to take us home."

"That makes one of us."

Fin reached over and weaved his fingers into hers. She squeezed his in response. "We'll find our way home, love. We have to."

"In the meantime, we'll have to find a place to hide."

"Agreed."

Fin sat back and watched Lizzy's world speed by at the pace of sixty horses. Cold air hit him from the vents in the car and dried the back of his throat.

It wouldn't be long now.

"By the way, great thinking back there." Liz stroked his hand with her thumb. "With the earthquake."

He smiled into her brilliant blue eyes with pride.

"I didn't think your gift would come in all that handy, but I was wrong."

Her admission took him back. It seemed they'd finally found a place where the two of them could speak their hearts without fear of retribution from the other.

"I'm glad you approve."

They settled into silence for a few minutes before Liz said, "Don't you find it ironic that your gift is to make the earth shake, and mine is to fly above the ground?"

He considered her words. "Opposites?"

"Yeah, yin and yang."

"What is that?"

Liz shook her head. "Nothing. Strange how things work out sometimes."

Fin didn't think she meant to voice her last words. "We work well together. Like the pipes the man at the store spoke of, one part male, one part female. Once a bond is applied they are inseparable."

When Lizzy squirmed under his stare and tried to move her hand from his, Fin held on firm.

"With everything being so crazy in our lives, do you think it's wise to talk about bonds?"

"'Tis because of the madness that we've found each other at all, Elizabeth."

"You'll have to forgive me for not praising Grainna's evil ass."

Even Fin couldn't take his thoughts that far. However, when his head lifted and he caught Lizzy's eyes briefly, he realized that he wouldn't want to be stranded in any time without her by his side. He'd thought endlessly about the possibility of having to stay in her time since they'd arrived. Although he'd miss his family, mourn their absence, he did feel he would survive. The same couldn't be said if Liz had returned here without him. He opened his mouth to tell her his thoughts before her hand broke free of his.

"Sonofabitch!" Liz angled the mirror and

studied it with a frown.

Behind them, a black-and-white car trailed.

"The police?"

"Crap. Are they following us?"

Fin turned in his seat and watched the other car's movements. "Perhaps."

"Mrs. Aaron must have seen us leave the parking lot. Okay, I'm going to get off the freeway." She moved the car to the exit and kept watch in the mirror.

The police car moved in behind them. Only one car separated the two.

"Shit."

Fin noticed the man in the seat, he spoke into a device.

"Stop staring, Fin. He'll see you."

He turned in his seat and leveled his eyes straight ahead.

"What are we going to do?"

Liz pulled into traffic with a jerk.

"Easy, love." Fin searched the road in front of them. Cars were parked along the side.

"Do the police stop to help others in need?"

"They're supposed to."

Fin sat forward and rolled down the window. Hot air met his cool skin like a furnace. "Slow down up here."

"Why? They'll see us."

"Trust me."

Liz brought the car to a slower pace and Fin focused his gift behind them. The earth gave beneath them and caused several cars to swerve. Once the one directly behind them slammed on the brakes he said, "Move faster."

Liz surged the car forward. The police car had no choice but to stop behind the other vehicle. Fin flicked his hand in the direction of a long pole and set fire to the box with wires stretching from it. Soon the space behind their car held sparks and skidding cars. Liz forced the car around a corner and sped past the houses until she managed to put much needed space between them and the police.

"That was close," she sighed.

"Too close."

"We need to ditch this car. They'll be looking for it."

"Where does one *ditch* a car when one wants to hide?"

Liz smiled and turned the car back to the freeway. "Call Selma back. Let her know we're on our way to LAX."

"The airport?"

"Maybe the police will think we've skipped town."

Fin was more than a little impressed. Lizzy's mind leaned toward the criminal a bit easier than he expected. "Brilliant idea."

"Only if it works."

Chapter Twenty-Three

"It's all I could think of. Besides, if anyone understands what it means to camp, it would be someone who lives five hundred years in the past."

Liz rubbed the back of her neck in frustration. Selma was right, but damn if she didn't hate the thought of sleeping on the ground...again. "I'm a transplant from this century. I like my box springs and down comforter."

"Your comforter isn't down. Bargain basement addition at best."

"Thanks for the reminder," Liz sneered.

"No one will look for you here. Who hides out at a state beach campground surrounded by families?"

Liz shuddered, already cold even though the temperature held in the seventies after the sun had gone down. They'd run nearly the entire day. Selma parked them at the campground and ran off to get supplies. Introductions were made to Selma's sister, Beth, who stayed behind at the airport to wait for more of Selma's family.

Their newest friend was calling in her own army. Selma's large extended family was flying in from all over the country. Cousins, once and twice removed, heard her plea for support and jumped on the chance to help her out.

Liz didn't understand it. How could people she didn't know give a damn about her and Fin? It wasn't them, she knew, but Selma they came for. Outside of the MacCoinnichs, Liz didn't know of any family with such fierce loyalty. Her own family, other than Tara, couldn't be bothered to stand by her side during the birth of her illegitimate son, let alone harbor her when she was wanted for questioning by the police.

Yet Selma's family came. From the sound of her estimates, by the dozens. Of course, she promised them a little magic and a show before the night of the eclipse was over. Maybe that was the draw. Free entertainment.

Fin fiddled with the poles to the tent and cursed several times. Even the sixteenth-century knight was having trouble with their deluxe accommodations.

The phone in Selma's pocket chirped as it rang. When she answered, she swiveled around, greeted yet another family member, and walked a couple of feet away.

A couple of kids rode by on their bikes, laughing. They were a couple of years younger than Simon and didn't seemingly have a care in the world. Liz swallowed the lump in her throat. Squaring her shoulders, she walked over to Fin, leaned down, and grasped one of the metal poles. "This is easier with two people."

"I can manage to erect shelter for us, lass."

Liz snorted a laugh. "As much as I'd love to watch you struggle with this thing for the next hour, I'd like to get inside and hide instead of standing here like an idiot waiting for someone to find us."

"Why not use your energy warming something to eat while I finish this."

Liz tossed the pole she held to the ground. "Don't start that sexist shit with me again, Fin."

Leaving the pole and tent aside, Fin stepped her way and placed his hands on her shoulders. Liz pulled out of his grip only to have him come closer and hold her more firmly. "I'm not battling you, Elizabeth. I too want to keep anyone here from seeing us completely. I can manage the tent, and if you hurry with a meal, we can escape the night quicker and avoid being seen."

What a bitch. What was wrong with her? She'd jumped down his throat and all he was doing was expediting their same goal. She covered her face with both hands and shook her head. "I'm sorry."

"We'll both rest easier when we're home," he told her as he gathered her close to the large expanse of his chest. Liz leaned into him, resting her head, and pushing back every what-if that entered her brain. She didn't want to think about the possibility of not returning, of never seeing her son again.

"This is going to be fantastic," Selma boasted as she snapped closed her phone.

"When are you going to let us in on your plan?"

Selma sat at the rickety wooden picnic table and waited for them to sit. Fin straddled the bench seat and pulled Liz back into his arms while Selma explained.

"You said that Grainna held the soul of hundreds of Druids."

"Yeah, so?"

"If I'm a Druid, then it's safe to say those in my family are too, at least some of them, right?"

Fin nodded.

"I've asked them to gather with me to help send you two back. I may not be able to assemble hundreds, but I can bring together a dozen members of my family in hope of helping."

"I doubt a dozen will be enough," Fin said, expressing Liz's thoughts.

"They can't hurt. Last night when we saw into the past, some window opened with only the three of us. The power of the moon, the eclipse, and my family may be enough."

Liz thought of Tara, Myra, and Amber and the hours they sat in a circle chanting spells and wielding their collective power. Together they were strong, could achieve nearly anything they set their minds to. They were connected by blood, either by birth or by ritual. Maybe Selma was right. Perhaps the right amount of weak power would generate enough strength to push her and Fin back in time.

"In order for your plan to work we need to do something first." Liz lifted her gaze to Selma and offered a smile.

"What's that?"

Around them, the campground grew quiet. Large bushes and trees hid their actions from any prying eyes.

"Fin, bring me your sword."

Before Selma could ask why, Fin brought his claymore to the table and sat it between the women.

"Tara, Myra, Amber and I have all shared this spell. A circle of Tara's blood forced Grainna through time before she regained all her power. I'm not certain that this ritual will help, but it certainly can't hurt."

Selma squirmed in her seat. "This is going to require me to bleed, huh?"

Liz chuckled. "Only a little."

Running a finger along the sharp edge of Fin's sword, Liz waited for Selma to do the same. Liz placed her elbow on the table and grasped Selma's hand until both their bleeding fingers touched and their blood mixed.

"In this day and in this hour, I call upon the sacred power. I choose to give my blood to thee, I choose you as a sister to me."

Selma gripped her hand and repeated her words. As the last one slipped from her lips, Liz's hand warmed and a shimmer of hope washed through her.

Before her newest blood sister let her hand go, Selma said, "When you two are safely tucked back in your century, I'm going to do a serious genealogy search. If I don't find a MacCoinnich in my heritage, I'll be shocked."

"I would be, too."

Wiping away a tear, Selma let go and stood.

"If you two are good here, I'm going to cut out for the night." Selma gathered her purse. "I'll call first thing in the morning. If anything happens, call any of the numbers in the phone and let them know where you are. I'll find you."

When Selma drove away, Liz turned toward Fin. "I'm going to miss her."

"We're forever indebted to her."

"Somehow, I don't think she sees it that way."

Fin returned to the tent while Liz placed a couple of logs in the fire pit. Making sure no one watched first, she lifted her hands and forced a spark of flame on the dry bark. Soon the logs caught and the orange glow of the fire warmed their small space.

Inside the waterproof container was a package of hot dogs, buns, a few condiments, and chips. Selma had tossed in a couple of sodas and had the good sense to add the makings for s'mores. After tossing a marshmallow in her mouth, Liz placed two dogs on the long metal stick and roasted them over the fire.

With any luck, this would be her last day in this time.

Damn, when had that happened? When did she stop thinking of the twenty-first century as her time? She glanced toward Fin who'd managed to erect the tent and now filled the inside with blankets and their things.

She would have done anything to return here months ago. She'd vowed to come home once Grainna was destroyed and she and Simon could do so safely. Would she try once that task was complete? Liz turned the hot dogs over and pondered.

If Simon were here, would she be working her way back?

Everything had changed. The family Selma had would have left Liz green with envy if she didn't feel the same connection with Fin and the others. They all counted on each other. Every day, every hour.

"What are you thinking about, love?" Fin sat beside her.

His deep, penetrating gaze burrowed into her. Her heart twisted. "What if we can't return?"

"We will."

"But what if we don't? Or what if the Ancients shift you through time, but not me?" Where had that come from? Having Fin with her was the only thing keeping her sane. Her mind shifted. For a moment, the loss of Fin, her son, and the others threatened to engulf her. She gasped and dropped the hot dogs in the fire. She started to shake.

"Stop." Fin gathered her in his arms. Liz clung to him like a life preserver for a drowning man. "We will return together. Please, love, don't cry."

But the tears came until she soaked his shirt. She pushed her mouth into his shoulder to quiet her sobs. Gentle hands stroked her back and allowed her to break down.

Once she quieted, Fin reached for her face and brushed the tears away. His tenderness no longer surprised her. Her acceptance of it did.

Liz leaned forward and captured his lips until the pain and worry lifted and blew away. Strong, capable hands pressed her closer.

Desire, never far from the surface whenever she was in Fin's arms, grew. When had she fallen so helplessly in love with him? Another sob tore from her throat.

Fin pulled away.

"Don't, Lizzy. Please, it tears me apart to hear you cry."

Forcing the knot down her throat, she met his stare.

Deep inside him, something sparked. Hearing her cry, feeling her anguish exploded his heart into a thousand pieces. He dipped into her mind softly, careful to only seek what she wanted him to see.

"Don't be frightened," he told her, knowing that was some of her worry.

"I am."

"We both are."

Her brows pitched together. "Really?"

"The uncertainty of tomorrow weighs on both of us. Don't feel like you carry that burden alone."

Her eyes shifted from his, their connection lost.

"You're talking about our journey back."

It wasn't a question. It wasn't what she worried about. "There will be many tomorrows for us both."

She started to tug away. He couldn't let her go. She didn't understand what he was trying to say. "Both of us together, Elizabeth."

Fin followed the path of her gaze, which landed on his sword sitting on the table. A dark patch of her blood marred the blade. She'd bonded with Selma and his sisters. There was no mistaking the power they held together.

"We are stronger together." As the words left his mouth, Fin reached for his sword and forced the blade into his palm. "In this day and in this hour, I call upon the Ancients' power. I choose to give my blood to thee…"

Liz sat tall, her eyes met his, and a grin splashed over her face. "If you say brother, I may have to hurt you."

He laughed. "I choose that you are bonded to me."

"What are you saying Finlay?"

"I'm saying that today, right at this moment,

you mean more to me than anything possibly could. That regardless of what may come tomorrow, I want you to be by my side so we can meet it together." The words no sooner left his tongue than he felt the weight of them nail into his soul. Did she know what he meant? Something told him that if he'd said he wanted to spend forever with her, she'd pull out of his grasp and hide. They were close, so very close to forever.

Fin held his breath, only releasing it when she reached for the sword and tore her skin against the blade. "In this day and in this hour. I beg the Ancients for their power. I choose to give my blood to thee, I choose that Finlay is bonded to me."

She grasped his hand. When their eyes met, she touched her blood to his. All the air left his lungs, his head grew dizzy, and the world tilted out of focus.

He awoke to Lizzy's lips on his. Fin crushed her to him and sealed their vow with a soul-searching kiss.

When he came up for air, Lizzy panted and stood. Reaching for him she said, "Make love to me, Finlay."

Her request humbled him.

After gathering a blanket from their tent, he led her away from the camp filled with strangers until he found a secluded section of the beach. Once he spread the blanket out on the sand, he beckoned her with one finger. "Come here, love."

The moon lit her eyes and sparked brilliant stars within them. He brought his lips to hers in a gentle kiss. She sighed and brought her frame along his until every part touched and molded together. Her hands wound around his back and down his hips and thighs. His body tightened, strained against the jeans he wore.

Bending her knees, he lowered her to the ground and pressed his body to hers. When her tongue swept into his mouth, all he could think of was how much he wanted to bury himself inside her. Her hand tugged at his shirt, Fin released her lips, brought his tongue to the lobe of her ear, and gave a gentle tug. Once she shivered, he knew he'd made her forget everything other than him. Her hips pushed against his. Liz wrapped her jean-clad thighs around his.

"I love your arse in these jeans, but pine for the ease of a dress."

Her fingers found the button of his clothes and popped them free. "Back at ya." Her fingers dipped inside his pants until she grasped onto his erection and sprung him free.

He gasped for air and forced control. "Careful, love."

She chuckled and helped him remove his clothes completely.

Only after she kicked her garment free of her legs, and swept her shirt and underclothes to the side of the blanket, did he cover her with his warmth again.

He feathered kisses over her lips. "The moonlight has never looked so good."

"You had me at *come here*. You don't have to quote poetry to me."

He trailed his lips over her breast and pulled one erect nipple into his mouth. Once her body went limp, he drew away. "I don't know any poetry." He bent to the other nipple.

"Oh, God. Yes, you do."

Her leg wrapped around his hips, her heated core pressed against his throbbing erection. If he slid home now, he'd hardly be able to control his seed from spilling. She wanted him to make love to her and he vowed to do so slowly, thoroughly.

Reaching between them, Fin palmed her mound until she rode against his hand and his finger slipped deep inside her wet folds.

A short span separated her breast to her navel. He met her skin, taking the path with his tongue. The salt air drifted over her wet skin. Her hands stroked his hair as he reached lower. He would taste her, explore her body until he knew every inch.

The musky sent of her sex met his senses before he forced her legs aside to make room for him. With the first pass of his tongue, Liz opened farther and pressed him closer. He wanted to laugh, not at her, but for her. She knew what she loved and had no qualms about asking for it.

He found the part of her body that made her breath hitch and her body weep.

"Fin," she moaned her approval and he felt her passion rise and met him. Her thighs pressed against his face until he heard her call his name again and again with her release.

Not allowing her body to settle, Fin crawled up her frame and sunk into her body.

She opened her eyes and wrapped her legs around his waist.

He moved inside her. Slow gentle strokes until he felt her body gripping onto his tighter. Perfect. His release soared through him, catching her a second time. Emotion caught in his throat. The moon really did shine in her eyes and helped him see his future.

Lord help him if she only bonded with him to return to her son. Because as far as Fin was concerned, Liz was his. Now and forever.

Chapter Twenty-Four

Eyeing the long cape Grainna wore, Tatiana listened to the witch bellow orders to her men. Something had happened. She was certain of it. The balance of power tilted in Grainna's favor, which she exploited mercilessly.

Two clans attempted to leave the Brisbane camp to find their numbers quickly depleted and their women and children returning to the safety of Brisbane's keep.

The fog from the sea never seemed to lift. The mist held the poison Grainna used to enslave the minds of her people. Yet Tatiana didn't feel the drug of Grainna's spell and didn't know why.

She hung her head in shame. Unable to stay away from the MacCoinnichs' youngest son would prove deadly to her or him, this she knew for certain. The way the witch studied her and raped her mind after their encounters violated her more than her uncle ever had.

She was a fool to have ever thought that being at Grainna's side would hold some redemption for her sorry existence.

Cian was everything good and pure. With him, Tatiana forgot who she was and the witch she served.

"I want each of you to bring me the severed hand of one of the knights protecting our enemies before the sun rises." Grainna gave her orders. The knights bowed their heads and lifted their swords to her.

Tatiana's lip trembled. "Would it not be better to capture them alive and whole?"

In painful slow motion, Grainna craned her

neck toward her. She blinked twice, once revealing pitch-black eyes that appeared blind, and then a second time to dark soulless eyes. "You question me?"

Tatiana lowered her eyes and cowered. "Forgive me."

She heard her approach, but didn't move. Why had she spoken?

Grainna reached a hand down and touched her face. Tatiana shook so violently her teeth chattered. She didn't dare close her eyes for fear she'd never be able to open them again.

"Where is your loyalty, my dear?"

"With you," she whispered.

One of Grainna's cold, pale fingers raked down her left arm, tearing her dress in its wake.

Tatiana's knees buckled as fear washed over her.

"I don't believe you."

"Please, forgive me," she wept.

Grainna knelt down and forced her gaze to hers. As she did, the stench of rotting flesh swam into Tatiana's nose and made her eyes water. Grainna's expression hardened. She clasped onto Tatiana's left hand and squeezed.

Searing pain burst through her hand and deep in her bones. She tried to pull away but couldn't.

Smoke lifted from her flesh. Tatiana didn't realize the unearthly scream came from her until after Grainna let her loose. She fell in a ball at her feet, cradling her broken and burned hand.

"Perhaps now you'll know never to question me."

As Grainna walked away, the stench left with her.

Before Tatiana could find her balance and seek herbs to relieve her pain, the witch spoke again. "If any knight returns without a hand, I'll take yours instead."

"Please, nay."

Grainna walked away laughing.

~~~~

The fugitive life wasn't something Liz could ever see herself living. She and Fin woke with the sun, packed their things, and shifted from one set of Selma's family's hands to another.

They hopped into one rental car then another so many times Liz lost count. Cars trailed behind and surged ahead, all watching for the police or any indicator of trouble. Sometimes they spoke to one another with cell phones, other times, walkie-talkies. Liz stashed a second set in her backpack just in case they returned to the sixteenth century. Radio waves were available in Fin's time, where cell service wasn't. Having the ability to communicate with a short wave radio would have its advantages.

The plan was to continue moving until nightfall, then meet at the Observatory where there were bound to be hundreds of stargazers gathered for the celestial event. Selma planned to hide Fin and Liz in the crowd and sprinkle her family into the crush of people in hopes of bringing them all together to welcome the eclipse. By the time any authorities could overtake them, Liz and Fin should be gone. With some planning, and a little luck, the plan just might work.

Sandwiched between Fin and Selma, Liz listened to yet another Mayfair cousin bringing Selma up to date on the family members who weren't a part of their little adventure.

"If you hadn't told us to pull out of the market when you did, we'd be in a heap of trouble now," Linda Mayfair, now Linda McBride said from the driver's seat.

"I'm happy you listened. I didn't think Stan believed in my gift."

"He didn't, but does now. Which is why I'm

here." The women laughed.

"Where do you live," Liz asked.

"Vegas. Stan runs three of the biggest convention centers on the strip."

"We appreciate your help," Fin told her.

"Please, a free trip to LA and a family reunion."

"Free?" Liz was wondering where all the money came from for Selma's family to jump on planes and make it to LA within twelve hours.

"I told you about the gems in the trunk. They were worth a lot of money."

"Enough to afford all this?"

Selma lifted a brow but didn't commit to saying she had enough money.

"Selma, tell me you aren't hocking yourself to the hilt for us."

"Stop worrying about me. I'll be okay."

Geez, she's going in debt. Liz wished she could get her hands on the money she'd put in the bank from the sale of the candlesticks Myra had brought with her in time. There was no way she'd be able to go into a bank and leave a free woman. Hell, there wasn't a guarantee there was any money there at all. Who would it go to? Without Simon or Tara to inherit it, who would the authorities give it to? There was only one answer to that.

"Let's find a place to stop for a while."

"Are you sure?"

"Yeah, I need to make a phone call." The call wouldn't be easy, but Liz didn't see any way around it.

Once they found a quiet park, they exited the car and stretched their legs.

"What are you thinking about?" Fin asked once Selma and Linda walked away.

Liz nodded toward Selma. "She's spending her money to make this happen. I'm guessing all of it. It's bad enough she may have some serious explaining to do once we're gone, if we manage to leave. But to bust her financially isn't right."

"'Twas her choice."

"Really? Seems like we forced her into this."

Fin leaned against the car and folded his arms over his chest. He'd shaved his face earlier in the day in hopes of not being noticed. Their pictures were already back in the news. Liz pulled the baseball cap further down her head, her hair tucked into it to hide the color.

"I may be able to give Selma something back."

"How?"

"My parents." She hadn't thought of her parents in months. Not since she'd landed in Scotland did she consider their thoughts once they found that both their daughters were missing.

Calling them and telling them to give any money that may end up in their hands from her account to Selma was the least she could do. There was no guarantee they'd do it, but she had to try. Then again, they would link Selma to her disappearance, and that may land her in even more trouble.

Fin voiced her concerns as if he'd read her mind. "If you tell your parents to give Selma money, the police will question her and possibly hold her."

"Would Jake let that happen?"

"He may not have a choice."

Liz started to pace. "There has to be a way."

"Is there anyone else you trust here?"

"Not on this level."

Fin scratched he head. "What of Tara's friend? The one who took her to the Faire?"

Her eyes lit up. She placed one very noisy kiss on his lips and backed away. "Cassy! Of course." Liz opened the phone and made the call.

Cassy was easy. Her part in Lizzy's plan didn't require anything illegal. Because she worried about tapped phones and everything CSI, Liz kept her conversation short and to the point. Cassy and Selma would never meet, never even know the other person's name.

Calling her parents proved harder than she thought. Part of her prayed for an answering machine, while the other part knew her luck wouldn't hold for that.

When her father's voice, weakened by his growing age, rumbled through the line, Liz felt the rush of every broken dream she'd ever had crash over her.

"Hi, Dad."

He didn't say anything at first, but Lizzy knew he was still on the line because the television blared in the background.

"Elizabeth?"

"Yes, it's me."

The volume of the TV quieted. She had his attention.

"Where are you?"

Like he really cared. "It doesn't matter where I am."

"You always were snotty. Do you have any idea what your mother has been through?" The disapproval in his voice overruled his concern.

"No, why don't you tell me? Tell me how either of you could possibly care what happened to Tara, Simon, and I."

"Elizabeth? God, Elizabeth where are you?" Her mother's tearful voice on a second line had Lizzy choking back. When Tara disappeared, neither of them bothered to travel to Orange County to join in the search. To think that either of them batted an eye at her and Simon's disappearance never crossed her mind.

"Hi, Mom."

Her mother sobbed into the phone.

"Stop it, Louise. She isn't worth it."

"Shut up! I'm sick and tired of you telling me how to feel. I've lost both my children and my grandson because of you, and I'll be damned if I listen to you now."

Liz lifted her chin, wished she could see the expression on her father's face. *Go, Mom!*

The phone clicked and Louise McAllister quickly said, "Are you all right? Where's Tara?"

"We're fine, Mom. All of us."

"I'm so sorry, Lizzy. Sorry for not being there for you. I thought you were all dead, gone."

"Is Dad off the phone?"

"Yes, he stormed out of the house. I need to see you. Where are you?"

A tear ran down her face. There wasn't time. "Listen, I don't have much time."

"What do you mean? Good God, is someone holding you against your will?"

"No. Please I need you to do something for me. For all of us."

"Anything," Louise sighed into the phone.

"Did you and Dad end up with my savings account?"

"Yes, as a matter of fact we did. Where did you get that kind of money, Lizzy?"

"It doesn't matter. Do you still have it?"

"Yes."

Good. "I need you to get the money to Cassandra Ross. She and Tara were roommates. Are you writing this down?"

"I am, but I don't understand. Don't you want it?"

"I don't need it." *Not where I'm going.* She gave her mother Cassy's phone number and address.

"Are you in trouble with the law?"

"No, Mom. We haven't done anything wrong. I can't explain what's happening and you wouldn't believe me if I did."

The pause on the other end of the phone had

Liz wondering if the batteries had gone dead on the phone.

"I'm never going to see you again, am I?"

Big, fat tears sprang from nowhere. Fin came from behind her and placed a hand on her shoulder.

"I don't think so," she sobbed. How unfair that she learned that her mother cared now only to say goodbye.

"I suppose this is the bed I've made. I didn't appreciate you when I had you, and now you're gone."

"I'm sorry I wasn't a better daughter for you."

Louise's voice grew stern. "You stop that right now, young lady. I'm the one who is sorry. Can you ever forgive me?"

"Yes."

"You and Tara were more than I ever deserved. I wish you both all the happiness in the world. Take care of my grandson."

The knot in Lizzy's throat erupted. "I love you."

"Oh, Lizzy, I love you, too. All of you. Be sure and tell your sister."

"I will."

"I'll forever be thankful to have had a chance at redemption."

Liz glanced at Selma who walked their way and made a rolling motion with her fingers.

"I've got to go, Mom."

"You be safe."

"I will."

The line went dead.

"We've got to go. Jake called, said the cell you're using is being tracked."

Without thought, Liz tossed the cell in the ivy away from the car. Selma jumped in the front seat while Fin opened the door to the back.

"Wait," Liz yelled before running over to a

232

massive oak tree.

"What are you doing?"

Liz placed her finger on the bark above her head and singed the bark until she made the shape of a heart. Satisfied, she followed Fin to the car.

"What was that for?" Selma asked while Linda started the engine and backed out of the parking lot.

"For you. Come back here in one month and dig. If you're being watched, wait until it's safe."

"What will I be digging for?"

Liz clasped Fin's hand in hers and smiled.

"About three hundred and fifty thousand dollars."

Chapter Twenty-Five

Unwilling to eat the food his falcon body or wolf form craved, Simon survived on stolen bread and water left in simmering pots. He spent the entire night and following day circling the camps in either wolf or falcon form. He'd stayed warm in animal skin and shifted easily from one shape to the other. His anger lifted, but not to the degree that he was ready to face the MacCoinnichs.

He sat atop the tallest tree. The moon lit the landscape below. With vision far beyond his human capacity, Simon witnessed more atrocities in the past twenty-four hours than he had in the entirety of his life.

Tatiana fumbled upon fallen trees as she made her way closer to Ian's stronghold. He watched, wondering how far she would go. When he'd told Cian that something about the girl wasn't right, he hadn't lied. Yes, he wanted to strike out at his friend for being so cruel, but the girl had an air about her that upset his stomach and filled his mind with dread.

Simon dipped off his perch and landed several feet from the girl. He tucked his falcon wings close and watched.

She held her hand against her body and risked injury protecting it. As a falcon, his sense of sight reminded him of Superman's x-ray vision. As a wolf, smell took over.

Simon flew to the ground and hit the dense foliage on four legs. He shook from head to tail and pressed his nose to the air. *Burned flesh.* He inched closer. Tatiana peered over her shoulder, hearing his approach. He kept to the shadows, avoiding her eyes.

Then the worse scent of all filled his brain with wicked memories.

Grainna.

The rotting flesh of the witch hovered over the girl like a plague. Simon had scented it the previous night before the witch gained consciousness. Fearful that she'd awaken and find him, Simon fled quickly, not looking back. He was a coward.

He should have done something to destroy her while she was vulnerable and weak. Cian would have. Fin, too. But Simon froze, unable to do anything but stare.

Fear rolled off Tatiana as she ran through the forest. Had Grainna hurt her? Was she fleeing to escape the witch?

The girl swiveled around, most likely hearing his approach. Simon didn't try to stay quiet. There was no need. She couldn't hurt him. She didn't have a weapon.

Simon bounded forward, making his presence known. Tatiana met his eyes and stifled a scream deep in her throat. "Please, nay."

She was petrified and attempted to walk backwards, her gaze never leaving his.

He considered shifting, letting her know she didn't have to fear him, but he wouldn't risk being discovered by someone who held Grainna's scent.

Behind her, a rock she didn't see blocked her path. Simon barked out a warning, scaring her further. Her ankle caught and tripped her to the earth. She landed on her injured hand, rent the air with a scream, and then passed out cold.

Standing over her in wolf form, Simon wondered what he should do. The camp wasn't far. In fact, Tatiana seemed to be heading that way when he'd found her.

Having more strength as a wolf than human,

Simon gathered the material of her dress with his jowls and dragged her along the forest floor. Her battered hand flopped on the earth, probably keeping her unconscious from the pain.

As the smells from camp reached his nose, Simon continued to tug and pull. He stopped before anyone could see him, moved several paces beyond the girl, and howled. Voices of alarm rose. He thought he heard his Aunt Tara call his name.

Men carrying torches moved in his direction.

"There," someone shouted.

Simon bound into the forest, leaped over rocks and trees and then sprung into the air on wings.

Cian ran past his father and fell at the head of Tatiana, calling her name.

Ian followed his son.

Tara called Simon's name, pleading for him to return.

~~~~

"Lay her down here so we can see the extent of her injury."

Ian watched Cian handle the girl as if she were made of glass. So this was the one Simon spoke of, the girl who'd captured her son's young heart.

"I saw a wolf drag her from the forest," Logan said from the mouth of the tent.

Those inside froze. *Simon.* Why had he run?

"Keep watch. If ye see the wolf again, call me or Duncan, but do not harm it."

"Aye, my lord. Though the wolf's behavior, 'twasn't normal."

"Nothing appears normal these past few days." Ian didn't concern himself with voicing his unease to Logan. Every one of his men felt danger in the air.

"Tatiana?" Cian stroked the lass's cheek as he coaxed her from her unconscious state.

Logan left the tent, leaving only family

behind. "Todd, see that no one enters."

Todd nodded and slipped away.

The girl stirred, bringing a sigh of relief from his son.

She moaned.

"Be mindful of her hand, Cian," Lora told him, already removing the soiled linen binding the obviously deformed bones.

"Cian?" Tatiana whispered. "'Tis ye."

"Shhh, quiet. Ye'r safe now."

The girl's eyes opened wide. "The wolf?"

"He's gone. Rest, lass."

"Nay, I can't. I've come to warn ye." Her gaze swept the tent. She reached for Cian's hand, pressed it to her chest and then turned her eyes directly to Ian. "Keep yer men close this night, m'lord."

Ian stepped toward her.

"Why?"

"They are not safe. She is collecting bodies, hands." The words left her mouth before she muffled a cry when Lora unwrapped the last of her bandage.

"Who do ye speak of?" But Ian already knew.

"Grainna."

Everyone grew still.

"How do ye know of her?" Cian asked.

Tatiana looked down at her hand, and back to Cian.

"She did this to you?"

"Aye. I spoke against her. 'Twas the result."

Ian squared his shoulders. "How do ye know her, lass?"

"She captured our caravan, killed those who didn't comply to her desires. I became useful to her."

"How so?"

Her gaze slowly shifted back to Cian.

Damnation. The lass used his son.

"I never meant to hurt anyone. I swear it on my life."

Cian backed away.

"Did she follow ye here?"

"Nay. I escaped when she was not looking. I came alone."

"Why?" Cian's voice held ice. His expression turned to stone. "Why are ye here?"

"I came to warn ye."

"And then?" Cian asked.

"Then flee."

Lora glanced at Ian and spoke to him in his head. *We cannot trust her.*

"Where does Grainna lurk?" Ian drew closer while Cian stood and put distance between them.

She sat up and cradled her trembling hand in her lap. "Grainna changes her form. I know not how, but I've seen her take the shape of a crow. She is everywhere. But that is not the answer ye seek." Tatiana's eyes followed Cian as he paced the far side of the tent.

"Tell my father where she is." Cian's harsh tone reflected his pain.

"Her camp is north of here, on the base of the cliffs. Her power there is absolute. To attempt defeating her there would mean death to any who tried."

These words Ian believed.

"Do ye know of any weakness?"

Tatiana closed her eyes and shook her head. "Her evil feeds her power."

"Why did she allow ye to be with me?" Cian asked.

Sorrow filled the darkness of Tatiana's eyes.

Amber knelt at Lora's side and placed a hand on the girl's shoulder.

Is she using her gift? Ian asked his wife silently.

Amber seeks the truth.

"I do not know."

"Ye do not strike me as dense, lass," Ian scolded.

"Nay. I am many things, but daft is not one of them. Grainna wants to destroy ye all, gain the powers ye yield, and rule all who cross her path. She did not reveal to me any goal of my knowing Cian." She bit her lip before continuing. "I cannot be a part of hurting anyone anymore. I cannot be a part of hurting ye, Cian."

Amber caught Ian's attention, stood, and walked toward him.

"Myra, Tara, fetch fresh water and have Logan bring me some ale." Lora directed the women and coaxed Tatiana into allowing her to tend the wound.

Amber lowered her head and her voice. "She is in such pain, physical and in here." She placed a hand to the center of her chest.

"Guilt does that."

"Aye, guilt and remorse. I think she speaks the truth. And the way she gazes at Cian reminds me of how Myra looks at Todd, and the way Duncan coos over Tara."

Ian had seen that for himself. The girl obviously held feelings for his son. Without a way of knowing if she were under a spell, trusting her was out of the question.

"'Tis no use, m'lady. The bones are beyond repair. In time the pain may go away, but I know I will never use it again."

"You cannot be certain of that."

"I can."

Tara returned with ale, which Lora gave Tatiana to drink.

"Nay. I will not be under any spell, with drink or by witch."

"But the pain…"

"Is not so great."

Cian, who had said nothing, now walked to the girl's side and calmly placed his healing hands on her.

Tatiana flinched.

"I will not hurt ye."

"I don't deserve yer compassion."

Cian said nothing, yet continued his task. He closed his eyes and held his breath in concentration. As they all watched, Tatiana's burned flesh slowly started to pull together. Several popping sounds, like that of wood crackling on a fire, flowed from her hand.

She gasped, but held perfectly still. With wide eyes filling with tears, Tatiana beheld the benefit of Cian's newfound gift.

Once he backed away, she flexed her fingers and palm. Her reddened skin still held scars, but the flesh no longer oozed blood and soot.

"Thank ye."

For a moment, the two of them stared at the other as if they were the only two there. Then Cian pivoted and left the tent.

"I should leave."

"Nay."

"I've caused enough pain."

"We've no way of knowing if you are a spy and are returning to Grainna."

"Then I have replaced one prison with another."

Ian tilted his head back and worked some of the growing tension out of his neck with his hand. "Our prison will not damn ye to hell. Grainna's will."

Before Ian could leave the tent, Tatiana's voice made him pause. "I have already seen hell."

Chapter Twenty-Six

"It won't be long now, love." Fin placed his hand to the small of Liz's back and led her through the crowd of people all staring off and into the stars.

The observatory was perched on a hill overlooking the city of Los Angeles. The twinkling lights below flickered as far as his eye could see. The sight would stay with him for his entire life. If he had to choose a perfect night to remember in Liz's century, this one would be it. He'd listened to a man who claimed to be a weekend astronomer explain why the lunar eclipse was taking place, and how often, or in all reality how rare a full eclipse was. He wished he could have spent countless hours poring over the inside of the planetarium to learn the wonders of the universe.

He knew how lucky he was, however. How blessed to have ever stepped foot in such a time and place.

"Do you think this is going to work?" Liz hunched her shoulders and drew the backpack higher onto her arm.

"I do."

"I hope so. I'd hate to think of Selma doing all this to watch our plan fail."

Fin leaned down and placed a soft kiss on her head. "There is something in the air tonight. I feel it." It wasn't simply the buzz of excitement rolling off the people around them either. His gut said they were going home.

"How much longer?" he asked, staring at the fullness of the moon. The actual eclipse took longer than he thought possible. The earth had cast a

241

shadow on the moon for nearly an hour already. The people who gathered there were focused on their telescopes and not paying much attention to them.

"About fifteen minutes until the moon turns red."

"We should change."

Liz jerked her head toward him, her brows slid together. "Into what?"

"Our rightful clothing."

"You want to run around here in a kilt and have me in a wool gown?"

"If we were to end up 'landing' in the encampment, surrounded by people, there would be enough to explain without trying to address these wee shorts." Although he did appreciate the look of Liz's arse in the garment she wore.

"I didn't think of that."

Selma stepped up, interrupting their conversation. "We're all ready. Beth is standing in the middle of the circle where she put your..." She glanced around and lowered her voice. "You know." Fin chuckled. Since Tara's blood sent Grainna through time before, they thought it would work again for them. One of Selma's family members was a nurse and drew blood out of their bodies with a needle and vial. It sounded as if the blood was in place and the night's journey was set.

"Then we should change."

"Change? Into what?"

"Our medieval clothes," Liz told her.

"Not the best way to blend in."

"I think once we start chanting and light a fire around us, blending in will be the last of our worries."

Selma laughed. "True. Goodness, I'm really going to miss you two."

Liz placed a hand on the other woman's shoulder. "We will miss you, too."

An emotional goodbye would cut into their last minutes, which felt suddenly short to Fin. "We need to change, lass."

Fin shuffled Liz to the women's bathroom and hurried into the men's. When he emerged with his kilt in place, mantle properly hung with his sword at his hip, Fin felt more at ease than he had since they'd arrived.

He received plenty of stares as he left the bathroom and waited for Liz by the door.

When she did, she didn't wear the handmade gown she'd arrived to their time in but instead wore a white spun linen with gold and silver threads. She'd brushed her hair free and it now flowed to her mid back.

"Why so fine?" Not that he was complaining. She looked like an angel.

"Something Selma said the other night had me thinking about how we could convince others to help once we made it home. This gown is part of my plan."

Fin gathered her hand in his, removed the backpack from her shoulder, and forced it over his with the second one.

As a crowd started to gather and stare, Fin drew Liz closer and headed toward their predetermined spot on the over-crowded observatory lawn.

As they approached Selma and the others, Fin noticed Jake standing by her side. Part of him tensed, truly unable to know if Jake was there to witness their departure, or keep them from leaving.

"Looks like you two are ready." The police officer wasn't wearing his uniform, and he didn't hold a weapon. When he extended his right arm to Fin, he grasped it firmly.

"We owe you our gratitude."

Jake nodded once. "If this doesn't work, I'm

going to have to take you in."

Fin didn't blink. He shook the man's hand and let it go. "I'll tell Todd of your loyalty to him and your friendship."

"You do that."

Liz pushed through the both of them and wrapped her arms around the man. "Thank you so much for everything."

A gasp waved over the crowd. Fin glanced at the sky and noted the color of the moon. Red. 'Twas time.

Liz quickly pulled Selma into her arms and whispered something in her ear. By the time they parted, both ladies held back tears.

Linda tapped her cousin on the shoulder. "We're gathering people. You guys ready?"

Fin and Liz nodded.

Liz glanced around at the strangers surrounding them before she removed the sacred stone and set it down between her and Fin. Selma spoke into the walkie-talkie and stepped away. *This is it. Or at least it had better be.*

People started to stare at them more than the celestial event in the sky. With so many people, Liz thought it would be difficult to get anyone's attention to listen to them, but Linda proved her wrong.

"As we bear witness to the complete eclipse of the moon, we here at the observatory would like to share with you a ritual that several Ancient people did in celebration of the event."

Liz held in her laugh. Linda had nothing to do with the observatory, but those standing around them wouldn't know that. Outside of a couple of security guards and a person operating the main telescope, there weren't any *officials* around to contradict her.

More than one head turned her way. A few noticed Liz and Fin and stood back when Selma ushered them aside.

"Sometimes, people would be sacrificed during the eclipse as a show of respect to the sun god for his generosity." Linda should have been an actress. Her voice carried through the crowd. Fin captured both Liz's hands and brought her attention to him.

"Are ye ready, love? The moon is red."

Jake caught her attention. He brought a phone to his ear and swiveled toward the parking lot. There, a few police cars pulled up with their lights flashing.

"It's now or never."

"Gather hands with your neighbor and send your thoughts to the gods. Ask them to accept our sacrifice as the Ancients did long ago."

The dozen plus members of Selma's family stood around and grasped hands. Others, strangers, probably toasted from the wine they drank or the weed they smoked, stood and held hands, too. Liz wouldn't complain, they needed all the help they could get.

Over Selma's shoulder, Jake was heading off the police. She couldn't hear what he said, but his colleagues didn't seem in a hurry to take them down.

"Light the ring," she told Fin.

With a flick of his finger, a ring of fire caught on their blood surrounding them. The crowd gasped, but not in the way of alarm so much as in awe.

Liz stared at Selma and mouthed the words *thank you*, then knelt down to touch the stone with Fin's hand in hers. The stone turned as red as the eclipsing moon. As she started to stand tall, the stone levitated from the ground until it sat at chest height between her and Fin.

Jake came forward with the cops at his side, his eyes wide.

Liz took a deep breath and began. "Within this

circle, we seek the power, to return in time with the Ancients' power."

"Okay, everyone, we need to break this up before someone gets hurt." The officer at Jake's side attempted to elbow his way between the people.

Liz shot out her hand in his direction and felt pulsating heat slip from her fingers. "Circle the people with a shield, show us the power that they yield."

The cop flew back. Jake sprang to the side.

Another cop attempted to move toward them and found himself on his butt in the grass.

The crowd around them gasped. Their eyes were wide and no longer stared at the moon.

Liz grabbed hold of Fin's hands again and willed their bodies to rise. The flame surrounding them grew with their assent.

"In this night and in this hour, we ask the Ancients for this power. Send us now across the sea, to be back with our family." Liz glanced to the moon, now completely red with the full eclipse.

Several feet below them the circle of people stared. "If the Ancients will it so, send us now and let us go."

The air thinned and the stars around them swirled until they appeared as streaks of light. Fin held her hands with such a firm grip she thought they'd break but didn't dare let go.

They were moving. Time shifting.

The cool air hit her senses first, then the quick thud of landing, which wasn't all that soft. They tumbled to the ground with such force, they released each other's hands.

When Liz's head stopped spinning, she opened her eyes to see the forest where she and Fin had made love prior to their journey in time.

They were back. She could feel it.

"We did it," she called back to Fin.

Expecting an instant response, her heart fell in her chest when he didn't.

She sat up and saw his frame a few feet away. "Good God, don't scare me like that. For a minute I didn't think we both made it."

Fin didn't respond.

"Fin?"

She hurried to his side. He lay there, eyes closed. Liz shook his shoulders, trying to wake him. Had he fainted during the trip?

"Fin. Wake up."

He didn't. Liz smoothed his hair out of his eyes. Something slick and warm coated her hand. Terror swam over her every bone. "Fin?"

She pulled the sticky substance to her nose, but she already knew what it was. Under Fin's head was a rock, covered in blood.

His blood.

"No. Please God, no."

Liz pulled their backpacks to his side, found his twenty first century T-shirt, and pushed it against his wound. "Come on, Finlay. Wake up. Don't do this to me."

She needed help, but had no idea where anyone was.

Simon! She yelled in her head. *Simon, where are you?*

Liz held her breath, hoping Simon could hear her. She didn't even see smoke from the camp. For all she knew, the MacCoinnichs had left.

"Please, Simon. Hear me."

A rustle in the trees brought the hair on her nape to a stand. She watched as a wolf emerged from the bush, its tail bent low. "Simon, is that you?"

Instead of an answer, Simon shifted form and walked from it naked and smiling.

He ran to her arms and started to weep. "I thought I'd lost you forever."

"Never," she whispered into his hair.

"What happened? Where were you?"

"Not now, Simon. Fin's hurt. We need to get him to the others."

Simon pushed out of her arms and bent toward Fin. "Stay here but keep quiet. There's a lot of danger in the forest tonight. I'll be back with others to help."

Something wasn't right with her son. If the forest was so dangerous, why was he in it alone? Before she could ask, Simon shifted into a falcon and took to the sky.

Once he was gone, she smoothed a hand over Fin's face. "Wake up."

The sleeve of her gown grazed his bloodied hair. She noticed the stain and looked down at her dress. She needed to change before she was seen. She didn't need anyone linking her in this gown to the image she wanted in the future.

After a quick change, Liz tucked the gown away, and searched the ground for the sacred stone. She couldn't find it. *Where could it have gone?*

"Can't anything go right?"

She stopped. Of course the stone didn't travel with them. The stone was already in this time, somewhere, either at the keep or in safekeeping with the MacCoinnichs. Six of them made it to this time, to hold one from the future would mean there are now seven, and that wasn't possible.

Forgetting the stone, Liz slipped beside Fin and carefully pulled his head into her lap and resigned herself to wait.

"We did it, Fin. Now wake up so I can kill you for scaring me like this."

He didn't so much as sigh.

Chapter Twenty-Seven

There wasn't time to waste, no pride to be had. Simon swooped into the massive tent, bringing a gasp from the only real stranger in the space. He knew who she was, didn't trust her in the least, but had little choice but to shift in front of Tatiana.

Each time the shifting grew easier, like riding a bike. He didn't even feel his bones pop and muscles pull any longer.

"Simon," Tara nearly cried his name as she quickly wrapped his naked body in a blanket.

Funny, he didn't even think of his nudity. Flipping in and out of wolf and falcon form made him forget he didn't wear a stitch of clothing.

"Where is Ian?"

"With Cian."

Simon's gaze fell on Tatiana, who sat in the corner with her mouth gaped open and her eyes wide.

"Are they near?"

"Yes. Simon, where have you been? We've been worried about you," Lora scolded.

Simon let his head fall for only a second, then whispered. "Call Ian. They're back and need his help."

"They? Who?"

Sliding a nervous stare to Tatiana then back, Simon didn't offer a reply. "Tell him to hurry."

Simon found some clothing, quickly changed, and then left the tent. He met Ian and Cian. Duncan and Todd soon followed.

"Where have ye been, lad?"

"No time. My mom and Fin are back and need help."

Simon started walking away.

Ian caught his arm. "What is amiss? Are they injured?"

"Fin isn't well." Simon forced his eyes to meet Cian's. "He needs your help."

Duncan stayed behind while Todd quickly gathered three horses before setting out into the forest.

Simon rode with Cian, although to do so hurt. Anger still boiled inside him. They had to slow down the horses once they started into the forest and thick brush.

"You were right about Tatiana."

Simon held perfectly still and said nothing.

"She is a pawn of Grainna's."

"Then why is she in our tent?"

"You could call her a prisoner now."

The sorrow in Cian's voice helped ease some of his own hurt.

"I didn't want to be right about her."

"And I should not have spoken to you the way I did. I hope one day you can forgive me."

Sucking in a deep breath, Simon sighed. "Life's too short to dwell." Way too friggin' short. The apology helped. A lot.

"Over there." He pointed to the left. *We're almost there, Mom.*

Thank God.

Is Fin awake yet?

She didn't answer right away. *No.*

Ian reached Fin's side first, followed by Cian. Simon placed a hand on his mother's back and watched.

"When we landed, he hit his head on a rock. Can you help him, Cian?"

"Or die trying," he said before placing his hands over his brother's head and calling his power.

Blue light pulsed and vibrated. The glow lit up

the space around them. Simon felt his mom holding her breath, watched her eyes widen and her lips tremble. When Fin sucked in a deep breath and stared to move, Liz all but collapsed against Simon's side.

When Fin's eyelids started to flutter, Liz pushed closer to him and wrapped her hands around his face. Cian sat back, giving her room.

"Are we home, love?" were his first words.

"You bastard, don't you ever do that to me again!" Instead of the slap or punch or some such aggressive move Simon expected, he watched his mom lean over Fin and lay her head against his chest and sob. It was as if she had held in her worry until she knew he was safe.

Fin lowered his lips to the top of her head with a tenderness Simon had never seen from him before.

"Welcome home, son."

"Hey," Todd yelled out.

Everyone stilled.

"We have company." Todd pointed to the east.

Simon's eyes shifted and peered into the forest. "There are three of them. Big men, carrying swords and splitting up."

"How can you see them?"

Fin forced Liz from his frame and sat up. Cian pulled his sword from his waist.

"I can smell them, too. Blood, lots of it."

"Theirs?"

"No. Others' I think." He knew it, but didn't want to frighten his mother any more than she already was.

"They're moving." Simon stood and removed his shirt and kicked off his leggings and jumped to the sky.

"Jesus Christ that was fast," Todd cried.

Simon, where are you going?

He silently flew above the men, noticed one

251

pull an arrow from his pouch.

Duck! he yelled in his head.

His mom shouted his order aloud to the others just as the man let the arrow fly in the air.

Tell Todd there is one on his left hiding behind the biggest tree. Another is watching and waiting for you all to stand.

Liz couched on the balls of her feet and told the others his observations.

Where is the third?

Circling behind.

With his mom in the middle, Ian, Fin, Cian, and Todd placed their backs to her and stayed low. The man with the arrow drew closer.

One is coming up on you with the arrow. If Todd has his gun, now would be a good time to use it.

He has it.

Good! Can you see me? Simon flew in the air and circled the man below.

Yes.

He's right below me.

Todd scurried next to a tree, closer to their enemy, and hid behind it. Simon watched the others as they closed in on his family.

Hurry.

Todd swiveled from the safety of the tree, aimed his gun, and fired before the other man could react. The blast in the air resulted in animals scurrying from their resting places, filling the forest with noise.

The man with the arrow flew back, the bullet caught in his shoulder.

Ian let out a warrior cry as a massive man charged him. Swords clashed. Cian held his sword ready to fight, Fin kept his back to his father watching for the other man.

Simon couldn't see him. He flew to another perch, searching.

Nothing.

I can't find the third guy anymore.

What about the one Todd shot?

He's backing away. Coward.

But from the fierceness of Ian's fight with the one man who charged, maybe the coward had the right idea.

When Ian's blade ran through his opponent's body, and before it fell to the forest floor, Simon heard the man utter, "Praise God!"

Then he saw the missing man, running to the west.

Once the men were out of sight, Simon swooped down, shifted, and said, "They're gone."

Ian stood over the body of the dead warrior.

Dressing as he walked closer, Simon stared down at the man. "He was being controlled by her." He told him what he heard the man say.

"I heard him, too." Ian placed a hand on Simon's shoulder as he spoke. There was no victory in the killing. Only sorrow for the soul lost at Grainna's hand.

~~~~

From the corner of the tent, Tatiana witnessed the reunion of two members of the family. Their hushed voices and frequent looks dug deep in her soul. Why was she still there? What was Grainna's plan?

Simon shifted like Grainna. The thought brought fear, but understanding as well. Grainna feared these people. Their collective power must be greater than hers. Yet they didn't wield it to master or control others.

Cian didn't look her way. He kept his back to her. She couldn't send him any blame. It was she who was wrong.

Resting her head in her hands, Tatiana tried not to listen to the others, although with nothing distracting her, she heard much of what they said.

"I spoke with Mom."

"You're kidding?"

The newest arrival, Liz, shook her head. "No. You wouldn't believe how sad she was. She told me to send her love. Can you believe that?"

Tatiana glanced to the sisters talking. Had they endured a childhood of pain like hers?

"And Dad?"

"Dad's an asshole. A real twit. You should have heard Mom tell him off."

The women laughed through what must have been a painful reality. At least they had one parent who cared and each other to turn to.

Their voices lowered, making it difficult to understand their words. Her gaze fell on Finlay, who looked so much like his older brother Duncan that up close they could have come from their mother on the same day of birth.

"Jake told me to give you these."

"Ammo."

"He risked his own freedom to help us."

"Jake was like a brother to me. I'd have done the same for him."

Tatiana lowered her eyelids, her mind drifted. She shivered and pressed her aching head into her palms. Cold slammed into her senses. She jumped to her feet, forcing several of the others to jump as well.

Tatiana held her head, nausea rushed from her stomach to her throat. "Nay."

"What is it?"

She covered her ears with her hands. "Don't say anymore. I hear ye all."

Cian approached her. She cowered away.

"She is in my head. I feel her inside my head." As the words tumbled from her lips, the pain splitting her head increased.

Traitor. Grainna's word echoed in her mind. Then she laughed and slipped away.

"Grainna listens?"

Of course, this was her plan. "She's let me go, but not completely. She reads my thoughts. I know it."

"A spy," Cian spit the word at her.

"Not by my will."

"How are we to trust you?" Cian's hands shook her shoulders forcing her eyes to open and meet his.

"Ye can't." She started to cry.

"Damn that witch. We need to find a weakness." Liz pushed past Cian and forced him to stop shaking Tatiana.

"Don't protect her."

"Knock it off, Cian. Can't you see the girl is hurting here?"

"He's right, m'lady. I don't deserve yer compassion."

"None of us deserve being led around by Grainna, but the witch finds a way to control all of us."

Light from beyond the tent signaled the rising sun. "She does not control ye."

"Really? Seems to me we're all sitting here now because of her."

The bold woman made sense.

"But it's time to put an end to her reign."

"How?"

Tatiana held up her hand. "I beg ye. Say no more in front of me. I cannot control her invasion in here." She tapped her fingers to her forehead. With careful thought, Tatiana moved around Liz and stared at Cian until he met her gaze. "I have no wish to deceive any of ye."

"No. I don't think you do." Liz's vow surprised her.

"Nor do I." This came from Amber.

Only after his sister's words filled the tent did Cian's face soften. Mayhap he believed her. She prayed he did.

"Do you know of any weakness?"

Tatiana shook her head. "Wait."

"What?"

"I think she met with a sword, or bow."

"What do you mean?" Ian asked.

"She held her arm as if it were wounded before I left. There was a smell, like decay and rotten meat."

"An arrow," Simon said. "She took an arrow in her wing. I saw her in the forest after."

"Was she still in the form of a bird when you saw her?"

"No. But her arm wasn't right. The arrow was gone, but some of the feathers still stuck out of her arm."

"How on earth did you get close enough to see that?"

Simon hunched his shoulders. "I wasn't that close."

Liz shook her head. "Well, I think we may have found a way to take her out. I've been working on a plan."

Tatiana panicked. "Stop, I beg ye. Say nothing in front of me."

Ian stepped forward, placed a hand on Liz's shoulder. "She's right, lass." He motioned to the mouth of the tent. "I'll find a safe place for you to rest."

Chapter Twenty-Eight

"Are you sure this is going to work?" Tara asked Liz as she dressed in the white gown she'd arrived in the day before. The eyeliner and glitter she added to her face only hid her identity so well. They would be relying on Ian stirring the clouds and the crowd's general unease over what she was going to ask them to do to keep her name from anyone's lips. Well... that and hovering above them like the angel she was trying to resemble. Who argues with a visitor from heaven? Wait a minute... She did. When Elise appeared to them right before they attempted to bring Grainna down the last time, she'd argued with her.

This time would work. It would have to.

"This has to work," Liz told her sister.

"I can't believe you can fly."

"Hover. I hover really well. Not ready to jump off a cliff and risk hitting bottom quite yet."

"Still freaking awesome if you ask me. I suppose we should have guessed you were the one behind the floating during circle time." Tara made a couple of air quotes over *circle time*, and then started to laugh.

Liz snickered with her before painting her lips hot pink.

"Geez, Tara, can you believe us?"

"Not really." Tara ducked behind her and ran a brush though her hair. "You haven't told me about you and Fin."

"Oh." What should she say? To tell her sister she'd slept with Fin would be a waste of words. Anyone with eyes could see their relationship had changed. Hell, it had before they even left. Now they were wrapped up in fighting Grainna and not giving much thought of what-ifs.

"What, speechless? You're never speechless."

"Pondering my choice of words."

"Ponder faster. Before Duncan and Todd return."

What could she say? They'd found comfort in each other's arms. Had amazing sex, bordering on power struggles. Okay, they were all out wars of the sexes with an amazing end. As a smug expression settled over her face, Liz shook it away.

"Was that wistful?"

"What?"

"Wistful, whimsy, bliss?" Tara nagged her and didn't let it drop. "Maybe Grainna sending you forward in time was a blessing in disguise? You're in love with him."

"Stop right there. Grainna's lived up to her title as queen witch. Her goal wasn't to bring Fin and I together, but to tear all of us apart. I'm glad to have found some peace with Mom and to let Dad put the final nail in that coffin. I know I tried, even if he's the same ass as always."

"Uh, huh."

"Uh, huh? What is that, uh, huh?"

"You didn't deny it."

No, she didn't, she mused. How could she? That would be like denying the sky was blue. But God, it was scary. Scary not knowing if Fin felt the same overpowering feeling toward her, scary not having a plan for tomorrow, and scary to consider all the unprotected sex they'd been having and her fertility rate with Simon.

Scary. Scary to the tenth power.

A crackling voice sounded from the walkie-talkie. The bell couldn't have rang sooner to save her explanations or lack thereof.

"You girls ready?" The voice belonged to Todd.

"Five minutes," Tara told him.

Liz pulled a long dark cape over her, hiding her dress, her hair, her twenty-first century makeup.

Tara lifted Briac into her arms and tickled his nose, and smiled at the resulting giggle.

"You can do all this and hold him at the same time?"

"Do I have a choice? I'm not letting one of the maids risk dropping him when the 'angel' comes. Besides, I'm a modern woman. Multi-tasking is my middle name."

~~~~

"Are you sure she can do this?" Duncan asked Fin as they took their positions.

"She *can* fly."

"Can she control it?"

"Her stubbornness alone will control it."

Duncan let his stoic expression slip. Amusement replaced it. "Ye know her well, brother."

"Verra well." She'd spun her plan to gather people from each clan to fight against Grainna and the men the witch controlled. Used some of the same tactics Selma used in the future. If Liz were a man, she'd be a warrior with skill and valor. If he were truthful with himself, he'd say she was a warrior now.

As Duncan crossed his arms over his chest, he said. "Your life with her will never be easy."

Fin tossed his head back with bellowing laughter. "Whoever said I wanted easy? I will never be bored with Lizzy."

"When will you tell the lass that you are to wed?"

"The future truly left no impression on your brain. I will *tell* Elizabeth no such thing."

Duncan lost his smile. "You do not plan on letting her go, do you?"

"Don't be daft. I will *ask* Elizabeth to be by my

side."

"And if she says no?"

Fin lifted a brow, considered his brother's words. "Then I will put her over my shoulder and remind her who is stronger."

"Not easy and never bored." Duncan slapped a hand to his arm.

Fin agreed.

~~~~

Tatiana sat next to the cooking fire, stirring the pot simmering over it. Ian did not put her in chains, and did not set a guard on her. When she'd asked him why, he'd answered, "I trust ye to do the right thing."

Why did he have any faith in her? How could he after all she had done? She forced her eyes to the ground, focused on the task of cooking and helping the maids.

Grainna hadn't forced her way into her head except the one time among the MacCoinnichs. For that, Tatiana was grateful.

She closed her eyes briefly, fatigue washed over her. She couldn't sleep, afraid of Grainna's invasion.

"Ye should sleep."

Cian's voice brought a skip in her heart. He appeared weary but more rested than she did. He wore his family kilt and mantle, a sword at his side. His hair was wet, as if he'd recently cleaned it. She smiled, unable to stop herself.

"I cannot," she told him. "She would find her way inside like weevils to wood."

"'Tisn't your fault. I know that now." He stepped close enough for her to smell the scent of soap on his skin. Clean, innocent, where she was not.

She backed away. "I beg ye do not. We can never be, Cian."

He placed a hand on her cheek, stroked her

skin. A sigh escaped her lips, and she allowed herself this one touch.

"My own father sees the good in you. And he hasn't opened his heart to you like I have."

Tears drew close, but she pushed them away. She closed her fingers over his hand and placed a tender kiss to his palm before moving away. Familiar tingles of awareness exploded inside of her. A vision in white filled her mind, peace hovered along the angel's side. Then there was pain, blood. Then nothing.

"Tatiana? Tatiana?" When her eyes opened, Cian held her. She's sunk to the ground, one of the maids came to their side.

"I-I am tired." Although, suddenly she wasn't.

"Fetch her water, Alice," Cian ordered.

Once her lips were moistened and Alice returned to her chores, Tatiana spoke. "An angel is coming."

"What are you speaking of?"

"An angel. I see her. She brings peace with her."

His eyes narrowed. "What have you heard?"

"I've heard nothing. I'm a seer, Cian. 'Tis why Grainna kept me alive."

"Why do you tell me this now?"

"Because I can." And she might not be able later. She kept that to herself.

"I need to find my father."

Tatiana nodded. "Go." *Don't look back.*

Before he turned to walk away, he helped her to her feet, kept his hand on her arm, and squeezed. "We will protect you."

"I never lied about my feelings toward ye, Cian. Never."

He smiled, dropped his lips to hers for the sweetest kiss he'd ever granted her, and then turned to walk away.

As he left, she pressed her fingers to her lips

and let the tears flow.

~~~~

As promised, the sky filled with clouds—thanks to Ian—with just enough light passing through to highlight whatever they desired. Myra and Todd stood beside her, Amber, Simon and Cian near the camp. Tara held court next to Lora and Ian in the center of the masses, while Duncan and Fin watched for her signals on the east bank.

The stage was set, and the film was ready to roll. Too bad she hadn't been part of the Hollywood scene while she'd had the chance.

"Ready?"

"No, but what choice do I have? This was my idea."

"A damn good idea, all things considered," Todd said.

Myra agreed with her husband with a nod. "You really can fly?"

Could she? Oh man, what if she couldn't? Instinct kicked in, giving her body a few inches off the ground. Myra gasped and Todd whispered some obscenity.

"Hover. I hover."

"Okay, hover-girl, you ready?" Todd brought a smile to her face. *No!* She was jitters from head to toe and suddenly petrified to think her plan would work.

"Stop that!" Myra scolded, obviously reading her expression all too well. "Solid plan! Todd told me that in your time, you'd have made a damn..." She sighed and upped her volume. "Damn good detective. You have the ability to lead people, Lizzy. Just look how you've taken control of all our powers, Druidry, spells... you make sense. This plan will work. I know it!"

Liz planted her feet on the ground and pulled Myra into a hug. "Thanks. You're a horrible liar, but thanks."

Todd tilted his head to the side. "Lying isn't her strong point. But she is right about your ability to lead and take control. Speak like a god and the people will listen. Then with any luck, and maybe a little magic, you guys can help the people forget once this is all over."

Todd was right. The plan was good. Her plan was solid, and the only one they had.

Simon, you ready?

His voice came back. *Ready!* Liz knew that her son signaled Tara who spoke with Duncan. *Wait for Ian to start.*

Okay. Even in her head, Simon's voice didn't waver.

"We're ready," she told Myra and Todd.

They held their breath, waiting.

One deep breath followed another, until the western sky lit up with lightning and the earth rumbled with the force of Ian's thunder.

Liz willed her body off the ground one foot, two. Myra grasped onto Todd and Fin's wrath shook the earth and people in the distance started to scream.

"Show's on."

Liz willed her body up, past the tree line, and beyond any possible hiding place.

Damn, how did Simon do this? She no sooner thought the words than Simon's voice rang in her head. *Don't look down and smile. It's hard to be scared when you're trying to smile.*

Liz spread her hands wide, in part because she thought it helped her balance, the other part because she wanted to appear like an angel and not a scared shitless wannabe.

She hovered, swam over the crowd below. Some dropped to their knees while others stared on. Myra and Todd slipped from the trees below and watched, like the other spectators only they focused on the people, the warriors who may feel threatened and want to strike.

Simon, signal Ian. Lizzy instructed her son as she lifted her hands to the sky. Lightning split and thunder roared.

"I come to you, ye from heaven above."

Several villagers made the sign of the cross and fell to their knees.

Fin's turn, Simon.

"Down here to rid ye of the evil that befell." Liz flexed her fingers and lowered her hovering frame a few feet.

Fin shook the earth.

She sprang up and swirled to make sure the others in the crowd listened. "A witch resides in the West. Her powers great. She has ripped yer families apart. She is the reason ye grieve. Together. 'Tis the only way to survive her wrath."

At the sight of the woman in white, Tatiana regarded her frame, considered her vision, and her knowledge. She was no angel. But those around her fell to their knees, their heads bowed, eyes refused to meet those of the hovering mass.

The clouded sky and sun sprinkling through the clouds gave Cian's family the power they needed.

Alice, the maid, whispered to herself. "What can we do for ye?"

It would take an army to defeat Grainna. The swarms of people would overwhelm Grainna's chosen four to one. The thoughts stilled, and Tatiana's head started to ache.

"Nay." She grasped her head in her hands. "Leave me." But Grainna swam in her subconscious, her insides turned cold.

Tatiana closed her eyes, refusing to allow Grainna to see through them. They opened, not by her will, but by the witch's. Forcing her hands to her eyes, she shielded her sight, turned and ran from the people and the woman posing as an angel.

Did you think I'd let you go so easily?

Pain ripped through her skull. "Nay, I knew ye would not let me be free, ever."

Turn so I can see.

Nay, she wouldn't witness anymore to grant Grainna knowledge or power. But her head split and swiveled on its own accord, or Grainna's will. Tatiana's eyes opened, blinked.

Grainna screamed inside her head.

"Stop." The word was not Tatiana's, but the witch's. As it rent from her lips, a few eyes turned to her.

"'Tis a miracle, lass. Listen to the angel." A woman she didn't know attempted to console her. She couldn't know that Grainna battled to see through her eyes.

Tatiana found her feet, turned from the crowd and ran. She stumbled over the cooking fire, her eyes landing on a butcher's knife. She grasped the hilt, stood and ran again.

Her breath erupted in short gasps. Pain split her sides. The people were well behind her when she reached the edge of the cliff.

Grainna forced her body to spin in a circle. When her eyes opened, she could not see through them. Tatiana knew someone else was in control.

"Nay," she yelled, pivoting toward the sea cliffs. She would not betray Cian. Not again. There would be blood, pain, peace, and then nothing.

There would not be betrayal.

She moved her foot closer to the edge and jumped.

No. Grainna's voice bellowed. Tatiana felt her body lifted from the air and thrust back to the grassland.

There was pain, but she ignored it, stood, and tried again.

This time, when Grainna pulled her back, Tatiana, with the blade she'd picked by the fire tilted toward her heart, landed.

Then the angel came. The true angel. Gold, brilliant, and gliding on the wind. "Shhh, my child." Her voice was that of thousands. Musical, magical. Peaceful.

Chapter Twenty-Nine

It worked. His mom's plan worked. She'd told the people to band together, listen to the lords, and defeat the witch together. The angel, his mom, would grant the people powers to defeat the witch.

The real angel, or in their case, the Ancient, Elise had told them months ago it would take all of them to defeat Grainna. Simon couldn't help but think they stood half a chance. Maybe more.

As the crowd settled, and Simon heard his mom's internal words as she changed clothes in the woods, he followed Cian and Amber back to their tent. They stopped by the cook's fire to find Tatiana gone.

"Where did the girl go?"

Alice shrugged and pointed to the west.

Simon caught Cian's eye. The three of them ran in the direction of Alice's pointing finger.

"She wouldn't leave," Amber yelled as they ran.

Simon wanted to agree, but couldn't be sure.

As they drew closer to the cliffs, the small frail body of someone lying on the ground started to come into focus.

There were skirts, and lots and lots of blood.

Amber halted first, trembling.

Simon froze in place along with Cian. When Cian sprang forward, Simon attempted to hold him back.

"Tatiana? Nay."

The mournful cry Cian let free from his lungs ripped Simon's heart from his chest.

He called his mom in his head, wished they'd hurry. Not that they could do anything for the silent, still girl in Cian's arms.

The three of them sat there, Simon holding Amber while she whimpered, and Cian rocking Tatiana's dead body, when the others arrived.

Cian had tried to use his power to save her, but the gift didn't raise the dead.

Ian reached his son's side. "There is nothing ye can do, lad."

"Why?"

"She suffered at the hands of Grainna. Her heart would not allow herself to betray you again. She said as much to all of us," Lora told her son.

Simon felt his mom's arms pull him closer. She still had shadows of makeup on, but the majority had been wiped clean. Eyeliner ran in streaks of black down her cheeks from the tears she'd shed.

Todd and Fin left, returning with tools to bury Tatiana's remains. Cian held her until Lora pulled him away. Myra and Tara wrapped her in a large cloth. The entire event took less than an hour.

Few spectators watched, all from well beyond hearing range. Simon had watched Todd, Fin, and Ian bury the knight struck down the previous day in the same manner. No official cemetery or box needed. According to Fin, during times of war, onsite burials were common.

Ian prayed over the grave and then led them all away.

Simon glanced from one family member to another and prayed they would all still be together when Grainna was defeated.

~~~~

Grainna clenched her teeth, waved her hand over her crystal, saw nothing, then cursed.

She didn't see the chit killing herself to save her boyfriend. What was wrong with people in love? It made her sick.

Wiping a hand over her wounded arm, Grainna flexed her fingers. She refused to acknowledge the pain. In turn, she didn't find the affliction to be a weakness. There would be no shifting into a bird again. Not if she could avoid it.

She could, however, call other animals to act as her army.

It was time to finish this war. Time to make the MacCoinnichs bleed. "Come, my little friends." Grainna closed her eyes and called out in her mind. "Time for dinner."

~~~~

Fin stood beside his father, Todd, Duncan, and every knight and lord in attendance. Lancaster and Brisbane's men were obviously uncomfortable alongside each other since the two lords were hardly speaking. Confusion and worry marked many faces.

"What do ye make of it?" Lancaster asked Ian.

"'Tis hard to ignore. The things the s-spirit said cannot be ignored. We are all missing men, are we not?"

A series of *ayes* erupted.

"Another from our camp last night. Mallick's older son was found this morning with his hand severed from his arm, and a knife through his heart. If our enemy comes from the western cliffs, 'tis time we find them and bring an end to this chaos."

Todd leaned over and whispered in Fin's ear. "No one has mentioned magic."

"The first one who does will be scorned, but the second one will be considered. Not until the heads of family nod their approval will anyone consider banding together against something so untouchable."

"The spirit—"

"Angel. She appeared as an angel," another man interrupted.

Fin lowered his head and smiled. She was beautiful. Earlier, when Lizzy returned to camp, giddy and swirling in circles with the success of their ruse, Fin told himself that he'd slept with an angel. With her, he'd found heaven.

"Aye, an angel. The angel said she'd gift some of us with the power to defeat the evil."

As predicted, some men huffed, ready to dismiss the notion.

"My own daughter woke not remembering her engagement," Lancaster told them. "She is not mad."

"The same day caused some madness over everyone here."

Voices all began speaking at once. All telling stories of what they'd seen, felt.

Fin turned his attention to Logan to see where the man stood. "Elizabeth and I found ourselves miles from here."

Logan smiled. "Are ye sure ye weren't just hiding to be with her?"

"If I need to be alone with her, I will take her away and tell my family."

"I wondered where ye disappeared to. Yer father said little."

"He didn't know where we were."

Logan glanced to the others and lowered his voice, not that he needed to many people all spoke at once. "Do ye think it was magic?"

Fin shrugged. "What else could it be?"

Ian lifted his voice above the others. "Quiet... quiet. There are many unexplained things. Nearly everyone here knows of one death or disappearance. Even before we journeyed here, we knew something was amiss in the Highlands. Brisbane, ye said yer men have fled in numbers too difficult to ignore. How many total?"

"Five knights from these walls. Three others were expected home last fall and never returned. Others are missing as well."

From Brisbane's village, over thirty people

were unaccounted for. Lancaster spoke of a dozen missing men, women, and children.

The numbers called out staggered Fin.

"What of ye, MacCoinnich?"

Duncan stepped forward. "We've buried two in as many days."

Fin sighed relief when the men nodded and went on to another topic. To tell everyone they'd lost none, would put suspicion on them. They didn't need that.

As the debate continued, Fin opened his mind and searched the room. There were other Druids among them. He knew there were. He met the eyes of one of Lancaster's knights, Donovan. He'd always wondered about the man, but would never openly ask.

There were others, peppered into the men. They kept quiet, listened intently.

"What should we make of the angel's prophecy to gift some with the power to defeat the witch?"

"She mentioned fire and rain. What does that mean?"

Fin glanced at his brother and nodded to the man who spoke. Duncan winked.

"Witches and powers. What nonsense," he said tossing a hand in the air. When he did, a ball of fire came from nowhere and fell to the ground.

"God's blood." The man jumped back and stared at his hand. He snatched his hand to his chest, looked at it again, and then shook it out. Duncan added a few sparks from across the room.

Fin wanted to laugh, but held it inside.

Someone beyond their council yelled and people screamed. They turned and peered into the space between the encampments. Within seconds, more screaming and crying filled the afternoon air.

Fin's eyes traveled to the family tent. Duncan slid beside him. "Tara says there are rats invading the camp."

"Rats?"

"Hundreds of them."

Fin felt the eyes of someone watching him, turned and noticed Donovan's stare. The man nodded to the left, away from the men. Duncan and Todd started toward the family, many of the other men fled as well.

"What do ye make of this?" Donovan asked.

Fin tilted his head, took a chance. "The same as ye."

"The *angel* bestows gifts, and we are to use them openly?"

Fin ignored the increasing screams. "I believe that is what the *angel* said. I imagine the *gifts* would disappear once the witch is defeated."

Just then, a rat two feet in length, ran at them without fear. It jumped onto Fin's leg. He quickly kicked it off. Before it set forward again, fire caught hold of it, stopping it in a flaming death.

When he glanced up, Donovan shook out his hand.

Fin extended his arm. "I have yer back, brother."

Donovan smiled. "And I have yers."

The women around them screamed, babies cried. Some of the rats were trampled to death while others latched on to legs and arms of anyone they could.

By the time Fin reached Liz and the others, hell had broken loose. Cian ushered him inside the tent.

"How can we fight this?" Liz held Briac in one hand, Simon and Amber held hands and grasped on to Liz's free arm. All four of them hovered in the tent, away from the rats.

"Stay here," he ordered.

"I planned on it," Lizzy shouted.

"Simon, can you call in a few cats to help us out?"

The boy enthusiastically nodded before closing his eyes.

Fin ducked beyond Cian, swiveled around and saw Duncan and Tara helping others destroy the rodents.

Alice screamed by his side. A rat latched onto her dress, she reached down to bat it off. Fin sent a spark from her hands, wounding the rat. Alice flinched, stared at her hand, then found a poker for the fire pit, and ran it through her four-legged enemy.

Duncan pointed to the edge of the forest. "They're coming from over there."

"Gather people, let them think they're setting them on fire."

Tara ran toward Myra as Duncan met with Logan and pointed toward the massive numbers of rats rushing toward them.

Fin found Ian and Lora and told them his plan. Soon, the camp was filled with small balls of fire and small measures of awe and celebration with every fallen rodent. When he met up with Donovan, the knight had a few extra people by his side.

"Where are they coming from?"

"Over there."

Duncan stood with six men, he managed to have each of them shooting fire, or think they were shooting fire, from their hands.

Fin ran to his side to help.

They dodged bites and threw fire, but the rats kept coming. As they managed to destroy one pack, another charged.

"Enough," Duncan yelled, spread both hands wide and lit the ground with fire in a steady stream. Some rats ran into the fire, others attempted to find the end of it.

Fin noticed the attention of one of the men that battled at Duncan's side. The virtual stranger mimicked Duncan's movement, Fin helped fire come, but not in the way of Duncan's talent. Fin nudged Duncan's hand when the stranger did it again. This time flames leapt and fire spread beyond them.

The rats retreated. Those inside the circle of flame were picked off one by one. Simon's cats chased, caught, and dismembered their share.

No longer hovering, Liz approached Fin when he returned to her side. She slipped into his arms and rested her head on his chest. He placed a kiss to her head.

"Is everyone well?"

"I won't sleep for a week, but we're all okay."

He laughed.

"Rats? Her mind is warped."

Fin had heard enough of her slang to understand her. "We should expect anything."

She shivered. "Make that a month. I'm not sleeping for a month."

Indulging in her warmth a little longer, Fin stroked his hand down her back. "Where is Simon?"

"He and Cian are helping Lora and Myra with some of the people who were bit."

"Any serious injuries?"

"Hard to tell."

Fin noticed Todd signaling him to come from across the camp.

Pulling out of Liz's embrace, Fin covered her mouth with a soft kiss. She purred, just a little and cuddled closer. He stepped away, placed a finger on her pert little nose. "Later, love."

Her lower lip stuck out in a pout but she let her hands drop from his sides and let him walk away.

~~~~

Liz dropped to her bottom, ignoring the dirt that would stick to her skirts. Her hair was a mess, her body in dire need of a bath. Not to mention she was so hungry she could eat a small mammal all by herself.

Tara fell beside her, followed by Amber and Myra.

"What a day."

"You're not kidding."

Liz glanced at her sister. "Where's Briac?"

"With Simon and Lora."

"What about Cian?"

Amber raised her hand and pointed toward the rocks overlooking the cliffs. The silhouette of someone staring over the sea stood out among the setting sun.

"Is he going to be okay?"

"He grieves, but he will survive," Amber answered.

Smells from Alice's stew had Lizzy's stomach rumbling. "Where are the men?"

"In council." Tara rubbed the back of her neck. "They're talking about sheltering all the women and children in the keep and having the men outside as guards."

Liz noted the size of the structure and the number of people. It would be tight, but they'd fit.

"We may be able to charm the walls, protect us and the others, out here 'tis difficult," Myra said.

"True." But she hated the thought of splitting up half the family. They worked better together.

Alice stepped forward with her pot and offered them dinner. They ate in relative quiet.

The calm before the storm. Liz hated that her thoughts led there, the cliché never felt more daunting.

As the ocean reached high tide, the fog swept over them. When the night closed in, the men returned and announced the decisions made by the men.

"Tomorrow we move the women to the keep.

We will send out scouts to search for Grainna's fortress."

"They won't come back. Grainna will take out a small party."

"I agree, but changing centuries of warrior tactics is impossible." Fin settled beside Liz and let her lean against him.

Simon stoked the fire. "Tatiana said Grainna resided close to the sea."

"Which will be her weakness. We need only to surround her halfway. She will have no place to hide."

"But she shifts, and flies." Simon kept his voice low and glanced around. Most of the people in camp slept, the guards kept watch around the perimeter.

"She's wounded. How, I don't know. If she suffered a wound that does not heal while in the form of an animal, she wouldn't attempt a shift again." Ian drank the ale at his side.

"Aye, father, I think you're right. Grainna is nobody's fool."

"Now what? We've banded the people together, we're all willing to fight the witch, but how? Running around starting fires is exhausting." Liz laced her fingers in Fin's as she spoke.

"But it worked. Something else happened with our... interventions," Fin told them.

"What's that?"

"Others came through. Others like us."

Ian sat forward. "I noticed that, too."

"How many?"

Fin shrugged and rambled off a few names. Ian added some more, a classroom of people. Not an army, but they would have to do. Maybe more existed but wouldn't expose themselves. If death loomed, they'd have no choice.

"I can help find the others like us." Amber glanced at her mother. "When we helped the

276

wounded earlier, I touched many hands. Some were Druids. I felt it."

Tara sighed. "Safety in numbers."

"Elise said it would take 'all of us' to defeat Grainna. All of us may be more than *only us*.

Those words sunk in while the fire in front of them dwindled to embers and smoldering coals. It wasn't quite midnight, the nearly full moon begged attention.

Damn, had it only been twenty-four hours since Liz had sat on the lawn of the Observatory, praying, chanting, and willing her and Fin through time?

What were Selma and Jake doing now?

Myra interrupted her thoughts. "I need to sleep."

Todd helped her to her feet.

"Wait," Simon whispered, yet everyone heard.

Liz narrowed her eyes at her son. "What is it?"

"Tomorrow, before the search party starts out, I need to go in front of them."

Fin shot up. "No!"

Ian agreed.

"Wait, listen before you think I'm nuts."

Liz peered into his face and eyes...eyes that seemed so much older than before Grainna's evil swept her to the future.

"I'll shift into a shark and find her."

"It's too dangerous."

"No."

"Simon, nay."

Liz listened. Her son's eyes never left hers.

"I can. I've already done it."

Her heart wept. She bit her lip and squeezed Fin's hand, but she didn't say a thing.

"Men will die if we let them go. Grainna won't find me in the sea, won't consider looking for me there."

"We don't know that, Simon." Fin's hand

clenched hers as he spoke.

"You have to trust me to do this."

While the other members of the family grumbled, Liz considered. She wanted to cry. God, she needed to bawl like a baby. No! God no! Don't let her baby go.

Simon stared at her.

Only her.

After a deep breath, she leveled her eyes to the fire and turned in Fin's arms. Before she spoke, tears sprang in her eyes and a knot formed in her throat. "I think... I think *we* should let him try."

Fin's eyes narrowed, the request for his opinion not lost. He shifted his eyes to Simon. "Can you do this, son?"

Liz felt a cry leave her lips.

"Yes. She won't know I was there."

Fin's gaze met hers.

Tears fell, but she brushed them away.

Fin's eyes glossed over.

"Then your mother and I approve."

Chapter Thirty

Liz, Fin, Myra, and Todd sat on the shore waiting. Simon had shifted and swam away under the light of the moon nearly an hour earlier. Every passing minute ate into Liz's confidence. Had she and Fin done the right thing by letting Simon go? They had no idea how far he'd have to swim to find Grainna's camp, or even if he would be able to see it from the water.

After fifteen minutes in the water, Liz could no longer speak with her son inside her head. Every minute since added to her anguish.

"We should have given him a time to return, even if he couldn't find her."

Myra reached for Liz's hand. "It must be difficult to gauge time under there. Even if you had requested him to come back, he may not be able to."

Simon? Can you hear me?

Silence! Damn quiet was entirely overrated.

A few rocks tumbled down the cliff. Liz glanced over her shoulder to see Cian and Amber walking toward them. Their eyes searched the waters.

"The men are starting to assemble," Cian said when he stood beside them.

Fin let out a deep breath. "Come, Simon. Hurry up, lad." Worry laced his stern expression. Thank God she wasn't standing on this shore alone. Maybe it was wrong to want to share the burden with others over the welfare of her son, but Liz was grateful for their combined concern.

Wow!

Liz glanced around wondering who'd said the

word. Her head shot to the sea. *Simon?*

Hey, Mom.

She slumped against Fin.

"What?"

She pointed to her head. "Simon."

You should see it under here, Mom. It's a whole world full of so many beautiful things.

Tell us about it on shore. How far away are you?

Not sure, hold on...

"What is he saying?"

"He's sightseeing."

Todd scoffed under his breath while Myra asked, "What is that?"

"Checking out what the ocean has to offer by means of beauty."

I'm coming around the peninsula now. You'll see me in about five minutes or so.

True to his word, Simon, in shark form, surfaced long enough for them to see him.

When he walked from the water, Fin covered him with a blanket to help dry him off.

"It's amazing under there. I wish you all could see it. I had no idea."

"Later, Simon. Did you find her?"

He shook his long hair out and smiled at Fin. "I sure did."

"How far?"

"How long have I been gone?"

"Nearly an hour and a half."

"So forty five minutes by sea. I swam quickly coming back. On the way over, I kept surfacing to search. I would say it took me about an hour to find her."

"It will be difficult to know the miles."

"I could sketch a map of the shore line. There were three peninsulas I swam around and one cove.

Simon slipped into his clothes and told them of

a couple more landmarks. Before they started back to camp, Simon moved next to Liz.

"Thanks for letting me go."

"You did great, sport."

"Not bad, kid," Todd added.

"We're all proud of you." Fin's words brought a smile from ear to ear.

~~~~

"We should go with them."

Liz agreed with her sister's words. "How do we convince these Neanderthals that women can help?"

"Ye don't, lass," Ian told her.

"All of us together. That's what Elise said."

"Like last time, you'll be with us in here." Fin pointed to his head.

"That didn't work last time."

"It will have to this time."

Liz stood and started to pace. "I don't like it. It isn't right."

"Our women are not accustomed to fighting. They will be a hindrance."

"If something happens to all the men, the women will get a crash course in fighting. Grainna isn't going to be happy until we're all dead."

They had moved into the keep. There were people everywhere. The men suited in armor and geared up for an all out war. Many of the women were more than happy to hide, but Liz had heard a few mumbling women questioning the wisdom of the planned approach.

"I'm coming with you." Liz declared.

"No, you're not."

"Yes, I am! Fin you're not going to win on this one. I'll dress as a man if I have to, but I'm coming."

"I am, too."

"I'm in."

One by one the women stood.

281

Ian started to speak and Lora held up her hand. "Don't ask me to stay and wait for word of your slaughter. If we all go, none of us will have regrets."

"If something were to happen to you, I'd have more than regrets," Ian said.

"Do you think it worse for me? The men should go in front, fight with swords and armor. We will fight the war with the witch. Together." Lora lifted her chin with her last word.

Ian crossed his arms over his chest, his face pinched in stone.

Liz held her breath. She knew without his support, they were screwed.

Fin glanced between her and his father. Duncan mirrored Ian's expression. Todd seemed a little more resolved with the idea. Then again, he'd worked around female police officers and knew women could hold their own.

"God's teeth," Ian muttered.

Liz allowed a smile to cross over her lips.

~~~~

The only tearful goodbyes were for Briac. Tara left him with the safety of Alice and the few capable knights at the keep. The rest of them headed out in the center of the men. Liz, Tara, Myra, and Amber all slipped on men's leggings and oversized shirts. Lora refused.

When they left their one designated room, dressed that way, a few women protested. To their surprise, a half dozen more complained, argued, and eventually joined them. From what Liz could tell, all of them were Druids.

As the keep slid into the distance, Liz turned in her small saddle. There must have been over a hundred of them, maybe more.

While in the open field, they brought their horses to a gallop but once they met the forest, they had to slow and spread themselves thin.

Donovan's sister, Emma found Liz's side. "'Twas ye, wasn't it?"

"I'm sorry?"

Emma lowered her voice. "The angel."

"Ah, I'm not sure I know what you're talking about."

She laughed. "Ye do, but I understand yer need for secrecy. We've all kept quiet."

Liz glanced behind her, noticed the other women speaking with her family. Worried glances were all around.

"I can call the wind and rain," she said while she stared ahead. "I'm not certain how I can help, but I'm willing to try so we can survive."

Liz noticed Myra turn in her direction and shrug her shoulders.

"Fire is easy...and well, you know the other thing I do." She couldn't come right out and say it. Maybe by the time all was over there wouldn't be a need to say anything.

Emma nodded, understanding. "What of the others?"

This was where Liz refused to offer more. "You'll have to ask them, but leave my son out of the questioning."

"I suppose I'd say the same if I had a child."

From there they rode in silence. At some point Myra and Emma switched places. Myra confirmed that the woman speaking to her had similar questions. In the end, Liz knew that all the women held some power. It would be easy to deduce that the men in the clans with the same name would have Druid blood as well.

That brought their number to over thirty.

No bad. Not great, but not bad.

After riding for over an hour, the lead knight brought them to a stop. Ian moved forward and hoisted his falcon from his arm. Simon rode alongside Fin. Her son's eyes were closed.

Are you looking through the falcon's eyes?

Yup. Can you move over to Ian and let him know what I'm seeing?

Liz guided her horse from beside the women. The men stared her way but paid little attention to her.

Oh shit.

What is it?

We're riding into a trap. There are at least a dozen men, some on horses, others on foot. They're spread out and not more than a half a mile ahead. Some look like they're starting to surround us.

Ian spoke with Lancaster and MacTavish. Between him and her were a dozen men. One pulled his horse in front of her when she tried to reach him.

"Ye may be dressed as a lad, but ye have no business up here."

Not a Druid, Liz decided. "Get out of my way."

He refused to move.

"Maybe you didn't hear me..." She flicked fire from her finger, hit the backside of the horse, and surged forward while the misguided knight tried to stay atop his mount.

The commotion brought many sets of eyes toward her.

"MacCoinnich." Liz pointed to the right and left. "I saw men on both sides of us."

The men in charge quickly surveyed the brush. This close to the sea, the low-lying vegetation gave them some security.

"Anyone in front?" Ian asked.

"Yes, several."

The men surrounding Ian didn't ask how she knew. They simply reacted.

Swords were drawn, shields raised. A hush went over the men. The women knew better than to utter a word.

A twig snapped. Eyes shot to the source.

Then hell broke loose.

Duck! Simon yelled in her head and aloud.

"Get down," she hollered at the top of her lungs.

An arrow lodged into a tree to Ian's left. His eyes slowly lifted.

Men scurried and the women banded together.

Liz felt no shame in retreating to her sister and the others. She would do better there anyway.

"What do we do? 'Tis our death. I know it," the woman next to Emma screamed.

"Calm down," Tara yelled.

Several of their men let out warrior cries and forced their horses forward to meet their enemy.

Liz slid from her horse, followed by Tara, Myra, Amber, and Lora. Soon the other women followed suit.

Arrows flew and swords met with the steel of the enemy.

Liz grasped Myra's hand.

Simon ran his horse in their direction, fell from his mount, and tumbled into their path. As soon as he managed to fall at her feet, Liz forced fire from her hands, forming a circle around the women.

Some gasped, probably out of surprise, but all eyes held understanding.

Amber reached for Tara's hand, then Lora's. Soon all of them stood holding hands.

"Give us protection within the fire, keep us safe in this day, in this hour."

The flames grew until they reached above their heads.

Liz's eyes grew wide, her heart beat so quickly in her chest the thought of it splitting in two distracted her.

She heard Duncan's voice calling a warning to Fin. More steel met with steel but they couldn't see a thing.

"Simon? Do you see anything?"

"No, nothing."

Liz pulled Myra's hand to Emma's who'd grabbed hers until she stood in the middle of the circle. She met Lora's eyes and yelled, "Come on."

"Where?"

Liz looked above her head.

Shaken, Lora nodded and followed Liz to the center of the women's circle.

With no time to waste, Liz grasped Lora's hand and the two of them shot into the air. Above the flames, and above the fighting, they found the top of the trees and witnessed the fighting below.

Duncan matched swords with an enemy but didn't hold back using his Druid gifts. Fin followed suit, each matching thrust for thrust. A man Liz didn't recognize was thrown from his horse. Lora threw out her hand until a ball of fire met the chest of the one aggressing.

"One of McLauren's men," she said.

Fire shot everywhere. Swords crashed. One man lay down in the center of things, but Liz couldn't tell who it was. Cian slid from his horse, found the man, and knelt by his side. Blue light lifted from the wounded until Liz noticed him moving again.

Her eyes found Fin again, fighting on the ground, his horse nowhere in sight. The man he fought was twice his size, but less agile. They moved beyond the trees one thrust at a time until Liz couldn't see what happened.

She held her breath, waiting for something.

Chaos filled the scene below them.

Lora continued to blast the enemy with fire for those who didn't have the gift. Most didn't think to look up to see where the spark came from, others did.

Fin finally emerged from the brush, his claymore in front of his face and ready for battle.

Some of Grainna's men started to retreat, knowing their defeat was certain.

Liz saw the calm before she felt it and lowered her and Lora's frame to the ground. Only when the noise beyond the protective circle dissipated did Liz will the fire to diminish.

When calm replaced chaos two of their men were wounded, one almost gravely, but once Cian tended his wounds, the grateful man lifted himself upon his horse and took his position a second time.

Fin came to her and Simon's side, dirt marked his face and blood splattered over his chainmail. "Are the women all right?"

"We're fine."

"How much farther to her fortress?" he asked her son.

"A mile, two at the most."

Tara mounted her horse and pushed forward. "Maybe I can help us find her easier."

Her horse drew up along Duncan's. The two of them exchanged a few words before they both moved forward in front of their party. Tara spread her hands and the brush parted a path to lead the way.

Liz watched Tara use her gift like never before. A clear path parted the forest floor, leading them to their destination.

~~~~

Grainna felt them long before they arrived, the large self-righteous lot of them.

She commanded her men to fall into position and then stood on the highest point of her towers to watch.

"You met my little four-legged friends, but what about these?" Lifting her hands above her head, Grainna swooped up every insect, bee, and creature she could control and told them to swarm.

Screams and yells came from the approaching party until lightning split the air and rain fell, dispersing the insects she called.

They moved closer.

Grainna called her dogs, some domestic, others wolves. They stood beside her men, waiting.

When the first horse penetrated the clearing, the hounds burst in their direction. The unmanned horses reared, fled and the dogs followed. In fact, Grainna couldn't see any of MacCoinnich's army.

She knew they were near, but couldn't smell them, taste them.

Wings flapped in the air in the distance, followed by chirping, squawks, and guttural cries of gulls. The sound increased until it gained the noise level of a jet airplane.

Grainna glanced behind her and dropped to her knees as the first of thousands of gulls flew over her.

The birds latched onto her men. Women in her compound fought off the flock, screaming.

Then the MacCoinnichs came.

She shouted a warning, willed the men to attack, then whipped her hand across the sky. Half the flock fell to the ground, dead or wounded. The other retreated, leaving the men to battle.

~~~~

"There." Fin pointed toward Grainna standing over them all. Her long black hair and signature black dress and cape fit the color of her soul.

Todd drew his gun from his satchel, pointed at the witch, and fired two rounds. One hit, but only pissed her off. She pushed her hands his direction and pulled him from his horse.

Fin heard Myra scream. Two things happened almost simultaneously. First Myra thrust both her hands in the air, forcing Grainna to a far wall. Even from Fin's distance, he saw Grainna crack her head on the bricks and slide to the ground. The second was Cian meeting Myra at Todd's side.

Grainna and Todd stood at the same time.

Before Grainna could let off another blast, the earth shook. Only Fin wasn't the one making the action happen. When he glanced to his right, he noticed one of Lancaster's knights spread his fingers to the earth. Fin smiled and added his own punch.

"Hold on," he yelled to anyone who could hear.

~~~~

Liz couldn't control her horse. She reared and tossed her to the ground. She scrambled out of the way of hooves and sprang to her feet.

Men pressed forward, swords once again crashed against each other and fire flew in the air. She ducked an arrow and found Tara huddled next to Amber.

"We need to get behind the fortress so Grainna can't escape," Amber told them.

"Is that her plan?"

Amber shook her head. "Aye, that and to kill us all."

Liz noticed one of their men struggling with an enemy and assisted him with a little magic. Myra scrambled toward them and pushed another man from his horse with a wave of her hand.

"What's the plan?"

"Over there." Liz noticed a break in the men and a clear path beyond Grainna's hiding space.

They started toward the entrance.

Wait for me.

The voice belonged to Simon, but when she looked down, he had already taken the form of a wolf. Before she could protest, he bounded forward and led the way.

Grainna wasn't expecting any approach from the seaside. Simon picked his way along the side of her fortress, Liz and the others followed. Once they reached what looked like an entrance they realized the door was only an illusion, most likely magical.

Liz beat her fist on the solid brick. "Dammit."

"What now?"

"We can't move to the front, she'll see us."

"Maybe we should retreat."

Lora gasped and pointed above their heads.

Liz stifled a scream. Above them was a vision in white. Familiar, but not the Ancient who'd visited them before.

"It's Tatiana," Amber cried.

"Ghosts? Oh, Christ." Liz shivered.

A floating cloud surrounding her sprit pointed farther beyond the cliffs and beckoned them to come.

"What should we do?" Amber asked.

Simon lunged forward and shifted from wolf to falcon in one leap. His wings caught the air and flew beyond the ghost.

There's a window over here, he told his mother.

How are we all going to get up there?

Duh! Fly. Hold everyone's hands.

Liz shrugged. She'd manage to hover during the rat attack, keeping four of them elevated.

Is the path clear?

Simon flew out of sight for a few seconds before telling her yes.

"Looks like we're going for a ride." She placed her hands out, palms up.

"Then what?" Myra asked. "We fly up there, find Grainna? Then what?"

Liz met her frightened eyes, her jaw set. "We kick some serious ass."

Myra started to comment again.

"No. No doubt. This is it, Myra. We've all felt it. Today this is over."

Tara nodded and said, "I can't go my entire life looking over my shoulder, worrying for my son's life."

Liz sent her sister a wry smile and accepted her hand in hers.

One by one, each of them nodded before

grasping hands.

"Don't let go."

Liz concentrated until all of them hovered above the sea cliff and found their feet planted inside Grainna's keep. The noise of the battle outside ran through all of them. Liz knew from experience, that neither Lora nor Tara would ask their husbands how the fight fared. Any distraction from them could prove deadly. Instead, their small party followed the ghost of Tatiana as she led the way through the maze of soggy passages to their ultimate enemy.

Chapter Thirty-One

Fin pulled his sword from the warrior who'd fought him. Like the others, victory only came when it wasn't your hide bleeding in the dirt and on the brush. These men didn't die for the greater good of their liege or clan. They had died in vain.

Drawing up beside him, Cian followed Duncan. The majority of men fell, some still fought, but the enemy's strength dwindled.

Fin's eyes shot to where they'd left the women. Some still stood, fire shooting from their hands and others appeared to be wielding some other gift. Peering closer, he realized that none of the women resembled Liz. He looked closer. His mother wasn't among them either.

"Where are *our* women?"

Duncan pointed to small gathering of ladies.

"Look again, brother."

Alarm filled Duncan's face, his eyes shot toward the keep.

Fin didn't wait for an explanation. He knew his brother spoke with his wife inside his head. Kicking his horse, Fin raced to the walls of the keep.

~~~~

Following the ghost of Tatiana through the dark chambers and long halls of the forgotten fortress prickled Liz's spine.

"Where are we going? Seems we're moving down and not up to where Grainna is."

They had been moving down several flights of stairs. Once in a while, they'd travel up one, but the majority were below the entrance they'd taken.

Tatiana hovered over a large ornate door. She

floated thought the wood, disappeared, and then shimmered in front of them again.

"In there? We need to go inside?" Amber asked.

Tatiana nodded and floated beyond the heavy barrier.

Liz grasped the handle of the chamber and pushed. Nothing happened.

She pressed her shoulder against it again.

Nothing.

"What's Grainna hiding in there?"

"Must be important."

Myra stepped forward. "Move back."

Liz obeyed.

Myra forced both of her hands over her head, springing the door off its hinge and across the room.

"Bitchin'," Liz cried, not able to contain her lift in her heart with the display of Myra's powers.

They entered what must have been Grainna's lair. No other way could describe her private chambers.

Layers upon layers of fabric ran the length of the walls, a massive bed sat in the middle of the room, but the mattress held no dip. Liz wondered if the woman ever slept. A fireplace filled one wall, another held shelves with flasks and containers holding untold things.

Tatiana waved a ghostly hand over a chessboard. There her wispy trails of smoke merged with a magical fog layered over the players.

Liz stared down at the game, eyes creased. She lifted her gaze to Tatiana. "What? What is this?"

Tatiana bent to the board, brought her hands to her mouth, and tried to blow. Without breath, nothing came from her lips. She repeated the action twice and then tried to wave a hand over the pieces.

The fog still settled. Never lifting, never moving.

"Blow?" Liz asked.

Tatiana tilted her head to the side and nodded.

Bending down, Liz opened her mouth and drew in a big breath. She spread the air across the board like a child blowing out candles on a cake.

The fog lifted but tried to come back.

"Do it again," Tara cried.

Liz blew a second time.

Lora called out, "The enemy is retreating."

"What?"

"Out there. Ian says their enemy is fleeing."

"Grainna is controlling the men with this. The game, the fog."

Tatiana nodded, and then her smile faded. Her head shot to the ceiling. Soon her spirit sprinted up and out of the room.

"What the hell," Tara yelled.

"Grainna knows we're here," Amber told them, her empathic ability never in question.

"We need to get out of here," Tara cried.

They ran toward the door.

~~~~

Fin noticed Grainna spring from her perch and knew she went to intercept the women. When the men in the courtyard and beyond turned their horses or simply ran on foot, he knew Grainna's hold on them was broken.

Duncan, Cian, Todd and Ian met him on the main stairs of the fortress.

"Where are they?"

Ian led the way, following the stairs to the west and down into the lower chambers. "Down there."

They ran, tripping over stones and debris until they heard a woman's scream. Fin hated that he couldn't tell whose.

Duncan ducked as something flew by his head.

Amber's voice yelled from behind them.

Fin swiveled.

"Hurry," he cried, pointing toward the sound of the scream.

Bounding down the stairs, Fin burst into the room to find Grainna holding her hand above her head. Liz and the others hovered above the ground, their frames encapsulated in an iridescent bubble.

Duncan shot fire toward the witch, breaking her concentration and forcing the women to the floor with a solid thud.

Todd shot off three rounds, catching Grainna in the chest before landing on the ground, unaffected. Her hand pushed the gun from his hand making it fall to the floor before Todd's body slammed against the wall.

Myra countered. Where the bullets had no effect, her force spun Grainna in circles, leaving her against the posts of the bed.

Grainna laughed, lifted her arms over her head, and disappeared in a cloud of gray smoke.

~~~~

"Where the hell did she go?" Liz screamed.

From the doorway, Tatiana appeared.

Cian's gasp brought all eyes to him. "'Tis you."

She nodded and pointed above her head before moving from the room.

"Wait," Cian yelled as he followed her spirit. Simon, in the form of the wolf, reached the top of the stairs first.

Hurry, Simon yelled. *She's trying to escape.*

Liz started yelling before she reached the landing where her son stood. "What's the matter, Grainna? Is the wicked witch afraid?" Maybe taunting her wasn't the brightest idea, but it seemed a better idea than letting her run away.

295

~~~~

Outside, Grainna turned at Lizzy's call, her words stepping on her last nerves. Why should she run? This was her world, her reign. These people were nothing.

Lightning split above her head, she batted it away with a wave of her hand. "I expected more of you, Ian." She tossed him off his feet.

The wind caught beneath her legs, she stumbled but didn't fall.

She drew a line of fire in front of the family and pulled in a deep breath. As she blew, the fire whipped and struck out at them.

Rain splattered down from above, stopping the flames as quickly as she could conjure them.

The women started grasping on to each other's hands.

"In this day and in this hour," Liz started the chant and the others followed. Ian grasped hold of his wife, his son, the others.

"We call upon the Ancient powers."

The air around Grainna thinned. She had to flee. She'd not be sent forward in time again.

Grainna lifted her hands and started to shift.

"Bring upon this witch every soul that she has taken or she has stolen."

Tatiana's ghost swam toward her, hands extended. Grainna forgot to shift and ducked the girl's dead fury. Another black ghost flew her way, and another.

Their weeping, cries, and sorrow followed rage and violence.

"Souls!" Liz yelled. "Take back your powers, every soul. Leave her empty, leave her cold."

The family advanced, united. Each one adding a chant, adding another layer of her demise. She batted away the ghosts. Slivers of spiny fingers racked her face and arms. Her skin started to tear.

Her body started to weaken.

"No more immortality, this is our curse from us to thee."

Grainna heaved a wail from her lungs. Lungs that breathed for five hundred years now sputtered dust. Her hands started to shrivel, her eyes fought to see.

As her body crumbled to the ground, Duncan lifted his hands, flames shot to her body, caught, and the pain of every death slammed into her black heart and took back what was theirs.

~~~~

When the flames cleared and silence replaced the screams, Liz's gaze settled on the pile of dust where Grainna had once stood. Tilting her head to the left, she saw Todd holding Myra's hand. To them linked Lora and Ian. Amber gripped a hold of Cian and Simon. On the right, Tara slumped against Duncan. Fin broke away from his place and stepped forward, wrapping his arms around her.

They'd done it.

They'd all survived.

Out of the corner of her eye, she saw Cian step forward, his hand reached out.

Tatiana was the only soul left in the room. She hovered close to Cian, her eyes filled with sorrow.

They hadn't all survived after all.

Cian's hand brushed around her image, caressing her.

"Mom," Simon whispered as he pointed above their heads.

"Elise."

An iridescent cloud of silver brought the stunning Ancient to them. "You have done well, clan MacCoinnich." Her voice, like that of an angelic choir, flowed like a river. She hovered over Grainna's ashes, and swept her hand above them causing them to disappear into a thousand pearls of golden light.

Elise settled her feet on the ground, walked out of her iridescent light, and materialized in front of them. Her flawless face was porcelain smooth, and her radiant smile was like a gift when she turned it on Liz. Simply looking at her gave Liz a glimpse of what heaven must be.

"Each of you fought with courage and valor. You brought together the future and the past in the only combination that could end Grainna's evil. We are all eternally grateful to you."

"We exposed ourselves to the others. Will we be safe?" Liz asked.

"Fear not, Elizabeth. We have filtered many images from the minds of those we feel would call you out or see your family harmed because of who and what you are. Others, like you, will remember."

"What of the stones? We have only the three."

Elise swept her gaze over to Tatiana who hovered above Cian. "Show them, m'dear."

Tatiana nodded and extended her hand to a chest sitting against the wall. Cian opened the latch and found the three missing sacred stones.

"They are entrusted to you, your family. As each of you go your separate ways, take one stone each."

"Separate ways? What are you saying? Are we going to be divided?"

Elise laid a hand to Lora's arm. "Only if you choose to do so, m'lady."

"Then our need to travel in time is over."

"Nay, m'lord. With Grainna gone, you can do so now with only one stone each."

Liz glanced at her son. They could return home if they wanted to. "Can we come and go as we please?"

"Everything has a cost, Elizabeth. Use the stones with caution. Do not attempt to return to any time that you've already been. The results would be...unpleasant." Elise directed her next words to Cian. "You cannot bring her back."

"Why? Why did she have to die?" His voice cracked when he spoke.

"Look again, Cian. Tatiana's soul is not dead. It lives on. Her redemption came from helping you all defeat Grainna. She has finally found peace. Peace she never would have had in this life."

"She's been taken from me."

"Her soul will live again. As will yours. Look around you, see the love that time has brought into your family."

When a tear fell down his cheek, Liz had to close her eyes. His pain, touchable.

"Come, m'dear. Comfort your love, tell him to live."

Tatiana hovered beside Elise. This time when she opened her mouth, she spoke.

"Don't weep, Cian. I have seen the future. Ye will love again. Yer sons will be honorable men, yer daughters beautiful and blessed with yer eyes."

He tilted his head to the side as her hand caressed his cheek. His face lost some of the strain of his grief.

The ghost of Tatiana kissed his cheek. "Goodbye, Cian. Thank ye for yer love, 'twas the only love I had in this life. I will forever be grateful for it." Tatiana soared above them all and disappeared into a wisp of wind.

Elise smoothed a hand over Cian's face, smiled and stepped to Amber and repeated the move. She touched each of them once bringing a wave of peace, enlightenment.

"Live long and valiant lives, m'dears. Love each other and teach your children what has happened here today." With those final words, Elise stepped back into her iridescent cloud and floated up and out of their sight.

"I think we've earned ourselves one hell of a

celebration," Liz said once they'd all taken a few deep breaths. She glanced at Cian to judge his thoughts. "Unless you disagree, Cian."

The young man looked up, smiled. "Nay. Tatiana's life is to be celebrated."

Ian placed a hand over his son's shoulders and led him from the keep.

~~~~

"You guys sure know how to party, MacCoinnich," Liz called out over the noise of the players filling the courtyard with music, while people danced and laughed over each other.

The band of warriors met with cheers and praise from those left at Brisbane's keep. A feast filled their bellies and wine and ale fluttered their heads.

Fin hadn't let Liz go for a moment once they bathed and changed back into proper clothing.

The women wore their finest gowns and adorned their hair with flowers. Tara danced with Duncan with her son in her arms and Myra taught Todd a few of their dances, stopping often to kiss him. Amber and Simon danced with children their own ages and even Cian laughed along with them.

Liz looked around the crush of people, searching for Ian and Lora. She noticed the couple sneaking off from the group, their heads pushed together. "Go Lora," she whispered, laughing at herself.

Tara stumbled over her way, dragging Myra and Amber with her. "Well, sisters, looks like we did it." Tara held her glass of wine up high.

"We did." Liz clicked her mug to the others and drank.

"We helped." The men came up behind them, squeezing close.

Fin's arms circled Liz's waist, her head fell back on his shoulder. "I can't believe this is all over. No more fighting, no more worry."

"It's like the sun is shining for the first time," Amber said.

Liz turned in Fin's arms. "I don't know about that. There's been a lot of sunshine in spite of, you-know-who."

Fin's lips sought hers, tender, brief. She moved close and when he tried to move away, she reached for his head and forced him into a much more enjoyable kiss. When he let go, her head was dizzy and she stumbled.

Duncan bellowed a laugh, the others joined in.

"Sunshine and moonbeams, love," Fin added.

"I heard that the wedding between Brisbane and Regina is on again," Todd said.

"Someone told me that Brisbane is requesting the ceremony tomorrow morning."

"He doesn't want her to get away again." Duncan rolled his eyes. "I don't know why."

They laughed.

"Maybe he loves her," Amber suggested.

Liz shrugged. "Maybe."

"Can we really travel back home if we want?" Simon asked.

Fin's hands tightened on her shoulders. The same wave of tension flowed down her back.

"That's what Elise said."

"Is that what you want?" Fin asked.

Simon stared at him, then caught Liz's eyes. "I guess that depends."

"Depends on what, Simon."

A smirk played across his face. "Depends on if you're going to make an honest woman of my mother."

Todd laughed outright. Tara smothered her smiling mouth with her hand, and Cian spit out the wine he drank.

The only two not laughing were her and Fin.

"Well?" Simon demanded.

"Simon!" Liz scolded.

"No, Mom. I have a right to know."

She started to tell him to stop being pushy, but Fin cut her off. "Tell me, do you approve of your mother and I together?"

Simon rolled his eyes. "Duh." The teenage attitude superseded his grown up question of moments ago.

"Well then, I suppose there is nothing more to discuss. Your mother and I will marry, and you both will stay here."

Simon's jaw dropped. "Really?"

Liz hit Fin's massive chest with her fist. "Excuse me. Are you forgetting a little something here?"

Sending her a look of pure innocence, Fin said, "Nay. I think we have everything covered."

"I don't think so, buddy."

"What's the problem, love? Simon has a right to—"

Liz grabbed hold of his shirt and pulled him away from the others. "This is just like you, Fin. What makes you think you can take charge of my life, my future like this?"

"Because," he said, moving closer and wrapping his arms around her to hold her still.

He felt so good, so right, even with the two of them splitting hairs.

"Because of this." His lips found hers, his tongue swept into her mouth and claimed it, marked it. She melted and let out a purr that brought a chuckle from deep inside him.

He drew away and waited until she opened her eyes before he spoke. "Because I love you. Because we belong together."

Her heart swelled, threatening to burst. "Those are really good reasons." Liz kissed him hard, making sure he knew how much she wanted him. "I love you."

"'Tis a good thing. Love makes a marriage so

much more enjoyable." He kissed her again, making her forget everyone around them, and showing her how wonderful their life was going to be.

###

HIGHLAND SHIFTER

BOOK FOUR

BY
CATHERINE BYBEE

Chapter One

Current Day, Los Angeles

Energy buzzed down Helen's spine until she shivered with the electrical current her gift created. The information she sought was close enough to taste, all she needed to do was touch it and she'd be one step closer to finding the missing boy.

Helen Adams shifted onto the balls of her feet, reached well beyond her five-foot six frame, and tipped the old leather bound text into her hands. As the book slid from its comfortable position on the top shelf in Mrs. Dawson's library, dust plumed off the sill in a cloud. The zap she'd been feeling for the last half hour eased into a nice, steady hum. The blanket of warmth that only came when she'd found what she sought brought a rare smile to her face.

"There you are," she whispered to the ancient book as if it were alive.

"Did you find what you're looking for?" Mrs. Dawson limped into the room, leaning heavily on the cane. Nearing her eighty-fourth birthday, Mrs. Dawson's battered, frail body appeared as if it wanted nothing more than to lie down and rest forever.

"I think so." Helen gently blew the layer of dust off the book and peered close to determine the title. Embossed into the leather was an old Celtic design. The scent of a fresh meadow after a cleansing rain settled over her. Helen closed her eyes and grasped the text hard. She heard the hooves of horses, smelled the sweet scent of

1

horseflesh. None of this experience came from the room where she stood, but from the book she held in her hands.

As the scents dissipated, Helen opened her eyes and gazed at the book in wonder. How could a book this old hold any relevance on a missing child's case in the twenty-first century?

"Do you have any idea where this originally came from?" Helen asked as she moved to the table and turned on a light to view the pages inside the book.

"My late husband collected boxes of books like that when he was alive. As you can judge by the dust, they've not been touched since his death." Mrs. Dawson eased herself into a chair, cringing as she sat. Helen knew her friend's arthritis would be acting up with the sour weather pounding the window outside. Helen also knew Mrs. Dawson wouldn't accept anything more than a sympathetic smile if Helen were to ask if she could help her sit or stand.

"Well, let's see what you have there."

Judging by the cover, Helen expected the text to be in either Celtic or Italian. She was wrong.

The title of Folklore, writing in a beautiful script font, splashed the front page of the book.

The book was written in English.

Helen glanced at the opening credits to see the publication date.

"This is over two hundred years old," Helen said, confused.

"What does it have to do with that boy?" Mrs. Dawson asked.

"I've no idea."

Mrs. Dawson was the only person who knew the extent of Helen's gift. Well, the only person Helen had told who hadn't laughed at her and passed her off as crazy.

Her work at a local antique shop had led her

down this path to Mrs. Dawson's library in search of a missing teenage boy, Simon McAllister. What the boy and the book in her hands had in common, Helen hadn't a clue.

Helen gently turned the pages and skimmed the text. From what she could tell, several different storytellers wrote the content. Illustrations dotted the pages with small captions explaining the pictures.

There were illustrations of Celtic symbols, Scottish kilts, warriors with broadswords, and women wearing long, flowing dresses.

What any of it had to do with Simon McAllister disappearing off the face of the earth without a trace was a mystery to Helen.

Releasing a long-suffering sigh, she flattened her hand on the table and twisted away in frustration. "This is useless."

Mrs. Dawson cocked her head to the side in a motion of concern. One of the shutters on the outside of the house ripped free of its lock and swung back, hitting the side of the old house with an angry bang.

Helen and Mrs. Dawson jumped at the noise and swiveled toward it.

Cold air blew into the room, and the drapes around the window flapped in protest from the outside elements.

An eerie screech whistled through the crack in the window, and the book to Helen's side started fluttering through pages like a deck of cards being shuffled in Vegas. The pages moved in a rapid pace, but the current of air in the room barely brushed her skin.

Unable to pull her gaze away, Helen watched as the pages of the book came to a sudden stop.

The air on her back blew colder, harder, but the pages no longer rustled.

Her chocolate brown hair started to come loose

from the tight bun on her head, but she ignored the tendrils falling in her face. Instead, Helen inched closer.

Two illustrations covered the pages. On the left was a Scottish warrior, broad shouldered and dressed in his plaid, as would any proud Scot of centuries past. In the corner of the illustration flew a hawk or maybe it was a falcon. Helen couldn't be sure.

The warrior's hand extended toward the opposite page, his face solemn with an expression of absolute desperation.

Helen let her eyes travel to the right page and time suddenly stood still.

"My God," Mrs. Dawson exclaimed.

My God indeed.

"That's you."

Helen peered closer, stared at the image, which certainly looked like her. The woman in the picture wore her hair long, past her waist. She wore a floor length dress with long, flowing sleeves.

Yes, it could have been a distant relative of Helen's. That alone gave her a sense of familiarity she had never experienced any other time in her life. Abandoned at a young age, Helen never knew her parents or any other relative.

Helen took in the features of the woman's face and gasped when her gaze landed on the pendant around the woman's neck.

Reaching a hand to her own neck, she pulled out an identical replica of the necklace in the picture from under her turtleneck sweater.

The breeze from the window stopped and the room started to warm.

"This lady must be one of your relatives," Mrs. Dawson said.

Helen nodded but couldn't voice any words. The necklace wasn't an heirloom. What did the picture mean? Who was the man on the opposite page, and what did it have to do with the missing boy she felt a need to find?

She had more questions than answers. Glancing at her watch, Helen realized how late it was. "I should leave so you can rest. Do you mind if I hold onto this book for a while?"

Mrs. Dawson patted her hand. "Of course not, dear. It appears to belong to you anyway."

Helen reached for the book, but Mrs. Dawson stopped her hand midway. Frail, wrinkled fingers touched the backside of Helen's hand and fiddled with the watch surrounding her wrist. Mrs. Dawson tapped the watch then lowered her same finger to the picture of the woman in the book.

There, in the pages of an ancient text, was a very similar timepiece on the wrist of the woman.

"Perhaps not a relative after all."

"What are you suggesting?"

"She looks exactly like you, Helen. That necklace, where did you get it?"

"I found it in a thrift shop." Her love for all things old brought her into thrift shops in search of hidden treasures. Lots of people threw their possessions away instead of treasuring them. The pendant had Celtic markings with a polished stone dead center. It was simply a well-polished rock set in a common metal. But the stone felt warm against Helen's skin when she'd put it on. Somewhere inside of her soul, she knew she was meant to own the necklace.

"This woman is wearing a watch. Your watch."

"That's ridiculous. It's probably a bracelet."

Mrs. Dawson pressed her reading glasses close to her eyes and peered down. "I see numbers."

Helen noticed them, too. But it wasn't possible. "What are you suggesting?" The woman in the picture was clearly garbed in a dress right out of medieval times, a time when watches weren't part of any woman's wardrobe. In fact, Helen knew wristwatches weren't invented until the early nineteenth century.

Mrs. Dawson stared deep into her eyes before she spoke. "To coin a phrase, 'a picture is worth a thousand words.'"

"Now you're throwing riddles at me." Her curiosity spiked, however, and she decided a Google search was definitely in order. What was the exact date the wristwatch was invented, and who were the authors of this book?

Glancing back at the curtains, Mrs. Dawson said, "Seems something else is throwing riddles at you, dear. I just happen to be the one holding the book with the answers."

~~~~

1596 Scotland

An unrelenting desire surged into the tips of Simon's fingers. If only he could toss a ball of fire onto the ass of his opponent's horse. But no, that would be cheating, and why hurt the innocent horse. Using his powers would be like bringing a gun to a knife fight. Besides, the warrior's sword arm was tiring. Simon felt it the last time the man's broadsword hit his shield.

Metal clashed against metal behind him, and smoke plumed above the fires in the encampment of the invaders who threatened MacCoinnich Keep. Night crept around the edges of light being cast off by the flames, bringing finality to the fight at hand.

Simon's opponent dug his heels into the flanks of the horse he rode, his sword aiming straight at Simon's chest.

Hold still, he whispered mentally to his horse. This skill, the one where he talked to animals, was one he'd mastered at the tender age of thirteen. Now, nearly thirty, Simon had complete command of any animal he came in contact with. Or, as his mother often said, he was a regular Doctor Doolittle.

The warrior charging him released an angry cry, his blade poised for a deathblow.

Simon waited, one hand holding his own weapon firmly, the other cradling a shield with the family crest engraved upon it.

A little closer.

Within a hair's breadth of the sword reaching his personal space, Simon urged his mount to lunge. With that momentum, he knocked the other man's sword aside and pierced his enemy's chest, laying it wide open, spilling the man's lifeblood.

A set of stunned eyes caught Simon's as the warrior slid from his horse on his final descent from life.

Simon paused for only a second to watch him topple before quickly spinning around to assess his next threat.

The enemy retreated to the west, fleeing the losing battle so they could fight another day. Duncan, his uncle by marriage, stood beside his horse, his chest heaving heated breaths as his brother, Cian, circled the fallen. He would determine if any still lived.

The bloody battlefield stunk of unwashed flesh and dying men.

"Do any still breathe?" Duncan called out to Cian.

Cian slid from his horse and carefully rolled one of their enemies over. Even from Simon's distance, he could see death on the man's face.

"Nay. None."

Several other battle-weary men gathered and awaited direction from Duncan.

"I'll send hands from the Keep to aid in the burial of these men," he told his men. "Did anyone see a leader?"

Simon shook his head. "No one stood out among them."

"None." A chorus of denial rose.

"Mayhap ye should send scouts to follow those who fled."

"Aye." Duncan's gaze settled briefly on Simon. An unspoken request lit his eyes. They would scout, but not with men on horses. Sending a small party, easily outnumbered and ambushed, was not the answer.

"I'll ride ahead and report to Ian."

This excuse would go unquestioned by the men. Ian was Laird of the MacCoinnich clan, and he would want to know the outcome of this battle. Instead of returning to the Keep, Simon would scout ahead alone and return without anyone knowing that he watched.

Duncan lifted his chin. "Tell my Tara I'm well."

Simon nodded, knowing he didn't need to say a thing to his aunt. Duncan and Tara had a special mental bond that made it possible for the two of them to communicate with their thoughts. Tara was probably in Duncan's head right now asking about his well-being.

Simon and his extended family were Druids, all of them. Each possessed special gifts—Druid gifts that aided them in life and allowed them to defeat their enemies, magical and mortal alike. He'd take the latter any day of the week. Magical enemies were much harder to fight.

Keeping to the forest, Simon reined in his horse away from any watchful eyes and slid to the ground.

He quickly removed each layer of armor and clothing and stacked them against a tree. "Keep an eye on my things, won't you, Kong?" Simon had named his very first horse King, a massive animal that served him well. Kong was King's son. The names were a constant joke between his twenty-first century family members.

Kong sniffed the air before moving to a patch of grass to graze. The horse was hungry and tired after the battle. Most likely, he'd eat and rest until Simon returned.

Stepping away from his horse, Simon spread his arms wide, closed his eyes, and envisioned the falcon.

Familiar energy gathered around him. The air crackled and the world started to pitch.

His limbs shortened and his skin erupted and morphed.

Pain started at his head and spread to his feet, but it was brief and gone before Simon could blink an eye. The entire change took only a few seconds before Simon became the falcon.

Kong offered a passing glance before returning to his meal.

Simon took to the sky.

Above the trees, Simon returned to the direction of battle. He noted the battlefield and Cian helping with the dead.

Simon let a falcon's cry fill the air and saw Duncan and Cian both turn their heads his way.

Duncan nodded at him then continued with his duty as Cian waved a mock salute.

Leaving his family behind, Simon followed the trail the enemy left behind in search of answers.

About the author

New York Times bestselling author Catherine Bybee was raised in Washington State, but after graduating high school, she moved to Southern California in hopes of becoming a movie star. After growing bored with waiting tables, she returned to school and became a registered nurse, spending most of her career in urban emergency rooms. She now writes full time and has penned the novels Wife by Wednesday, Married by Monday, and Not Quite Dating. Bybee lives with her husband and two teenage sons in Southern California.

Connect with Catherine Bybee Online:
Website: http://www.catherinebybee.com
My blog: http://catherinebybee.blogspot.com
Facebook:
https://www.facebook.com/pages/Catherine-Bybee-Romance-Author/128537653855577
Goodreads:
http://www.goodreads.com/author/show/2905789.Catherine_Bybee
Twitter: https://twitter.com/catherinebybee
Email: catherinebybee@yahoo.com

Discover other titles by Catherine Bybee

Contemporary Romance
Weekday Bride Series:
Wife by Wednesday
Married By Monday

Not Quite Series:
Not Quite Dating

Paranormal Romance
MacCoinnich Time Travel Series:
Binding Vows
Silent Vows
Redeeming Vows
Highland Shifter

Ritter Werewolves Series:
Before the Moon Rises
Embracing the Wolf

Novellas:
Possessive
Soul Mate

Erotic Titles:
Kiltworthy
Kilt-A-Licious

30391192R00184

Made in the USA
Charleston, SC
14 June 2014